Hedging

Other Five Star Titles
by Annette Meyers:

Repentances

Hedging

A Smith and Wetzon Mystery

Annette Meyers

Five Star • Waterville, Maine

First Edition
First Printing: February 2005

Published in 2005 in conjunction with Tekno Books and Ed Gorman.

Set in 11 pt. Plantin by Minnie B. Raven.

Printed in the United States on permanent paper.

Library of Congress Cataloging-in-Publication Data

Meyers, Annette.
    Hedging : a Smith and Wetzon mystery /
by Annette Meyers.
        p. cm.
    ISBN 1-4104-0199-5 (hc : alk. paper)
    1. Smith, Xenia (Fictitious character)—Fiction.
    2. Wetzon, Leslie (Fictitious character)—Fiction.
    3. Women detectives—New York (State)—New York
—Fiction.   4. Executive search firms—Fiction.
    5. New York (N.Y.)—Fiction.   6. Amnesia—Fiction.
    7. Mystery fiction.   I. Title
    PS3563.E889H44 2005
    813'.54—dc22   2004063671

For Lynn Hall

Acknowledgments

Special thanks to Marianne Coughlin, Vice President for Program Development, Mount Sinai Medical Center, who gave me a thorough tour of both the Department of Psychiatry and the ER. To Jean Mensing, retired, Former Director of Admissions, Mount Sinai Department of Psychiatry; and to Allison H. Stier, Nurse Practitioner, Psychiatry Outpatient Department, Mount Sinai. To Ami Gantt, Ph.D., Deputy Director, Social Work, Psychiatry, Bellevue Hospital Center. To Sybil Kaufman, RN, MSN, CS. And to Robert Davis, MD.

To Special Agent Joseph Valiquette, FBI, New York Division. To Linda Ray for Mississippi and Wall Street lore, and Marty, who always gets the first edit. And to Bob Capri, mime extraordinaire.

Finally, I would like to thank everyone I worked with at Five Star/Gale, in particular, Ed Gorman, Mary P. Smith, Pat Wallace, John Helfers, and Ed Vincent for their caring professionalism.

Author's Note

After 9/11, storage lockers were removed from New York City bus and train stations. As the first draft of *Hedging* was almost finished and this is a work of fiction, I have taken a liberty by allowing storage lockers to exist in the Port Authority Bus Terminal.

"Running a hedge fund is not for sissies. It's a blood sport. You have to be tough, you have to believe. It's a go for the throat business. All risk. Great rewards. But you can burn your ass in an uptick, and no one, but no one thinks it can happen, until it does."

—Former manager, hedge fund, in recent headlines

"Here's my formula for success: Camp by the money river and good things happen. Don't be afraid to go out on a limb. That's where the fruit is."

—Andy Campanero, V.P.
Financial Consultant
Bliss Norderman

Chapter 1

The impossible chirped. Beside her. Another chirp. Louder: an urgent bleat.

Phone, she thought. Phone. She groped for the receiver. Fumbled it to her ear.

"Two. Gray car." The accent was . . .

Not now, she told herself. Move.

Sound enclosed her, roaring. The walls groaned. Her eardrums thundered. The bed quaked. In the murky darkness, she was sharding, splintering. She pressed hands to ears. Her eyelids twitched, eyes tearing.

The roar faded to a deep hum that made her throat tremble.

They were coming. She was trapped.

Subtle motor, different from the roar. She knew what had to be done with exquisite clarity. She opened the bathroom window and ground her coat sleeve back and forth on the warped frame to catch enough black threads, and with hardly a second thought, pulled off a shoe, grit-sticky, and dropped it on the floor.

No sooner had she thrust herself under the low slung mattress, dragging along the voluminous coat, than they exploded into the room, winter with them. And light. The door, off its hinges, lay at right angles to her. Stop breath.

"Fuck, she went out the window. There's her shoe."

"Muthafuck musta warned her."

Pancaked under the bed, nose to dusty carpet, she didn't know reality from nightmare.

13

"She couldna got far with one shoe." They were moving around the room. Black Gucci loafers in her face, one gold stirrup dented. Shiny. New tips. She could have misted them with her breath.

"See that?" They were bent over the bed.

"Yeah. You got her?"

"Nicked maybe. Not enough blood."

A blast smashed her.

"You shot the fucking mattress!"

"Felt like it."

"You're a fucking idiot! You wanna leave a trail? Dig it out and let's get going."

The weight of the man on the bed pressed her face and chest deeper into the carpet, drained her lungs of air.

"Can't get ahold of it."

"Forget it."

Time dissolved. When she came back, they were gone.

She inched out, cheek scraping prickly fibers. As if terror had made her swell. Breathing pain. On her knees, dry-heaving. Her back, one long bruise, crackled. Crackled? She groped under her skirt. Documents, printouts. God, that's what they were after. No time for this. She thrust them under the bed.

Move. Move. The sheets were torn and bleeding, the mattress shredded. She blinked. Don't think. She wrapped the coat around her, pulled the wool beret over her ears.

Her shoe lay across the room, on its side. She was on her way.

Night fell on her when she stepped over the toppled door. Icy snow sliced her bruised face. She made her way to the manager's office. The door was open. He lay sprawled on the floor, the chair over backward, his turban a slipped bandage. Blood. Labored breathing. She had to get out of there before they came back. He'd tried to help her. 911. Phone smashed to crumbling pieces. She pulled drawers open, looking for a cell phone. Panic, a wilderness threatened. She pushed it back.

Check his pockets. Success. She made the 911 call. Where was she? On the desk, a billing book. Golden Blossom Motel. Somewhere. "Assault. Murder." She threw down the cell and fled. She was not stupid. If she kept it, used it again, it could be traced.

She ducked into the shadows. A taxi came up the drive to the motel and stopped in front of the manager's office. A woman got out carrying an overnight bag. Another car followed. A gray Mercedes. They were coming back. The woman's scream thrust her in motion.

Two-lane highway, snowy brush on the side of the road. A tower of Texaco lights ahead. Plane circling, lights blinking, lower and lower. Hideous droning sound. She was near an airport. If she could just get to the gas station without being seen.

It didn't matter. Closed. Two cars and a truck sat dark and empty on a side lot. They would find her now. She had nowhere to hide. Unless one of the vehicles was unlocked. It was possible. Before going for the lot, she checked the road again.

Coming down the highway, through the swirling snow, headlights. A bus. It pulled to a stop in front of the gas station and two swarthy men in work clothes got out.

"On or no, lady?" the driver called to her.

She got on.

"Where to?" The bus pulled away from the gas station and onto the highway again.

She let out a ragged breath. It was going to be okay. "What's your last stop?"

15

"Port Authority, New York."

"Okay."

"That's eleven-fifty."

"I—" She put her hand to her face and felt crusts, like scabs. Her hands were free. No purse. Had she left it in the room? Where was she going to get money? Helpless tears. She groped in the deep pockets of the big coat. No tissues, bills. A lot of them. She shook one loose, drew it out, and uncrumpled it. A twenty.

The driver handed her a punched ticket and change without taking his eyes from the treacherous road. She stuffed everything back in the pocket.

The bus was crowded, hot, stinking of perspiration and wet wool. Light dim. Still, she felt herself examined with more curiosity than she wanted. No seats. She kept moving. In the next to last row, an empty window seat. Not empty. A dog, a golden retriever, sat up and yawned.

In the same instant, a man said, "Do you want to sit here? Come, Nora. Let's let the lady sit down."

The golden—Nora—was a seeing eye dog. With her owner's help, Nora climbed down to the aisle and shook herself, giving off a spray of moisture, as if she, too, had been out running in the snow. Instead of settling in, the dog began to nuzzle and sniff under the voluminous coat.

"Nora, stop, down," the man said. The dog lay down, chastened. "Here, let me help you."

The man was younger than she'd thought at first, although his hair was gray.

She closed her eyes and leaned back in the seat. The lingering smell of the dog was somehow comforting.

"Are you all right?" the man said.

Could he sense she wasn't? "Yes, thank you." She could barely whisper it. What she needed was sleep. She turned her back to the man and began emptying the pocket with the bills, drawing out bill after bill: twenties, fifties, hundreds. She folded them and put them back in the pocket. Why did she have so much money?

She curled up in the seat, shifted, tried to find comfort. Damn, she must be sitting on stones. The coat was voluminous, black, cashmere. Not hers. Not a woman's coat. Why was she wearing it? She straightened and slipped her hand deep into the other pocket. Stones. Real stones. A pocketful of loose stones. What the hell—? She pulled out a small handful and opened her palm.

"Miss?" The blind man was staring at her again.

"I'm okay. Please." She closed her fist around the stones and peered out the window. The gray Mercedes was riding even with the bus in the second lane. Her cringe was involuntary. They'd seen her get on and were following her.

The man next to her shifted in his seat.

She turned her attention back to the stones in her hand. The beam over her seat caught the glitter. The stones in her coat pocket were diamonds.

Chapter 2

What was that song—a pocketful of something or other—
she had a pocketful of it. Right. Miracles. She hunkered
down inside the coat. A magic coat that produced money
and diamonds. She bowed her head and covered her eyes.
Two men with guns in a gray Mercedes were trying to kill
her. The trembling came again and she couldn't stop it.

"Maybe I can help." It was the blind man again, voice
muted. "You're in some kind of trouble."

She thought, you're not just whistling Dixie. How could
a blind man help me? What I need is Superman.

"I'm a good listener," he said.

"You can't help me." Her voice came out scrappy, as if
she had not used it in years.

Wiry salt and pepper threads sprouted from under a
wool tweed cap. "I would say I can feel your pain, which I
can, but that remark seems to have become a joke."

"Please." She turned away.

"I was in law enforcement," he said. "Until this—" His
hand went to his eyes. "Macular degeneration. When we
can't see, our other senses become sharper."

"Look, I don't want to be rude, but I'm going to be. You
can't know and you can't understand—so please, let me
be."

The dog whimpered and licked her master's hand. "It's
all right, Nora," he said.

Why did she have to go and feel guilty now? It was her
life. Yes. Or her death. One of them would be waiting for

her in the Port Authority, the other in the car. How could a blind man protect her?

"Two men with guns in a gray Mercedes are trying to kill me." The man said nothing and she wondered if he'd heard her. He was a big man with huge shoulders and thighs like hams. When he'd had his sight, he must have been formidable.

"Why?"

Why, she thought. The big question. Why? "I don't know. But I'm sure one of them will be waiting for me to get off the bus at the Port Authority, and the other will be in the car outside."

"Are you sure they're not—"

She interrupted. "Cops? No, I'd know if they were on the job." How? How would she know? What did she have to do with cops?

Above his thick, tinted glasses his eyebrows were white bristles. "Are you Feeb? DEA?"

Some adjustment had been made. He was acting as if she was a colleague.

"I'll help you," he said.

"How? He'll be waiting when we get off the bus."

"You get off the bus right behind me. The minute we're off, Nora and I will create a diversion. People will crowd around. You take off behind the buses. Just be careful of the ones pulling out or coming in."

"Thank you, Mr. . . ."

"Marty. Just call me Marty."

The atmosphere changed. Sound more compact. They were in the tunnel. They would exit the tunnel and enter the Port Authority, and it would start all over again. She pulled the beret over her brows. She was ready.

As they pulled into their slot, Marty rose. The dog was

already standing, alert. She gathered the big coat around her and followed him into the aisle.

He bent his head toward her. "Do you want me to call someone for you?"

"Uh. Three seven four five five—" She had no idea where those numbers had come from.

He was nodding. "Go on."

Go on? What was he talking about? She shook her head. The well had gone dry.

"Give me a name."

She racked her brain.

"Your name?"

She didn't answer. She couldn't.

"Get ready." He stepped off the bus, she on his heels. The dog barked. Marty began yelling, then fell to the ground.

Amidst the confusion, she ducked behind the bus, and ran. A door marked EXIT. She opened it, clambered up the stairs, opened another door. Light so bright it hurt her eyes. The crowded lobby of the Port Authority Terminal, everyone moving fast, faster.

To her right, a Krispy Kreme doughnut shop. An ambulance siren blared and the crowd parted for the EMS people from the Fire Department. She ducked into the sweet-smelling shop and bought a doughnut, had them put it in a bag, and asked for her change in coins.

She had to get rid of the diamonds. She stopped at another shop and bought a pair of sunglasses. Next stop, a ladies' room.

Behind the door of the stall, she stuck the doughnut in her mouth and emptied the diamonds into the Krispy Kreme bag, shoved the bag back in her pocket. She ate the doughnut in ragged gulps.

When she stepped out of the stall, there was a line of women waiting, everyone in a hurry. The water, the harsh soap, stung her hands. She saw cuts and burns, torn, bloodied nails. She glanced into the mirror over the sink and jerked back. The woman in the mirror had a deep rose rash mixed with dirt encrusting her face. She removed the dark glasses. Her features were sharp, her face drawn, her eyes bloodshot, deeply circled, gray. Fascinated, she pulled off the beret. Curly hair black as jet tumbled out, stopping at her shoulders.

She had no idea who she was.

Chapter 3

Terror, which she had till now successfully subdued, became a second self, ricocheting through her, having a thrill at her expense. She thought, soon I'll wake up.

The insistent crackle of the paper bag in her pocket gave her the impetus to push away inertia. A locker. The diamonds could stay there until . . .

A maintenance man directed her to the lockers. She put in the coins and pulled out the plastic card, then opened the door. Pausing, she checked the area. Everyone self-absorbed. She took the bag from her pocket, pushed it all the way back in the locker, and slammed the door, testing that it was locked. She held the card in her tight fist.

The flow of humanity through the terminal was incessant, uneven, swirling, at once menacing and yet not. She couldn't spend the night here, hiding. The subway was downstairs. She took a breath, hat over her ears, head down, and stepped out into it, pushing back the random thought that, yes, the subway was downstairs, but where would she go?

Something cold nuzzled her ankle. The golden. Nora. She knelt, causing a discreet clearing. "Nora," she whispered into the dog's coat.

"She led me to you," Marty said. "I thought you'd be long gone."

Nora's growl was an alert. Too late. She saw the shoes first, the damaged stirrup. She hugged the dog, garnering energy, fingered the leash. She had to get rid of the locker card. The gunman had one arm across Marty's shoulder, the other held his gun against Marty's side.

"Leave him alone," she said. "He has nothing to do with this." She slipped the card into the pocket of Marty's coat.

With a ferocious growl, the dog sank her teeth into the gunman's calf, the gun went off. Marty fell hard. She scrambled to him, cradled his head. Bubbles of blood formed on his lips.

"Where are you hit?"

He groaned. "Shoulder."

The screaming was shrill, louder than she could stand. Someone lifted her and dragged her from the building, her cries blending into the rest, squandered.

On the street the snow was thick and fine and the gray Mercedes was waiting. He shoved her into the back and climbed in the front, then leaned over and smacked her hard on the side of the head, slamming her against the window frame. The Krispy Kreme slopped down the coat in undigested clumps. Vomiting will keep a rapist away. Was that true? She tried to jump start her brain, but the numbness was taking over. Fight back. You have to fight.

"Fuck, she's barfing. She's ruining my car."

"Shut up and drive."

The car made the turn on Eighth and headed uptown.

She thought, I've killed someone else. That nice man, or his dog . . .

"Hey, what's that? You get shot?"

"Dog bit me. Hurts like hell. You got a bottle somewhere?"

"Look in the glove compartment."

"Okay, okay, I got it."

"Don't do it here, for crissakes."

"Well, fucking pull over."

"Wait a minute. Let me make the turn."

The car pulled over, the locks clicked, passenger-side door opened. "Fuck, I can't see a goddam thing."

"Just get it over with." The driver was leaning across the seat, intent on his partner.

They'd stopped near the park at Columbus Circle. She felt around on her door for the lock, let out a moan, threw open the door. But the driver grabbed her as her feet touched the ground, getting tight hold of the coat. Slipping out of the coat was easy.

She dodged a taxi, just, feeling the whish of the wind and the splatter of moisture. They were shouting at each other. She laughed. It was wonderful. The park beckoned to her. It was her special place. She flew through Merchants' Gate, dancing on the soft white footpath, leaping and pirouetting in the snow. Perfect *jeté* passes.

I'll protect you, the park said.

She knew it would.

Chapter 4

Chocolate. She smelled chocolate. It floated in the air around her. She got up from the bench, searching. The streetlamp splayed light on a bus shelter where a black woman, bulked up by coat, scarf, and hat, stood waiting, looking up the street for a bus. As she came near, she saw the woman was taking bites of something she held in bakery paper. A chocolate croissant.

"Don't you come any closer, y'hear!" the woman yelled. "I got pepper spray—"

A bus came and stopped in front of the bus shelter. The woman got on, shaking her fist at the specter holding onto the side of the bus shelter. The door to the bus closed and the bus moved on down the street, taking the smell of chocolate with it.

Confetti began to dance in the light of the streetlamp. Pieces glanced her face, her arms. White confetti like snow. Snow. It was snowing. What was she doing in the snow without a coat? She must have left it somewhere. The bench. She'd been sitting on a bench. Where was the bench? She went up and back on the sidewalk, frantic. Now she'd lost the bench.

She knew the bus shelter. She returned to it, trembling violently, and squirmed into a corner to keep warm.

A car passed, and another, and another. She counted them, reached eleven, started from one again, then lost count. The noise was filling her head.

"There she is! Pull over."

25

Tires screeched. She made herself invisible.

"Where?"

"There. The fucking bus shelter. Hey!"

"Shit!"

"Miss? Are you all right?"

She shrieked, but no sound came out. Make the noise stop. She could hardly open her eyes. Hiking boots. Brown corduroy knees knelt beside her. A beard blurred. Spearmint. She closed her eyes. A hand touched her shoulder and she thought, turtle, and did just that.

"She's gone fetal." A woman's voice, very close. "What a mess." Warm breath drove a wedge into her shell. "She's hypothermic. Can you hear me, Miss? We're going to help you."

"Here you go." Warmth. "Jeeze, she's like an ice cube." Hands lifted her. "Try to relax, Miss. We won't hurt you. Just want to get your blood pressure." The strap pinched her arm. "Where'd you find her?"

"Seventy over fifty-eight."

"In the bus shelter around the corner on Fifth."

"Miss? Do you hear me?" His voice was tinny, from way off. "Was she like this when you found her?"

"You mean the blood and stuff? Yeah. Like she was laying in it. We're going to leave now."

"Okay. She have any ID on her?"

"Nothing. We're outa here."

"BP's moving. Come on, honey, lie on your back. We just want to see where you're hurt."

Someone lifted her eyelids and shone a light in her eye. "Miss? I'm Dr. Coughlin. You're in the ER at Mount Sinai. What's your name?"

They were raising her arms, her legs, touching, pressing.

"God," she whispered. "Make them stop the noise." Her skin shivered, pulling away from her body. The space filled with clattering, moaning, a woman crying.

"Get someone from psych over here."

"Contusions, burns, nothing serious. Looks like she put up a fight, but she took quite a beating. On the back, side of her head. Nothing broken, but let's get some X rays. Cuts and scratches, facial abrasions, eyes bloodshot, but nothing that would cause all that blood on her clothes. We'll do the works and see what we get. But she's hypothermic, disoriented. Keeps saying, 'Make them stop the noise.' She was fetal when they brought her in, found her huddled in the bus shelter on Fifth. No ID."

"Rape?"

"No bruising in the groin area. We'll check. And we bagged her clothes."

"What's she said?"

"When I asked what her name was, she said, 'God,' then 'make them stop the noise.' "

But they hadn't done it. It was going around and around in her brain. And she hadn't said her name was God. Why were they saying that? The shaking began again. Her fingers clawed the blankets they'd wrapped her in.

"I'll see what I can get." Someone took her hand and calmed her clawing fingers. "I'm Rachel Hirsch. I'm a doctor. Dr. Coughlin's going to make sure you don't have any broken bones. I'm going with you to keep you company. Don't be afraid."

The quiver of release flushed through her, forced her eyes open. A woman in a white coat, open over a shirt and tailored trousers, young, vivid blue eyes, and ringlets of red hair surrounding her freckled face. "Is that okay with you?"

She squeezed Rachel Hirsch's hand. She tried to speak, and this time she heard a voice, presumably her own, though she didn't recognize it.

"Good girl," Dr. Coughlin said. "Do you think you can sit up? Hey, Manny, get us a chair."

She saw them exchange nods, Dr. Coughlin and Dr. Hirsch. As if they had a secret they weren't going to share with her. Dr. Hirsch put an arm around her shoulders and she sat up with some difficulty. Her skin felt raw, and every muscle in her body ached. They lifted her off the table and into a wheelchair. She was drowning in blankets. Someone tucked another one around her like a hood. She came back, conscious of the pain and stiffness in her shoulders, the ache in her head. And the noise, around and around. She pressed her hands over her ears and rocked. It didn't stop.

"Do you know where you are?" Dr. Hirsch asked, as Manny wheeled the patient down the hall to the elevators.

She took her hands from her ears and stared at Dr. Hirsch. "Mount Sinai Hospital." The noise stopped. "It stopped."

"What stopped?"

"The noise."

"What kind of noise? Music? Subway?"

"I don't know." She tried to run her fingers through her hair, but her hair was matted, tangled in knots, her fingers raw. "It was there, but I couldn't hold onto it . . ."

Dr. Hirsch looked thoughtful. "Do you know how you got here?"

"No." Had there been an accident?

"Some people from Project Help found you huddled in a bus shelter and brought you in. Do you remember?"

She searched her mind. Nothing. Nothing. She heard the noise again, muted, far off. "No." She began to shake.

Tears burned her eyes, her cheeks. "No, no, no. Please. You have to tell me. Please."

"What do you want to know?" Dr. Hirsch said. She motioned to Manny to keep moving and placed a soothing hand on the slight, trembling shoulders as the elevator stopped and the doors opened.

The words came in a hoarse whisper. "Who am I?"

Chapter 5

A woman was singing, somewhere in the distance, a song so sweet and sad, she felt the tears creep down her cheeks.

She opened her eyes. The singing stopped but the sadness lingered. She was in a chair in a green room, walls bare. A window faced another building. No blinds. The sad song seemed to have replaced the noise in her head. She was grateful.

"Can you hear me?"

She started. The voice was faint. Someone. A small, dark-haired woman was sitting opposite her, pen in hand, a sheaf of papers on her lap. The papers rustled. Why hadn't she noticed before?

"Can you hear me?" the dark-haired woman said again. "I'm Barbara Bullard."

"Yes, I hear you, but not well. Where am I?" Her head, even her cheekbones, throbbed; her eyes burned. She pulled the blanket closer.

"You had an accident. You're in Mount Sinai Hospital."

She moved her limbs slowly, testing. Her head hurt. "What kind of accident?" Something like what happened to the woman when the homeless man hit her with a brick? "What happened to me?"

"You were found in Central Park during the snowstorm, without a coat, cut and bruised and suffering from burns and exposure."

"I don't understand. How long have I been here?"

"Three days."

"I think I'd like to go home."

"Where do you live?"

"I—" Where did she live? "I live on—" The itch started behind her ears, traveled to her neck and arms. She tugged at her gown, washed her hands in air, then groped around her on the floor. "It's in my wallet. Where's my bag?"

Barbara Bullard made notes on one of her papers. "You didn't have it when they brought you in. That's why you're here. You had an accident. If you'll give us your name, we'll get in touch with your family."

Well, of course, wasn't that ridiculous? "My name is—" She didn't know her name. She staggered up, hands flailing, knocking over the chair. "I don't know my own name. What's happening to me?" Fear clumped in her breast, choking her. She gasped for air, straining her throat, tears streamed.

"You're hyperventilating," Barbara Bullard said, righting the chair and helping her sit. A paper bag materialized and was held over her patient's face. "Breathe now, slowly and deeply. It'll stop."

It did stop, but the terror didn't. It broke over her in gigantic waves. She surrendered.

She awoke in sunshine, remembering the woman in her dream, standing up high, singing her sad song. The song faded. She lay still, getting a sense of herself, the odd metallic taste in her mouth. The bed was not hers. The room was not hers. The walls were a soft green. Her mind was empty.

"Good morning. How are you feeling this morning?"

The woman who came into the room had curly red hair and freckles.

"You're Dr. Hirsch."

"Good, you remember. We gave you something to calm you and you had a good night's sleep."

"What time is it?" Her stomach gave a fierce growl.

"Eleven o'clock. You must be hungry."

"I guess." She tried to raise herself, but her elbows were sore and she was shaking again. "What I am is scared. What's wrong with me? Why can't I remember anything?"

"You remembered me. You remembered my name. What you have is a dissociative disorder—temporary amnesia—caused by some kind of trauma."

She fought back the tears. It seemed that was all she was doing. Crying. "I'm sorry to be such a baby. What am I going to do? I have nowhere to go."

Dr. Hirsch handed her a tissue. "First, you're going to have something to eat, then I want you to sign yourself in voluntarily. You'll stay here. We're going to help you find your way back."

"I can't believe this is happening to me. Where is my bag? Was I mugged?"

"You had no ID when you were brought in. Nothing in your pockets."

"In other words I am Jane Doe." Bitter words. She forced herself to sit up.

Dr. Hirsch reacted. "You get a gold star. Until we find your name, we'll call you Jane, temporarily. Do you mind?"

"Do I have a choice?" She threw back the blanket. "My God, I'm wearing a hospital thing. I can't just lie here. Where are my clothes? I want to get dressed."

"You were wearing a black dress and black pantyhose. They're not in good shape. We'll have to find you something for the time being."

"Not in good shape?" She tried to remember. They'd

mentioned her clothes . . . something about blood. "Blood! It was blood!"

"Your clothing was covered with dried blood and other matter."

"Blood? Mine?"

"You had no wounds that would cause that much of it."

Temporary Jane put her hands over her eyes because the tears had started again. "What if I killed someone and I don't remember?"

They were interrupted by the arrival of a tray full of stainless steel covers and the smell of toast. Covers were removed, revealing a bowl of oatmeal, pats of butter, small containers of milk and orange juice. Coffee.

"I hate oatmeal, and I don't drink milk." She buttered her toast.

"What do you eat?" Rachel Hirsch asked. She pulled over a chair and sat down.

"Bagels and black coffee."

"Where do you get your bagels? H & H?"

Temporary Jane savored the buttered toast, her hands shaking. "Never! They put sugar in their bagels."

"I didn't know that. So where do you go for bagels?"

"Zabar's." Jane paused, hand halfway to her mouth.

Rachel Hirsch smiled. "Yes. You see. It's coming back. In all probability you live on the Upper West Side. The most important thing is to relax and try not to be afraid."

"I'll try, but I can't stand feeling so . . . so . . . helpless." She took a sip of the coffee. "This is terrible coffee."

"I'm afraid you're right."

"How am I going to pay for all this?"

"Don't think about it. You probably have some kind of insurance, and if you don't, we will absorb it. It's the law in this state."

"That's a relief. Did I have shoes?"

"Yes, but they were sodden. They'll be of no use to you."

"Sodden? Blood?"

"That and snow, too. I'll get you some booties."

Temporary Jane waited until the door closed, then she got to her feet, gingerly, and padded to the door. She opened it just a crack. Fairly quiet. Where were the other patients? A man wandered by in pajama bottoms, a hospital robe hanging open. Hairy belly, barefoot. He was talking to himself. He looked crazy. She shut the door.

What did she look like? She became aware of her own hair, touching it. It was long, falling over her shoulders in what felt like straggles and snarls. There were no mirrors on the walls. No paintings. It came thundering down on her: this was the psychiatric floor. She could feel the panic building again, short erratic breaths.

"Here we are." Dr. Hirsch was back carrying a pair of green booties. She set them on the table near the bed. "Your shoes were black patent leather with fabric bows. Nice shoes. You have good taste."

Jane felt her breathing moderate. "They're Ferragamos. That's what I wear."

"Do you feel up to finishing our interview?"

She nodded, walking around the room, her energy askew. Pausing, she said, "Do you want me to sign that paper?"

"Yes." Rachel Hirsch took some folded papers from the pocket of her white coat and put them on the table next to the tray. She handed Jane her pen. "You are signing yourself in."

The pen was heavy in her hand. She didn't move, except to rock back and forth slightly. "Just like that?"

"Until you know your name and where you live, or—" she smiled "—someone in your family takes custody."

"What do I sign? Make an X?"

"Sign in as Jane Doe. Go easy on yourself. When you feel the anxiety coming, take deep breaths."

She signed the papers. "What if my memory never comes back?"

"It will, and sooner rather than later." Dr. Hirsch took the papers and put them in her pocket, hooked the pen to the breast pocket of her coat. "I'll see what we can come up with in the way of clothing, okay?"

"Okay. And a comb and a mirror, too, please." She-who-was-now-Jane watched Rachel Hirsch leave, then she scurried to the door and once more opened it a crack. An elderly man passed by wearing normal clothes. Was he a visitor?

Voices came to her from beyond the door.

"You're Dr. Hirsch?" a woman said.

"Yes. You wanted to see me?"

"I'm Detective Holly Hogan. I want to talk to your Jane Doe."

Chapter 6

Holly Hogan was a hefty woman, and tall, her sturdy body forced into clothing that looked a size or two small. She wore pants that stopped at the ankle, thick-soled running shoes, a bulky sweater, and a navy, quilted down vest. Her light brown hair was tied back in a ponytail. She dwarfed the chair.

"Do you feel up to answering a few questions?" She gave Jane a reassuring smile and reached into an inside pocket.

"If I don't know who I am and what happened to me, how can I answer your questions?" Irritated, Jane focused on Holly Hogan's physical action of removing the notepad from her pocket, then on the notepad itself. It was a familiar process, a familiar object. She was sitting on the edge of the bed, feet dangling. "I'm sorry. I guess that sounds rude, but how else can I put it?"

Rachel Hirsch arrived with another chair and a warning to Detective Hogan in her eyes, which her patient registered.

"What *do* you remember?" Hogan asked.

"Nothing before the emergency room and even that is hazy."

"You don't know how you got all that blood on your clothing?"

"No. Can you check to see if anyone's reported me— someone like me—missing?"

"I will. I'm going to take your clothing to the lab and see what they come up with."

"The lab? Oh, God, was I raped?" She looked at Dr. Hirsch, horrified. "I don't feel raped. Could I have been raped and not know it?"

"You wore pantyhose. Blood had seeped through from your dress. Not evidence of rape. You're wearing a ring."

Jane touched the rolling rings on the ring finger of her left hand. Why hadn't she noticed them before now? Maybe because they hadn't been on her finger? Could someone have slipped them on while she was sleeping?

The room began to undulate, the sad song obliterated by a blast of sound.

"Catch her," someone said.

"Breakfast."

She rolled onto her back and pulled the covers over her head. "Not now." Every muscle in her body screamed.

Dishes rattled nearby. "There's a bathroom a short way down the hall, on your left."

"I know where my bathroom is," she said, annoyed. The smell of buttered toast and coffee filtered into her nostrils. It was a while before her limbs would obey orders. Finally, she sat up with a jerk and looked around, remembering only not remembering. Her back ached and the light hurt her eyes. Whoever had brought the tray was gone. She ate the lukewarm toast greedily; she was starved.

Afterward, she ventured from her room to the bathroom. A youngish woman in a chenille bathrobe was coming out. She made eye contact with Jane for an instant, then looked away and scurried into the room next door. She looked like any normal New Yorker except for the bandages on her wrists that glanced from under the sleeves of her robe.

The bathroom had a toilet and a stall shower. No mirror.

Oh, for a hot shower, she thought. She would ask for one.

When she got back to her room, she saw someone had left some clothing on the bed. Black leggings, bulky sport socks, a big red sweater, a tee-shirt, and cotton panties. Worn Keds rested on the floor next to the bed. She leaned against the wall near her door, away from the window, which had no blinds, and quickly put on her new clothes. Everything was a little too big, but it didn't matter. It felt right.

She touched the wall with her fingertips and slipped into first position. Yes. Now second, third, *releve, plié*. Again. The door opened, catching her in mid-*plié*.

Dr. Hirsch said, "You're a dancer."

She finished the *plié*. "I'm a dancer," she repeated. "I am a dancer." She twirled around the small room. "Yes! I am a dancer!" She sank into a chair, her burst of energy dissipated, her anxiety replenished. "Thank you for the clothes."

"I brought them from home. My sister knitted the sweater."

The sweater was unusual; it had a design knitted into it: little black Scotties. She rubbed her fingers on the dogs. Something . . . She jumped up and rushed to the door, where Dr. Hirsch blocked her way. "My dog. I have to go home."

"You can't go home until you remember where home is. You have a dog?"

"Yes." She came back to the bed and threw herself down. "Who's going to feed my dog?"

Dr. Hirsch touched her shoulder. "You know you're a dancer, you probably live on the Upper West Side, and you own a dog. Your memory is coming back."

"Tell me again, how long have I been here?"

"You came in late Saturday night. Today is Tuesday."

"She'll starve."

"She?"

"My dog. What am I going to do?" She sat up, plucking at her new clothes.

Dr. Hirsch took a packet from the pocket of her white coat and shook a small pill into her palm.

"I don't want it."

"It will ease your anxiety."

"It will make me groggy and leave an unpleasant taste in my mouth. I have to be aware of what's happening to me."

"The anxiety is normal in this kind of situation. If we let it go on, it could develop into panic."

"I won't let it."

That brought an immediate smile to Dr. Hirsch's face. She slid the pill back into the packet. "Too much control is not helpful either. Barbara Bullard is going to work with you today. I don't want you to do too much. Tomorrow morning we'll get your eyes checked and your ears. Are you still hearing noise?"

"It comes and goes. I wish I could make out what it is. And there's the woman singing—"

"What woman?"

"I don't know. She's on a hill, some place high up. I can't see her, but I hear her singing."

"What is she singing?"

"I don't know. Just that it's very sad."

"It may be connected to what happened. It'll become clearer as your memory returns."

"Black."

"White."

"Sand."

"Beach."

"Dog."

"Cat."

"Cold."

"Hot."

"Dancer."

"Me."

"Dog."

"We did that already."

"Go with me. Close your eyes and take a deep breath. Work."

"Play."

"Bagel."

"Zabar's." She was tired. Her eyelids had grown heavy, heavier. "I want to lie down now."

"Just one more, okay?"

"Okay." Her chin nudged her collarbone.

"Dog."

The room began to spin. "I can't—"

Hands held her still. "Try. I'm holding you. Dog."

"Dead."

Chapter 7

The tunnel was long and brightly lit. She felt like an inmate with an attendant. She *was* an inmate with an attendant. They followed a circuitous route up some stairs, down some other stairs, through an atrium, into another building. Pedestrian traffic, a few patients, but mostly health professionals, all with plastic labels—doctors, nurses, social workers, administrators—rushing. No one strolled. Everyone seemed to know everyone else and Barbara Bullard was no exception.

"What is that?" It looked a lot like a library or bookstore, right in the middle of the hospital.

"It's a library," Barbara Bullard said. "I'm planning a visit this afternoon. Would you like to come? You can pick out something to read—like a book on dogs— that may help jog your memory."

Dr. Gillette, the ophthalmologist, bore an uncanny resemblance to the actor Michael Fox. He was light-haired and preppy in a navy sport coat and gray flannel trousers. His yellow oxford cloth button-down was very Brooks Brothers. He read the material in the folder Barbara Bullard handed him, then said, "Okay, let's have a look at you. I'm going to put these drops in your eyes to dilate your pupils." He was chewing gum.

His moving jaws made her testy, as did the procedure, but Dr. Gillette didn't seem to notice her pique. When the first drop hit, she gasped and brushed his hand away and, hugging herself, rocked back and forth. She was on fire.

"Keep cool," he said. "It'll subside. I have to do your other eye."

The pain was agonizing. "I can't," she cried, coming out of her chair.

"Keep blinking," he said. "I promise it will subside."

She sat down again. "I've had these tests before but never this pain."

"You remember eye examinations though?"

"Just a sense of it." She responded with more ease as the pain receded. These people were her lifeline. How stupid she would be to alienate them. It was better to be docile, yet somehow she knew that docile was not her basic nature.

"Do you wear glasses? Contacts?"

"I don't know."

"Don't think so. Look up. Okay. Don't move your head, just your eyes. Look right . . . left. Been seeing spots last couple of days? Headache?"

"Doesn't that come with a bad bump on the head?"

"Sometimes, not always. Let me see it." He ran his hand lightly over the back of her scalp, the side of her head.

"Ouch."

"Okay. No double vision?"

"You ask me that after you put the drops in?"

Dr. Gillette chuckled and tilted his head toward Barbara Bullard. "Any allergies? Your eyes are bloodshot, very irritated."

Well, duh, she thought. Didn't you just do that? "How would I know? My eyes tear. Maybe it's from the pill they give me to keep me from being agitated."

"I don't think so," Bullard said. "And you haven't had a pill since Sunday night. It's now Wednesday."

★ ★ ★

A Dr. Pentil was the next stop. His speech was so thick and incomprehensible, Temporary Jane whispered to her escort, "He's going to check my hearing? You have to be kidding."

Still, he was able to pronounce her eardrums bruised but with no permanent damage, and by the end of the session, she was beginning to be able to understand what he was saying.

"What about the noise I keep hearing?" she asked.

"Is it static noise?"

"I can't make it out."

"It's the result of the blow on your head. Is it less than it was?"

"Yes."

"It will go away."

Detective Hogan was waiting in her room when they got back, staring out the window at the snow.

"She needs some rest," Barbara Bullard said.

"I won't be long. You're looking a bit better. How are you doing?"

"I'm tired. They just tested my eyes and my hearing." Hogan was a blur. "I can't see you clearly because of the drops." She lay on the bed, exhausted from the morning's activities.

Bullard pulled the blanket over her. "You have to stay warm."

"Did you look at the missing persons stuff?"

"Nothing that fits your description through yesterday. I'll check again this afternoon."

"I have a dog. I remembered that. She needs me. Who's going to feed her?"

Hogan made a note in her notepad. "I'll send a notice to the Twentieth and the Two-four precincts on the Upper West Side to be alert for a barking or howling dog. We'll find her."

"My clothes. The blood." Sleep was beginning a slow drip to her veins.

"Your dress had a Donna Karan label. That's high-end designer merchandise."

"Which means . . . I have money—or a rich lover." Her words were squashy to her ear. She was holding on, but barely. "The blood?"

"Not yours. Not just one person's either."

"I'm Candy Pandolfi," the woman said, a half-eaten tuna fish sandwich in her hand. "You're the one who's got amnesia." It was a statement, not a question, and it came from the woman with the bandages on her wrists. "Sit here." She pointed to the chair next to her. "The tuna is passable, forget the rest."

She didn't want to sit with the woman, but she didn't want to offend her either. It was a question of living in the same area, and who knew how long that might be? The only other person in the dining room was the man she'd seen wandering around yesterday, or the day before, in pajama bottoms. He was muttering to himself.

Sandwiches were stacked near the coffee urn. She picked out one that was labeled tuna, then filled a coffee cup, picked up a plastic spoon—no forks or knives in psychiatric—and brought it all back to the table, where Candy was leafing through *People* magazine.

Candy rolled up the magazine and slipped it under her sweater and into the waistband of her slacks.

Watching, Jane shivered, thought, someone's walking

over my grave. The eerie sensation was gone in a moment but a shadow remained.

"There's ice cream in the cold tub, and sodas."

"I'm okay." Tuna on white bread. She hated white bread. Institutional food for the institutionalized. She peeled back the bread and used the spoon to eat the tuna.

"That's why you're so thin." Candy got up and took two cups of ice cream from the tub. "One for you and one for me."

"Thank you." It was chocolate. She liked chocolate. If only she could stand back dispassionately and watch the onion as it unpeeled. She had money, she wore good clothes, she had a dog, she was a dancer, she lived on the Upper West Side, liked coffee, bagels, and chocolate, and didn't like white bread. And something terrible had happened to her.

"I'm a real estate broker," Candy said. "I guess you don't know what you do." She got up and took another cup of ice cream. "Want seconds?"

"No to more ice cream and I don't know to what I do."

"My husband left me for the babysitter."

"I'm sorry."

"Oh, that's all right. He was a putz anyway. No loss except to him. I'm going to make him pay through the nose. They'll never live together happy."

"You have children?"

"Two. My mother has them." She took a photograph from her pocket. "See." Pressing her lips together, she said, "We'll be all right." The picture showed a more attractive Candy Pandolfi with two dark-haired, laughing little boys.

She thought, I don't have any children.

"Okay, who wants to go to the library?" Barbara Bullard

came into the dining room and helped herself to some coffee.

"I do," Candy said.

Temporary Jane stood up. She threw the detritus of her lunch in the trash bin.

They took the elevator downstairs and went through the tunnel to the library.

She felt immediate comfort in the library. It was cozy and warm. People were browsing in the stacks. Others were sitting at tables reading. She requested a book on dogs, with pictures. If she saw a dog that looked like hers, it might bring everything back.

The books about dogs were all together on one shelf. She picked out the one that listed the breeds with photographs and took it back to a table. It was Wednesday. Did she have a job? Had someone fed her dog? No one had reported her missing. Where was her husband or lover? Why wasn't he looking for her?

"You can take it out and look through it when we get back." Barbara Bullard relieved her of the book and went to the desk, where Candy had an Agatha Christie waiting.

In the tunnel, they followed a small group of well-dressed men and perfectly coiffed women, led by another woman who was talking about the design of the new building.

"Who are they?" Candy asked.

"Trustees, probably, philanthropists, whatever. Deep pockets," Barbara Bullard commented. "They're getting a tour of the new psychiatric floor, so we'll just follow along behind them."

Every footfall grew more leaden. The hum of the voices of the trustees surrounded her. Almost there, almost there. When they arrived at the bank of elevators, the visitors had filled one entirely.

Bullard motioned them to wait for the next one.

As the doors were closing, a man called out, "Wait!" Too late, the doors closed.

Another elevator arrived. They got on. Up they went to the fifth floor. Off on the fifth floor.

A man in a dark gray pinstripe was waiting. Under his thin, styled gray hair, his face alive with expectation. He didn't look at Barbara Bullard or Candy Pandolfi. He was looking at her.

"My dear," he said, "don't you know me?"

Chapter 8

"What happened?"

"It's one of the trustees. He knows her. When he spoke to her, she fainted."

I didn't faint. I'm awake. I hear you. She tried to force the words into the open, but her brain wouldn't connect.

"Mary Lou . . ."

"Excuse me, sir—"

"What's wrong with her?"

"Let's get her back to bed. Someone call Dr. Hirsch."

"Dr. Hirsch. And you are—"

"I had no idea. I was getting the tour when I saw her."

"You know who she is?"

"Of course. Her name is Mary Lou Salinger. She's my niece. What is she doing here? She looked right at me and didn't seem to know me."

Mary Lou Salinger.

"She came in Friday night. She was found in a bus shelter on Fifth. She was hypothermic and has dissociative amnesia—"

"Amnesia? How could that happen?"

"Memory loss that's not drug induced, and hers wasn't, can come from a trauma of some sort, either psychological or physical. It's usually a short-term condition."

"My God. She didn't know me."

"Possibly she had a spark of recognition. Whatever, she's very fragile right now."

"I want to talk with her."

"Well, let's see how she's doing. Please stay outside, Mr. . . ."

"Gold. Lewis Gold."

Mary Lou.

The hazy cotton cocoon kept her ensnared. But she could hear what they were saying and they weren't even in the room. When she tried to open her eyes, the room careened like a carousel gone nuts. The woman was singing, high and sharp.

Nuts. That's what she was. The man who knew her, what had he called her? Mary Lou something. Mary Lou. Yes. Mary Lou Salinger. Easy as pie.

She opened her eyes. The spinning slowed, then drifted to a halt. The singing stopped. Dr. Hirsch was standing beside the bed, taking her pulse.

"Mary Lou?"

"Yes."

"You know your name?"

"I think so. That man knows me. Is he a doctor?"

"He's a big donor. His name is Lewis Gold. He says you're his niece, Mary Lou Salinger."

She shook her head, eased herself up. The room did not spin. "I didn't recognize him."

"He wants to talk to you. Do you feel up to it?"

She was afraid, patted her hair nervously—did she need a comb?—bit her lips. "Will you stay with me?"

"Yes, I'll be here with you."

He had a thin smile and cold brown eyes, was younger than she expected. His gray suit was expensively tailored. Her fingers worried the rolling rings.

"Mary Lou, my dear," he said, pulling a chair close to the bed. His black Gucci loafers looked out of place with his suit. "What happened to you?"

"How do you know me . . . Mr. . . . Gold?"

He looked at Dr. Hirsch. "Uncle Lew," he said. "You were married to my nephew, Richard."

She looked at him with horror. "Married? Richard?"

"Richard was killed in an automobile accident six months ago."

His gaze was so intent, she looked away, her eyes tearing. He took her hand and brought it to his lips. Revolted, she pulled her hand away from him.

"Mary Lou." Dr. Hirsch rose. "Perhaps we should let Mary Lou rest for now, Mr. Gold."

"I understand. I'd like to arrange for Mary Lou to come home."

"I don't think that would be a good idea just yet."

"I don't mean to her home. She can stay with me until she's well again."

"I don't want to leave here."

"We'll see, my dear," Gold said, smiling. He picked up the phone next to the bed. "If I may, I'd like to let our lawyer know where you are."

No!

"It hasn't been connected, Mr. Gold," Dr. Hirsch said blandly. "There's one in the visitors' lounge." She steered him toward the door.

"I'll see you tomorrow, my dear." To Dr. Hirsch, he whispered, loud enough for Mary Lou to hear. "She's been despondent since Richard's death. What really happened to her?"

"Whatever it was, she can't remember. But it will come back."

"Wait," Mary Lou said. "I have a dog."

Lewis Gold hesitated in the doorway, turned back to her. "No, Mary Lou. You're allergic to dogs."

Tears crept down her cheeks. He was wrong.

Dr. Hirsch paused. "Stay still, Mary Lou. I'll be right back."

She nodded. Confused, she got up and went to the window. The snow continued to fall, the texture of fine sugar.

She had no memory of what had happened to her, but knew one thing for sure. She was not Mary Lou Salinger.

Chapter 9

"What's troubling you, Mary Lou?"

White light surrounded her, cushioned her as her eyes filled with it. She flattened hands and face against the window. The woman began her sad song.

"Mary Lou?" A hand lodged gently on her shoulder.

With languid inertia, she pulled herself away from the hypnotic radiance.

"Too much excitement," Dr. Hirsch said, steering her to the bed. "Are you still hearing the woman singing?"

"Yes."

"She sounds a little like the Lorelei."

"The Lorelei?"

"Yes, you know, the legendary seductress on the cliff who drew sailors to shipwreck with her sweet song." She patted Mary Lou's shoulder. "Rest now."

Obedient, tucked in, almost immobile, she closed her eyes. Yes, she would rest. Her breath became slow and deep. She opened her mind to her thoughts. And as they swirled, she gave each thought value, even those that frightened her. When she finished her meditation, for this is what it was, and she recognized that she was comfortable with the process, she understood what she had to do.

The dinner trays were delivered at five o'clock. Mushroom barley soup and stewed cod with rice and vegetables. She saved the saltines and wrapped the roll in napkins. She would need them later. While she ate the bland food, she turned the pages of the book on dogs. Her whole existence was uncertain, but she knew she owned a dog.

After dinner, she closed the book on the photo and description of the Labrador retriever and strolled down the hallway to the nurses' station.

In a small glass-fronted room off the station, a nurse called Lucy sat at a desk yawning over paperwork. The nurse at the station was on the telephone. She looked up. "Do you need anything, Mary Lou?"

"No. Just getting some exercise." They both looked tired; their shift changed at ten o'clock. She'd watched and clocked them, not yet certain how it would work. The great escape.

When they came around with the sleeping pill, she took it without protest, slipping it to the side of her mouth, and then into a tissue as soon as the door closed.

All she had to do now was wait until the lights in the corridor were dimmed and the footfalls of both patients and staff ceased and the uneasy institutional night settled in.

There was a script for this. She'd seen it in movies. You take the extra pillows and blankets from the closet and shape a body, drawing the covers around it. In the dark it looks like a sleeper.

She didn't know what time it was when she opened the door a crack. Time here was not real anyway. The corridor both ways was empty. No one was at the nurses' station. No one. She knew Lucy usually hit the bathroom before she went off her shift.

A dark blue down jacket was hanging from the back of a chair in the small office. "Sorry, Lucy." She put it on. She needed it more than Lucy did right now. There were gloves in one pocket and a woolen ski cap in the other. And a wallet. The moral dilemma held her for only a moment. She took the cash—sixty dollars—and the MetroCard. That was all. It was bad enough she was stranding Lucy without a coat.

But she had no choice. Her life was in danger. If she lived, she would find some way to make it up to Lucy.

Down the hall to the elevators. Total quiet here. She pressed the down button, pulled the knit cap over her ears. If she made it to the lobby without seeing anyone, she'd be home free, or at the least, on the street. She had no thought of anything else, otherwise she might have wondered what she would do on upper Madison Avenue late at night without a place to go. Or maybe even if her loss of memory, her trauma, had made her so paranoid that she wasn't thinking straight.

The street was a wide, white ribbon in spite of the occasional car and the surreal lights of a bus heading uptown. Snow reeled lazily in the wind, dazzling her eyes, fuzzing the light from the streetlamp, the night crystal like frozen tears. The gloves were wool and stretched to fit her hands.

She started walking. Some coffee shops were open twenty-four hours, but where? Bus and train stations. Grand Central Station. She would wait out the night over a cup of coffee and maybe by daylight she would have a plan.

She hurried along Madison Avenue, passing only a few pedestrians, some protected by umbrellas, all with heads down against the icy wind and snow. It would be safer, she thought, to cross over to Lexington on Eighty-sixth Street at this time of night. That gave her pause. Her real life was definitely here in New York. She was familiar enough with the city to think of Grand Central Station and to know that the bus went downtown on Lexington. Maybe things would begin slipping back to her. She would be sitting with her coffee in Grand Central Station, and pow, her memory would be back and she could just go home.

By the time she got to the bus stop on Eighty-sixth and Lexington, the Keds were sodden and her feet were icicles in her sopping socks. An elderly woman, her head covered by a hood, had flattened herself against the window of the Hot and Crusty to take advantage of the narrow eave. She held two shopping bags high, trying to keep them from getting wet, but she wasn't succeeding.

"Have you been waiting long?"

The woman shrugged, her eyes glued uptown, desperate for a glimpse of a bus. A small sigh, then the hazy headlights of a bus came out of the mist moving slowly toward them.

Lucy's MetroCard got Temporary Jane on the bus without a problem, and there was enough left on it for two full rides. But when she took it from the machine, the blue ID hospital bracelet slid into view. She pulled the sleeve of the ski jacket over her wrist and as she moved into the bus, she tried to tear the ID off. She took a seat, tried to chew it off. No luck. She needed scissors or a sharp knife. She tucked it out of sight.

In the front of the bus the old woman settled herself behind the driver, bunching her wet shopping bags on the seat next to her. In the sudden warmth, the bags relaxed and began to drip.

A couple of Hispanic kids were murmuring and necking in the back of the bus. Otherwise, it was empty. As it made its way down Lexington, more people got on, but as is often the case in inclement weather, each person becomes too involved in his own comfort to even notice another.

She left the bus at the Grand Central stop and made her way into the terminal. Shops and coffee bars were scattered around the entire area, though not in the magnificent main terminal. Some of the shops, the produce stands and places that sold meat and fish, were closed. But the terminal was a Mecca for night people, some going to work, some homeward bound, some going nowhere, like her. And no one took any notice of her as she walked around looking for a place where she could sit over a cup of coffee.

Main Street Coffee was only a sliver, four stools in front of a black granite counter, two tiny tables with chairs only small-bottomed people would find comfortable. Here's your brew and what's your hurry.

A slight young woman stood behind the counter, scrubbing the surface with a wet cloth. Her hair was a deep walnut, a mass of shimmering sausage curls banded, for the health department, on top of her head, but irrepressible nevertheless. She had gold studs in her nose and lobes, and thin wires lining the outer edge of both ears.

She looked up and stared. "Hey, dude, don't I know you?" she said.

Chapter 10

"You know me?" She tried to keep her voice low, the question casual.

"You sort of look familiar. What'll you have, dude?" The pierced one's eyes were wide set, charcoal in color, and highlighted dramatically with black liner. Her nose was barely a button. She had another stud in her tongue. On her hands, thin surgical gloves.

Temporary Jane sat on the stool. "Coffee, black. How late are you open?"

"All night. I'm the night shift." A cup was produced, filled, and placed on the countertop.

"Isn't it lonely?"

"I don't mind. It's a job. I have a real career. It's just starting to build. So whatever pays the rent."

The steam was rich with aroma. It filled Jane's nostrils, left a gentle film of moisture on her cheeks and the tip of her nose. A calm settled over her. She took off the knit cap and her hair tumbled around her face.

"Hey, dude," the young woman said. "I would have thought you were a blonde." She grinned. "I'm thinking of going that next."

"Your hair suits you. I hope you don't mind my saying, but you make me smile when I look at you."

She jumped straight up in the air, grinning, her arms undulating wings, and came down almost in slow motion. Her curls were puppet limbs following her descent. "You're supposed to smile. Mimes bring that out, among other emotions. I'm part of a troupe. We're just starting to get paying gigs. I'm Zoey, by the way."

"Pleased to meet you, Zoey. I like your name."

"It's from a book, like in Franny and— My mom was into Salinger."

Salinger. J. D., not Mary Lou. Was she real, this Mary Lou Salinger? "*Franny and Zooey*," she said. "Zooey was a guy."

"They wanted a boy."

"So you became Zoey."

Zoey was giving her that stare again. "What did you say your name was?"

She took a sip of the coffee. It was as good as it smelled.

Temporary Jane, she thought. T.J. Yes, why not T.J.? "T.J.," she said.

"T.J., like Teresa Judy?"

"Or Tillie Joan."

Zoey giggled. "Or Tabitha Jill."

They both laughed.

A workman went by outside the shop and the flash of his blinking worklight filled the small space. Zoey froze, stared off into the distance. Her eyes rolled back. She slipped out of sight.

Stunned, T.J. leaned over the counter. Zoey lay on the floor, thrashing, her head rigid. A seizure. Projecting herself off the stool, T.J. squeezed into the small space behind the counter. She raised Zoey's head slightly, and stroked her cool forehead. Spittle oozed from the corner of Zoey's mouth.

She'd call 911, but there was no phone that she could see and she didn't want to leave Zoey. A minute or so might be okay. A minute or so went by and the twitching began to subside. Color came back to Zoey's face.

Zoey's lids fluttered, opened. She sighed. "I'm sorry, dude."

"Just stay still. I'm going to call 911."

Zoey clutched her hand. "No, you can't. Please. I'll lose my job."

"But you've had a seizure."

"I have epilepsy. Help me sit up. I'll be okay, honest. I just have to sleep for a little while."

"I'll close the shop then."

"No, please. I don't know you, but you seem so nice. Could you just stay behind the counter for me and pour coffee if anyone comes in?"

"I can't—"

"I know it's asking a lot, but please. The coffee is ready. All you have to do is pour it and take the money. I need to close my eyes for a few minutes." She stripped off the vinyl gloves. "Here, put these on. We're supposed to wear them."

"I don't know how to work an espresso machine."

"Say . . . broke down." Zoey's words were thick and mushied. She threw off the packages of napkins on the shelf under the counter, and even before T.J. had finished helping her onto it, Zoey was asleep.

She listened to the even breathing, then rose and took off the down jacket. Temporary Jane was now temporary counterperson.

With shaking hands, she straightened the fingers of Zoey's gloves and inserted her own, smoothing the gloves into a second skin. She refilled her coffee mug with regular coffee and wiped up the spill. She would need the caffeine and a steadier hand. It was going to be a long night, and maybe, just maybe, after a healing sleep, Zoey might remember why she looked familiar.

Chapter 11

"Where's the other one?"

T.J. snapped awake. A burly man in a yellow plastic hardhat was grinning at her. "I'm sorry." She blinked. Coffee. The coffee bar. As coffee bar tender, she said, "I'm filling in for Zoey tonight. What can I get you?"

"The top of the line. Tall, black, and leaded, to go."

She slid the cardboard collar on the steaming tower and handed it to him. "Would you know the time?"

"Almost six," he said. He waved off the change from his two dollars and left.

T.J. knelt down and gave Zoey a nudge. "Zoey? Are you okay?"

Zoey sighed, stirred.

"What time does your shift end?"

Eyes glued shut, Zoey crawled out from under the counter. "Six."

"It's almost six now."

"Shit." She listed against T.J. "Thanks for covering for me, dude."

"Can you open your eyes? Ah, there you are."

"I'm okay," Zoey said.

"You look a little fragile."

"Fragile. I like that." Zoey's smile was full of sleep. "But you can leave me now. I'm really okay."

Leave? She had nowhere to go. She came out from behind the counter and sat on one of the stools. "I'll have a cappuccino," she said. "To stay."

60

Zoey made cappuccino, for two. "Maurice is late."

"Maurice?"

"He's here from six. He should have been here by now."

The skin under Zoey's eyes was dark, bruised. She bent down and returned the items on the floor to the shelf.

"Where do you live, Zoey? I think I should see you home."

"You don't have to—"

"I'll feel better if I do."

"What about you?"

"Ah, that's another story," T.J. said. "You see, I'm running away from home." She removed the vinyl gloves and dropped them into the trash container.

The tardy Maurice, pumped with adrenalin, made his entrance on Zoey's giggle. Dry snow flaked his nylon quilted ski jacket, added luster to his round, black cheeks. "You won't believe it! Do you know what's going on out there?"

Grabbing her down jacket, T.J. tucked her hair into the knit cap. They were looking for her. She had to get away. But wait, she told herself. Slow down. They couldn't know where she was.

Zoey stepped out from behind the counter. Three people were waiting to be served. "I'm tired. I'm getting into a cab."

"You'll never get a cab." He shrugged out of his jacket, reached under the counter for an apron and gloves. "Be with you in a minute, folks." Aside, he said, "There're ambulances all over the place and cops. Bus skidded into the Hyatt and they closed off the street. Just get on the subway."

See, T.J. told herself, you're not that important. But she had to find a place to stay until she figured out what to do next.

Zoey grabbed her arm and steered her out of the coffee bar, calling, "Bye, Maurice," as she struggled into her black duffel coat. The corridor was getting crowded, people rushing to work, lining up for coffee. "You're running away?"

T.J. nodded. "I have no place to go."

"Come with me," Zoey said. "I need you to. I'm scared."

Not as scared as I am, Zoey, she thought.

They got out of the subway at Astor Place and trudged through the snow to Fifth Street.

The building was old and squat, eight stories of flat, gray stone that had once been white. Its entrance was unattended and Zoey let herself in with a key. A rickety, unmanned elevator left them on the sixth floor. "I'm house sitting," Zoey said, as she unlocked the door. "It's a good deal for me. All I have to do is take care of the cat and water the plants until they get back. They'll be gone about three more months." She stepped inside and turned on the light and called, "Chat?"

"What about your apartment?" T.J. followed Zoey, taking in the small space, the closet of a kitchen, the tiny living room. Her eyes began to prickle. She sneezed once, then again.

"I don't have one, dude. I'm a professional house sitter." Zoey threw her coat on the small sofa. "Make yourself at home. I have to feed Chat." When T.J. sneezed again, she said, "I hope you're not allergic."

"I don't know if I am." Her so-called Uncle Lew had said she was allergic to dogs. That is, Mary Lou Salinger was allergic to dogs.

T.J. hooked her jacket on the knob of the front door. She

stood in the doorway of the kitchen as Zoey opened a can of cat food and emptied it into a bowl. A ball of gray fur shot past, right for the bowl.

"I was wondering where you got to," Zoey told the cat, putting down some fresh water. She straightened, swaying. "I'm crashing. There's food in the fridge . . ."

T.J. caught Zoey by the waist. She put Zoey's arm around her shoulder and half walked, half dragged her to the open door beyond the living room. An even smaller bedroom, big enough for a double bed, unmade, a dresser, and a TV with cockeyed rabbit ears. She helped Zoey to the bed, took off her shoes, and covered her with the quilt. Zoey had passed out. But her breathing was even and her color was okay.

In the tiny bathroom, T.J. took off the sodden Keds, the stiffened socks, and her clothes, laying her leggings on the hot and sputtering radiator. The damned blue plastic ID was still with her. She wrapped herself in a towel and in the kitchen, with a paring knife, rid herself of the bracelet. The hot shower was respite, albeit transient.

Afterward, she rinsed the socks and her panties in the sink and hung them on the shower rod. She stuck the Keds under the radiator and pulled on the warm leggings. The floorboards creaked under her feet as she returned to the bedroom to check on Zoey. Sleep so deep. If only she could sleep as Zoey slept.

If only.

She walked to the window and closed the metal blinds against the bleak sunlight. A thin blanket lay on the floor near the bed. As she picked it up she knocked over a wicker wastebasket, spilling out used tissues and a rolled up newspaper.

The newspaper, the blanket, it was a sign. Maybe she

would sleep like Zoey. She lay down on the sofa in the tiny living room and covered herself with the blanket. It brought an involuntary sigh. She unrolled the newspaper, the *Post* it was, and flattened it so she could read the headline.

It said: *IT WAS MURDER! Four Known Dead in Mysterious Explosion.*

But it was the photograph that stopped her. There she was, the same face, but smiling and happy. Under the photograph:

Mary Lou Salinger. Missing and feared dead.

Chapter 12

Mary Lou Salinger. The man who claimed to be Mary Lou's uncle had told the truth. T.J. stared at the photograph in the newspaper. Mary Lou might be a real person, but I'm not her. And there was something really slimy about her uncle.

She searched her poor confused brain, hoping for a sliver of memory. Anything. Why had she found Mary Lou's uncle so frightening?

What if she'd been there at that explosion and the shock had caused her loss of memory? Why hadn't she read the rest of the article? Afraid? Yes.

The rest of the article was continued on pages two and three. An explosion on a private jet. Horrendous photos of the burned-out plane. The pilot dead and several others dead. The jet belonged to Jason McLaughlin, a financier. His flight plan was taking him to Italy. His companions were an assistant, this Mary Lou Salinger, a business manager, a secretary, as well as a chef who doubled as co-pilot. There had been people seen at the airport with McLaughlin before the explosion but they had not as yet come forward.

If she'd been there, in New Jersey—Teterboro Airport it said—how had she gotten back to the city? What was she doing wandering around Central Park without a coat and her dress saturated with blood . . . She covered her eyes. The more she thought about it the more anxious she became.

Someone had to have brought her, someone who'd been

there. Maybe someone involved in the explosion. Uncle Lew wanted something from her. She'd escaped. And he found her in Mount Sinai. Now she'd escaped again. She was safe here, for the time being. She tore the story from the newspaper, folded it, and tucked it into a pocket of her jacket still hanging from the doorknob.

A shrill shriek jarred her awake, eyes wide. She took in the blanket, the sofa, the small room. Panic subsided. She was safe wrapped in the blanket on Zoey's sofa. It was only a kettle whistle. She sank back and closed her eyes. The sensation of being watched penetrated her calm. She opened her eyes cautiously. Sneezed. Like the Sphinx, the gray cat lay on top of the back cushion of the sofa studying her.

"She likes you, dude," Zoey said. "She hardly ever comes out except when she's hungry."

T.J. threw off the blanket. Ebullient in a stretched and shapeless red sweater thrown over a leotard and black leggings, Zoey showed no sign of stress from the night before. "How do you feel?"

"Great!" She looked away with a careless smile. "I always feel great after one. Best sleep in the world."

"Don't you have medicine to prevent an attack?"

"Takes away my energy. Makes me feel like a zombie." She ducked back into the kitchen. "Coffee's almost ready. Hope you don't need milk."

"I don't. But, Zoey, isn't it dangerous? What if you have a seizure on a subway platform?"

Zoey shrugged. "You saved my life last night. What can I do for you?" She handed T.J. a mug of coffee.

Chat jumped down from the cushion, stretched, yawned, and curled up on T.J.'s lap. T.J. sneezed.

"You said you're running away from home." Zoey sat down next to T.J.

"Sort of."

"You can hide out here with me for as long as you like. I just don't have enough money to feed two of us."

"I'll get a job. If I can. I don't have any ID."

Zoey grinned and her abundance of curls bounced about her face. "Down here, that's not a problem. They don't want anyone on the books anyway."

"I'm going to need to change how I look."

"That's easy. I'm a whiz at that. You think I really look like this?" She jumped up. "It'll be fun doing a make-over."

"You're not asking me about my trouble."

"That's your business. Tell me if you want, when you want. You went out of your way for me. I owe you."

"You'll have to clothe me until I get a job."

"We're about the same size. But why don't you take a shower while I see what's here for breakfast besides stale muffins? Then we'll start with your hair. When we get finished, no one will recognize you. That's what you want, right?"

"Right." But T.J. saw it was a catch 22. If no one recognized her, she would be safe, but if no one recognized her, she wouldn't be able to find out who she really was and what had happened to her.

She dried her hair with Zoey's dryer, flipping the long dark hair over her face and drying the nape hair first.

"Hey, dude," Zoey said, surprise in her voice. "You know what?"

T.J. stopped the dryer and shook out her hair. "What?"

Zoey was scrutinizing her, puzzled. "Maybe I was wrong. Go back to what you were doing." When T.J. did, Zoey drawled, "So I guess you were just having a little fun with me."

Her fingers stopped the power. She faced Zoey frowning, fingers pushing the hair back from her face. "I don't know what you mean."

"Oh, come on, T.J., your hair is dyed right now. Your real hair color is coming through underneath and it's blonde."

Chapter 13

With deliberate care, T.J. handed Zoey the hair dryer and sat down on the edge of the tub. "I didn't know."

Zoey was all but indignant, more puzzled, standing there hands on hips. "How could you not know?"

T.J. groped for sense among the jumble filling her head. "I don't know because I don't know who I am."

"T.J., you said your name was T.J. and that you were running away." Zoey parked the dryer on its wall hook, draping the cord around it.

"T.J.—for Temporary Jane. They called me Jane Doe in the hospital."

Zoey was getting it. "You ran away from the hospital."

T.J. nodded.

"You don't remember anything?" There was awe in Zoey's voice.

"Nothing. They found me wandering in Central Park without a coat or ID. Then a man came to the hospital and said he knew me and was coming back the next day—today—to take me home."

"You didn't want to go with him?"

"I didn't like him. He scared me."

The phone rang.

"Where'd I put the phone?"

"Coffee table, I think," T.J. said. She followed Zoey into the living room.

"Maurice? Hi . . ." Zoey looked at T.J., eyes widening. "So, listen, what did you tell them?"

They were getting close. She could see it on Zoey's face.

She brushed past Zoey to get the down jacket from the front doorknob, but Zoey's hand caught her arm. She shook her head at T.J.

"Thanks, dude. I owe you. She's my friend . . . yeah, well, it's a long story." She pressed the off button. "Two cops came around because someone spotted you when you were filling in for me, said you looked like the missing girl."

"I've got to get out of here," T.J. said. "They weren't cops. They're going to kill me." She grabbed the jacket.

"No, no, wait a minute. Maurice told them I was the only one working there at that time, that I'm Zoey Kantor, not Mary Lou what's-her-face. Look at us. We're the same height, same coloring. Just the hairstyle is different."

"But they'll come here and find me."

"Maurice didn't tell them where I live. He doesn't know anyway. And he didn't give them my phone number. But he thinks they'll be back when it's my shift."

T.J. leaned against the front door, winded, afraid. "What am I going to do?"

But Zoey was elated. "First, we'll do your hair like mine, and then we'll talk to David. He'll know what to do. He always does."

"Who's David?" She didn't move from the door, didn't take off the jacket.

"He's our master."

"Master?" T.J. thought, what am I getting myself into?

Zoey giggled. "Chill, dude, we're not an S&M cult, we're mimes. We work out of David's loft on Avenue A."

The loft was in a former commercial building, its fundamentals hidden under a century plus of soot and layers of black paint. Tall, almost cathedralesque windows looked blearily down on Avenue A. The entranceway was stubby and narrow, walls institutional gray, floor laid with colorless rubber squares, so threadbare that the concrete beneath was visible.

An elevator designed for freight rather than people took Zoey and T.J. to the fourth floor.

"Just follow me," Zoey said. "David's at the other end."

To get to the other end of the floor, they had to walk a circuitous route through open areas, crowded with furniture, belonging to other residents. No privacy here.

"Shouldn't we be dropping crumbs?" T.J. asked.

"Huh?"

"You know, Hansel and Gretel."

Zoey paused, looked back at T.J. "Oh, I get it. It's a joke."

I guess, T.J. thought. Whoever I am, I have a sense of humor.

They came upon a large open area, sparsely furnished, except for the man who stood on his head in the middle of the floor, watching them. Some mattresses lay along the far, windowed wall. On all the other walls, mirrors, including the one set behind a makeshift galley kitchen. The smell of good coffee scented the air.

When the man righted himself to face Zoey and T.J., the motion was fluid. He was short, but well built, with lean hips. His tight Gortex shirt showed well-developed chest and upper arm muscles. His gaze was potent.

"Les Deux Columbines," he said.

"David," Zoey said, "this is T.J."

David bowed with a flourish. "Welcome." All the while T.J. felt his eyes on her. He'd seen the newspaper.

"T.J. has a problem, David."

"I should think so," David said. He took three mugs

from a cabinet and set them on the galley countertop. "Coffee is almost ready."

"See, I told you," Zoey said. She hung her coat on one of the wall hooks and gestured for T.J. to do the same. "David just knows. Tell him, T.J."

T.J. hesitated. Besides amnesia, did she have, she wondered, some other brain injury that made each day a totally new experience, as if she were constantly stepping off the girder of a tall building under construction? Yet what else was she to do? She couldn't go back because there was nothing there. She had to go forward.

She hung her jacket next to Zoey's coat and reached into a pocket for the newspaper clippings. She handed the clippings to David, who put them on the counter without looking at them. He poured coffee into the mugs and expertly brought all three to the center of the room, set them on the floor, and lowered himself tailor fashion. Zoey and T.J. joined him in an almost identical motion.

"We're having a pow-wow," T.J. murmured to the tune of "We're Having a Heat Wave." She took a sip of the strong coffee, didn't know where to begin.

Again, the sharp, contemplative look from David.

"T.J. doesn't know who she is," Zoey blurted. "She woke up in Mount Sinai and ran away because someone scary came and said she was this what's-her-face?"

"Mary Lou Salinger," David said. "This morning's news said there's a reward for information. We can use the money."

Chapter 14

Despairing, T.J. wilted over her crossed legs, registering Zoey's, "David!" So he had known. It was over. Mary Lou had won. She hid her face in her hands.

A roar filled her ears, her brain. She was flying through the air, tumbling, rolling on tarmac. A soft landing, soft and giving, blood sodden, mewling—

A gentle hand capped her head. The frightening images vanished.

David said, "But we know you're not Mary Lou, don't we?"

She raised her head and his hand slid away. "I don't know who I am, but I know I'm not Mary Lou."

Zoey cried, "Damn it, David, you really scared me."

T.J. watched both warily. Was it an act?

"The papers said you were found wandering in Central Park covered with blood, that you were identified as the missing woman from the Teterboro explosion. You don't remember anything?"

"Bits of things not related to what happened to me, like I prefer Zabar's bagels to H & H's and that I own a dog and that I may be a—"

"Dancer," David finished for her.

"How do you know?"

"The way you move, the way you folded yourself up just now."

"Yes, you're right. It's instinctive. About that explosion—I think I was there because when I thought you would turn me in, I heard a terrible noise and felt myself flying and falling—"

"Go on." His gaze was penetrating.

She shuddered, got up, walked a few paces, turned back to them. "I landed on something soft and squishy."

"Gross," Zoey said. She jumped up and held T.J.

David collected the mugs and set them on the counter.

"They told me at the hospital that I would start remembering, in isolated moments, or large chunks. I want to do it with—forgive me—strangers, who won't lie to me about who I am."

"They're looking for her, David," Zoey said. "They came to the Main Brew this morning because someone spotted her with me last night and told. What can we do?" She made no mention of her seizure, staring hard at T.J. as if to say, *don't tell on me.*

His response, if he intended one, was lost in the dramatic arrival of a trio, an inordinately tall woman and two men, filling the huge room with "good mornings." Their curiosity colored their movements as they sent quick glances in T.J.'s direction while draping their coats over the wall hooks. They were all dressed in black, long-sleeved, tight-fitting tops and black, equally tight-fitting pants.

David settled his arm around T.J. shoulders. "I wasn't kidding about the reward being offered," he whispered, his breath cool in her ear. She stiffened. "But we can hide you in plain sight, can't we, Zoey?"

"Oh, David," Zoey cried, "of course."

"Come," he said. He stepped toward the three newcomers, pulling T.J. with him. "This is T.J., and these splendid characters are the rest of the Lumare Mimes. Mona—" Mona made a quick swirl. "—Jeff—" Jeff did a back flip, and bowed. "—And Eric." Eric sprang forward, went down on one knee before T.J., and lifted her hand to his lips.

T.J. suddenly found herself in the midst of a pirouette that ended with an elaborate curtsy. How on earth—she rose self-consciously, feeling the rush of heat to her cheeks. Zoey clapped her hands. David had a smug smile on his face.

T.J. thought, he's a man who has to be right.

"I don't have to tell you, T.J. is a dancer," David said. "We're going to add her to the troupe and see how the dynamic changes."

"What about this afternoon's performance?" Mona sat on one of the tall stools and reached into her backpack. In no time at all, she was smoothing white makeup over her face.

Eric and Jeff did the same.

Clown white, T.J. thought. It was something she knew.

"T.J. can make up and watch us work, then . . ."

"Grab a stool, dude," Zoey told T.J. "I'll show you."

Zoey's makeup kit was a pale green tool box. She snapped it open. The pungent odor of stage paint was a madeleine. T.J. closed her eyes, inhaled deeply.

She was on stage, a line of dancers, laughing, curtain up, music up, the taps glory. The joy of it, the intense joy.

The window closed.

"Don't move your head," Zoey said. "Lean back against the mirror. When I turn you around, you'll be surprised."

"The face is a cartoon," David said. "The eyes and eyebrows darkened. And Columbines have high brows. Wide-eyed innocence."

"Chin up," Zoey said.

Eric, fully made up, peered over Zoey's shoulder, puckered over-sized red lips, outlined in black. Palms together, he laid his cheek on his hands.

Zoey giggled. "He wants me to give you smoochy lips."

Mona looked sad and hung her head.

"Please don't be sad, Mona," T.J. said. "I'm not in love with Eric."

Mona's huge red lips smiled and she leaped into the air, clicked her heels, and came down on bent knees.

Now it was Eric who looked sad. He pointed to his outlined teardrops under his eyes.

"Once the mouth is painted on, the mime does not speak again," David said, "until he's out of makeup."

The Lumare Mimes' engagement was at a senior center on East Sixty-seventh Street. They took the Lexington Avenue subway to the delight of most of the riders, as Eric smiled and flirted with every female, young and old.

Taking care on the sand-strewn steps, they came out of the subway, Eric and Jeff carrying a small whimsical pirate trunk. They walked single file on Sixty-seventh Street, one hand on the shoulder of the one in front. Shoveled snow lay in still-white, crusty piles framing the sidewalk.

A tall man with deep pouches under his eyes stood on the steps of an old building watching their progress. His smile almost drove away the mournful expression on his basset hound face. He crossed to a car in front of the building and bent to unlock his door on the driver's side. Straightening, he watched them pass by.

T.J. following Eric, Jeff's hand on her shoulder, felt drawn to him. Her eyes caught his. He did a double take and she smiled her distorted smile. He didn't move. He didn't get into his car and drive away.

Jeff nudged her, because she'd stopped. He nodded to the building from which the man had come. Carved in the stone above the door were the words: Twenty-first Precinct.

Chapter 15

The man with the basset hound face was a cop. And she had smiled at him. Well, a grotesque tease of a smile. But he couldn't have recognized her. When they arrived at the senior center, she stole a second look back. He was still standing where he'd been, talking into a cell phone.

Was she testing herself? Was she the kind of person who did dangerous things? Like getting involved with people who blew up planes?

They were greeted enthusiastically by an authoritative black woman in a plum-colored knit suit, a cream and plum striped silk scarf around her neck. "I'm Midge Walton, the program director. We've been looking forward to your visit, and performance," she told David, smiling at the troupe, who responded to her with exaggerated bows and curtsies.

It was a small, low stage, perhaps a step off the floor, with a pull curtain, which was now open. Folding chairs were arranged in rows and about half of them were filled with elderly people, some in wheelchairs.

Jeff and Eric carried the trunk out onto the stage as if it held bricks, and the audience applauded when they set it down stage left after almost dropping it several times. Jeff mimed opening it but was unable to and was finally replaced by Eric who did so with a grand gesture. More applause. At once all the mimes, except T.J., crowded around the trunk. T.J. hung back, playing shy, eyes downcast, knees together, pigeon-toed, finger in her mouth. Almost automatically, she'd fallen in with the routine.

The mimes began pulling things from the trunk. What looked like an old-fashioned phonograph, but was really cardboard. Eric mimed winding its handle and a kind of circus marching tune began to play. A belled jester's hat with bells was claimed by Jeff; Zoey tied a piece of black tape, from which bells were suspended, around her waist and proceeded to flounce about the stage, magnifying her puzzlement about where the tinkling was coming from.

T.J. edged over, still keeping her eyes down. They surrounded her suddenly, tied a ruff around her neck, and thrust a tambourine in her hands. Then they all had tambourines. The music changed to a ballad and violins. They began acting out a love story. Mona, a married lady, loves Jeff, a dashing captain, and is determined to take him away from his true love—Zoey, as Columbine. Eric, Jeff's friend, the sly buffoon Harlequin, pretends he's Jeff and exposes Mona's wickedness.

And T.J., not quite knowing where she fit in the scenario, found a place for herself by reflecting her horror at Mona's behavior and her amusement with Harlequin and her sadness over Zoey's plight.

The happy ending came to the accompaniment of tambourines. From a red velvet bag Harlequin threw showers of confetti. Then bows to the applause. T.J. looked out into the audience. To her horror, standing in the back was the cop with the mournful face.

"Grouch bag duty," David told them, patting the drawstring bag hooked to his belt. "Get everything back in the trunk and I'll meet you in the lobby. Remember, T.J., we don't speak while we're mimes."

T.J. nodded. The mournful cop seemed to have slipped away, which was good. Maybe he just liked mimes.

Except for the confetti, everything was returned to the trunk: the props, the belts and bells, ruffs, hats and caps and tambourines. Movement was exaggerated and no one spoke.

She felt buoyed by the experience. For the first time since she'd awakened in the hospital, she had a sense of solace. It was all too brief. In the lobby, waiting, was the mournful cop, and when he saw her, he headed right over.

"Excuse me," he began, but he got no further. The others closed in around her.

David appeared, sized up the situation, and tapped the cop on the arm. "Can I help you? I'm David Lumare. This is my mime troupe."

"Yeah, I'd like to talk to one of your troupe." He turned and looked at T.J.

A quiver ran through her. She knew him. His name was . . . it was on the tip of her tongue. It got stuck in her head. Was he one of the good guys or one of the bad guys? She couldn't take the risk.

"Mimes don't speak when they wear their makeup," David said. "I'm their voice right now. Which one of my troupe do you want to speak with?"

"That one." He pointed to her. He smiled. He was being friendly. Why hadn't he said he was a cop?

"Well, why don't you give us your card and I'll have T.J. call you when she's out of makeup."

"T.J.?" The cop looked puzzled. He pulled out his wallet and handed David his card.

David read it out loud. "Detective First Grade Arthur Metzger, Twenty-first Precinct. That's you?"

"Yes." Detective Metzger stood well above the others, even Mona, and his gaze was so blunt, T.J. lowered her eyes.

"This is police business?" David asked.

"Not yet. Right now it's personal. Give me your business card and I'll get in touch."

"Why not?" David patted his pockets amiably. "Guess I forgot to bring any."

Not very likely, T.J. thought, watching the charade. David liked being master in more ways than simply mime master.

The detective didn't seem surprised, or annoyed. He directed his words past David. "I'd like you to call me . . . T.J. It's about someone we both know. Someone named Leslie."

Chapter 16

"I don't know anyone named Leslie," T.J. said, dabbing at the few remaining streaks of white makeup that had settled around her hairline and upper lip. "Though there was something about that cop Metzger . . ."

"I wanted to be a cop once," Mona said, hitching her backpack onto her shoulder.

Eric howled. "I'll bet."

"I did, but it didn't work out."

"Why not?"

"Too big for the breeches," Jeff said. They high-fived each other.

"Oh, you guys. Did we get cash this time, David?"

David reached into the grouch bag and took out a wad of bills.

"Twenty each." He doled out the bills "This was our first institution, and feedback should be good. We'll do better when we get to hospitals and schools."

After the others left, Zoey gathered up the greasy tissues and cotton balls and threw them in the garbage. "Didn't T.J. do great, David?"

"Yes." He'd put the drawstring bag away and was rinsing out the coffee pot. "Want to join the troupe, T.J.?"

"I'd like that, but I have to get a regular job. Besides, do you really think I'm ready?"

"You can be. I'll work with you. Tomorrow we can go to the zoo."

"The zoo?"

Zoey laughed. "You'll see. Listen, dude, it's dark outside already. We should go. I have to get some sleep before my shift tonight."

"T.J., why don't you stay and we'll work through some exercises?"

Zoey, who was gathering up her things, paused, her back to T.J. and David. On the surface of the pause was an unnatural tension. She had brought T.J. to David. Did she resent David's response?

It was enough for T.J., who had her own qualms about working in David's intense sphere. "Too much stimulation for me for one day, David. It's not even twenty-four hours since I ran away from the hospital. And Zoey and I had—" she looked at Zoey "—no sleep at all last night. And tomorrow I have to see about finding a job in the neighborhood."

"Be here at noon tomorrow," David said, "and we'll go to the zoo."

"That cop," Zoey said. "He didn't seem half bad."

"I forgot to take his card from David." T.J. stopped at a newsstand and bought the *News* and the *Post*, folded them under her arm. Better to read the stories in Zoey's apartment than on the street.

"David will tell you he lost it."

"David didn't like him."

"David likes you."

"What?" T.J. was startled.

"He likes you. You'll be part of the troupe."

"He likes me for the troupe, you mean." She was uneasy.

"No, more, I think." Zoey stared straight ahead. "He was different with you."

"How different?"

Zoey thought for a moment. "I don't know. Tender, sort of."

"Zoey, this is all wrong. I'm not sure I can handle any of this. It might be better if I left."

"No, please don't go." Zoey clutched her arm. "It'll work out all right."

She sighed. "Where would I go?" But it was in the front of her mind that she might have to leave, sooner rather than later. She could call the cop, Metzger. She didn't need his card. David had read the card out loud. The Twenty-first Precinct. It was personal, he'd said. About Leslie.

There was some good news: her photograph on the front page of both newspapers had shrunk to the size of a passport photo. No one could think it looked like her. But there was a little more to the story. Yes, a ten-thousand-dollar reward was being offered for information leading to Mary Lou Salinger, the only known witness to the explosion of the executive jet on the Teterboro runway. The explosion had now been pronounced deliberate sabotage. Four bodies had been recovered but not yet identified.

"It says I either escaped or was kidnapped from the psychiatric ward of Mount Sinai and was spotted in Grand Central Station at a coffee bar during the night."

"If they come looking for you tonight, they'll find me," Zoey said, yawning. "That should take care of it."

"I hope so." She read on. "Calls have been coming in from all over the city with sightings."

They both laughed. "Like Elvis has left the building. Let's get some sleep," Zoey mumbled. "You can look for a job tomorrow."

But sleep for T.J. was not easy to come by. She lay on the sofa staring up at the ceiling. Her eyes began to itch and she sneezed. "Chat," she whispered. "Come out, I know you're here."

Before long she felt the warmth settling at her feet. It was strangely comforting, and at that point she must have drifted into sleep. The comfort ended quickly.

She was running, somewhere, anywhere, away from the noise and blood. But it followed her, swooping down, forcing her to her knees. Up again, running, the huge overcoat tangling her feet. Fear parched her throat, numbed her lips.

She was dreaming, knew she could stop it, but if she did, she'd be back to T.J. So she let it run with her. Bells rang. She was under a mattress. They were standing on it, crushing her. She couldn't breathe. Then the shot—

"Damn!" Zoey said.

T.J. woke shuddering. Chat was heavy on her chest, purring.

Zoey stood over her, pieces of broken crockery in her hand. "I woke you. I'm sorry. I dropped a mug." She dumped the pieces in a garbage bag.

T.J. pushed Chat off and sat up. "I'm glad you did. I was having a horrible dream."

"I'm leaving now. Go back to sleep. We're out of coffee, I'm afraid."

"Zoey, will you be okay?"

"Sure." She smiled a crooked smile. "Last night was just last night. It won't happen again. At least not so soon."

After Zoey left, T.J. found teabags and made herself a cup of tea. She cut the articles on Mary Lou and the explosion from the newspapers and read them through again.

A phone number was provided, for information, which if

it were correct, would get the caller the ten-thousand-dollar reward. A local number. She folded the articles and put them aside. Unfolded them and looked at the number again.

The phone was in the bedroom. She took it back to the sofa with her and punched in the numbers from the article.

"NYPD Hot line." A man's voice. Bored.

"Hello, I have some information about Mary Lou Salinger," she said. "I know where she is."

"Hold on, I'll patch you through."

Patch me through? Who was going to take the call? Mary Lou's pseudo uncle? The burr of a ring.

She started to hang up, stayed when the burr stopped and a woman answered, "Special Agent Blue."

"Special Agent Blue?" Code blue. Judy Blue. Judy Blue? Where had that free association thread come from?

"Yes."

Who call themselves special agents? Only the FBI. Well, that makes sense. It was an explosion. Maybe it was an international terrorist thing.

"Yes?" Special Agent Blue prompted.

"Um, I think I saw that woman you're looking for."

"Where?"

"Grand Central Station. This morning. Leaving a coffeeshop."

Special Agent Blue paused, as if she was thinking. "And you are?"

"Special Agent Blue, what is your first name?"

"Judy. Judy Blue."

Her hands spasmed. "I can't talk any more. I have to catch a train." Maybe they were tracing the call. "Just tell me, what has she done?"

"It's okay," Special Agent Blue said. "It's okay to come in now."

Chapter 17

She walked eastward at first, toward the river, then uptown, savoring the sun on her face, trying not to think about how she could have known the name of the FBI agent, Judy Blue. What had Judy Blue said? *It's okay to come in now.* What did that mean? Was she an undercover agent for the FBI? Or was it like Robert Redford in *Three Days of the Condor*? Did they want her to come in so they could get rid of her? Were those two men chasing her FBI? CIA?

Her mind was as mushy as the melting slush piles of snow. It wasn't fear she felt, but a small kernel of anger. And maybe this was good. It was part of her character, being slow to anger.

She stopped in her tracks. Part of her character was slow to anger? Hold on, she told herself. It's coming back.

She needed coffee and a real breakfast, bacon and eggs and a toasted bagel. The Big Dipper was a small restaurant-cum-coffeeshop on Avenue B, near Tenth Street. It had a sign in the window: HELP WANTED: NIGHT CASHIER, PLUS.

She sat at the counter, behind which was a myriad of liquor bottles, and ordered the breakfast special. "What's the plus mean?" she asked the counterman when he came back from the kitchen. He was an aging, freckled, biker type with a buzz cut and a couple of gold hoops in one ear.

"You know, fill in when it gets busy at night." He gave her the once-over.

"I need a job."

"You're hired." He set the coffee mug down in front of her and grinned. "Minimum wage and you keep your own tips." He gave her a sharp look. "I pay cash, no benefits."

"What are the hours?"

"Six till closing. I try to close around one, Monday through Thursday. On Friday and Saturday, I'll need you till two or later. My girlfriend does Sundays." He returned to the kitchen and brought back her breakfast.

"Okay. When do I start?"

"You can start tonight. I'm Wally, Wally Dipper." He held out his hand. "Dress hip."

"Hip?"

"You know, cool. Show a little."

She grinned, shook his hand. "Pleased to meet you, Wally. I'm T.J.," she said.

"T.J. what?"

She hesitated. "Just T.J."

"Yeah. Okay, T.J. Go on and eat, it's on the house."

After breakfast, she wandered around the neighborhood looking for a place to buy used clothing, but didn't see any. She didn't have much money left. She'd have to borrow something from Zoey until she had her own money. And she had to replace the money she'd stolen from Lucy at the hospital.

On First Avenue, she found an Army-Navy store and bought camouflage pants and used jeans, each in as tight a fit as she could handle. After adding a black tee-shirt to the mix, she was close to the end of her money. Maybe Zoey would have a sexy top and slides so she could dress up the costume. Afterward, she wandered through the big drugstore discounter, Duane Reade, and found a package of three cotton panties, an eyeliner pencil, and mascara. That left her with just ten dollars, a pocketful of change, and the MetroCard. She stopped at a small grocery and bought a can of Melitta coffee.

Zoey was sleeping, but Chat greeted her, nestling against her legs, purring. T.J. put food out for the cat, stayed with her black leggings, but added the new black tee-shirt, and borrowed joggers from Zoey. She made a pot of coffee. David had said twelve. There was no point in antagonizing him, and besides, she'd rather enjoyed herself as a mime.

He'd been waiting for her, although his surprise was artful. He wanted her to like him. She saw that was the way it would be. She hung up her jacket, aware this gave her some control of her situation.

He took her hand. "Here," he said, indicating one of the stools in front of the mirror wall, "let's see how you do with the makeup." He set a makeup kit—his own—on another stool and stood aside to watch her.

Her hands did the job; they knew how. The white mask.

"The mime," he said, "works from the outside in, kinetically. We use both sense and physical memory."

She drew on large, red Kewpie doll lips and puckered up for David, who laughed. "Very good," he said. "Remember, the face is a cartoon."

The last step, dark eyebrows, eyes and lips outlined in black.

"You're a pro, T.J.," he reflected. "Someone in the biz would know that you're not Mary Lou Salinger or . . . that you are."

She shook her head at him emphatically and held her palms up in front of her. She did not have to wonder what *biz* meant. He meant show business.

"But you don't want to know. Not yet." He took a long

black coat from one of the hooks. "Wear this." The coat came down to her ankles. "And this." He tucked her hair under a black and red jester's cap. The bells tinkled.

They walked toward Astor Place and the Lexington Avenue subway, T.J. bouncing beside David. She didn't have to get with the program, she was the program. And David was pleased, at ease. A few people turned to watch her, smiling, but it was New York and didn't everyone look like T.J. from time to time?

As they crossed the Bowery, David suddenly grabbed her arm and began tugging her. "Faster," he said, till they were almost running. He raced her down the subway stairs and it was all she could do not to fall over the coat tails.

A train was coming into the station. He had to use his MetroCard twice because hers was in her jacket in his loft.

They just made it onto the train. She raised her arms and brows at him. Why?

He watched the platform. The doors closed, the train began to move. He let out a breath. She followed his gaze.

The mournful cop Metzger was on the platform running alongside the train looking in the cars. When the train entered the tunnel, he was left behind.

Chapter 18

She was no longer hidden. Now, in mime makeup, the whole world saw her. She couldn't disappear in a crowd, that was for sure. When they switched to the N train, the car filled with a group of preschoolers who clustered around T.J., giggling and chattering. It took her mind from the cop following her. She stood up and pretended she was Marcel Marceau. The kids loved it. It was as if she'd been born to it.

David was a watcher, eyes, body language assessing her. Much to the children's excitement, they all got off the train at the same stop: Fifth Avenue and Sixtieth Street. The earthy smell of animal waste hung in the air. She played Pied Piper as they trailed her through the entrance to the Central Park Zoo.

"Bid them adieu," David said, *sotto voce*.

She turned and faced them, made a sweeping bow, and followed the fast-moving David.

The sun was brilliant, glistening off the melting snow, the winter landscape disappearing into near spring. It was March, she realized. The storm had been winter's final slashing blow.

David stopped in front of another entrance and counted out seven dollars for two tickets. Beyond the turnstile a closed door announced the RAIN FOREST. He knew where he was going. She was along for the ride, or so it seemed.

A warm mist enveloped them. The smell was animal and it was rich.

"Give me your coat," David said. Once off, he slung it

over his shoulder. She was not incognito. Everyone saw her. Children pointed, adults whispered.

They walked on wooden ramps lined with lush greenery on one side, glass enclosed exhibits on the other. Up a flight of stairs, through vertical strips of canvas, and lo, the monkeys.

David's voice in her ear: "Watch their movements, watch how they react to you."

COLOBUS, the card said. They had black faces, flowing coats in black and white, their tails luxurious. They scrambled on rocks and trees, paying no attention whatever to the children and adults watching. No attention, that is, until one of them spotted T.J. and stared, looping closer to the window that separated animals from humans.

T.J. cocked her head and made eye contact with the creature. She forgot about David and everyone else. At once the other Colobus swung their way to their cohort and began a kind of showing off for T.J., as T.J. mimicked their antic movements.

Outside again, on the rocks beyond a heated pool, they found the pink faced, cuddly snow monkeys and once again, they were attracted to T.J.

"It's the face and the movement that are the magnet," David said. "To them, one human is like every other, and then the mime comes along."

The exercise had been exhausting. She could hardly put one foot in front of the other as they returned to David's loft. She'd get her jacket and take the makeup off at Zoey's.

But David was insistent. "Sit and rest and I'll take off the paint." He rolled a paper napkin around her collar and began to remove the greasepaint. "You have it, T.J. You're a quick study. Don't speak yet." Gentle fingers brushed her cheeks with the cotton balls, once with cream, once to wipe up. He tilted her chin to look for places he'd missed. Finally, he removed the paint from around her mouth.

His kiss was a glancing caress.

She sprang from the stool, toppling it. "No, I can't, you're not playing fair." She grabbed the ski jacket and ran. He didn't follow her.

In front of the building she paused for a moment to catch her breath but the panting continued. An anxiety attack, that's what it was. She looked around to see if anyone was watching. People were wrapped up in their own lives and weren't paying any attention to her. Across the street a man was trying to walk a rambunctious little white dog that kept howling and tugging on its leash.

See, she told herself, starting to walk, no one has even noticed you.

Zoey was awake and the apartment smelled of coffee. The television was blaring. "Hey!" Zoey was leaning over the TV set.

"I got a job," she told Zoey, hooking her jacket on the doorknob. "At the Big Dipper. Evenings."

"That's great, but you've got to hear this. They just promo'd breaking news about Mary Lou Salinger. Maybe they found the real one."

It was too much. T.J.'s knees gave out on her and she slumped down on the sofa, shaking. What could it be? She was sure it would only complicate, compromise the little peace she had.

Zoey sat down beside her and held her hand. "Don't be afraid."

"The mystery only deepens," the newswoman Roz Abrams said. She quickly retold the story of the explosion, the missing financier and his assistant, Mary Lou Salinger, and the woman assumed to be Ms. Salinger who appeared to have amnesia and had fled from the Mount Sinai psychiatric wing two days earlier.

"They're just rehashing the same old shit," T.J. said, beginning to unwind.

"Shsh," Zoey said. "Here it comes."

A glamorous woman with short dark hair and glossy red lips came on the screen, sitting at a table, a microphone in front of her. She fluffed her hair several times, obviously enjoying the attention. T.J. studied her. Was this someone from her past? She hoped not. This woman loved herself.

"Boy, is she gorgeous," Zoey said.

Roz Abrams spoke again. "I'm here at the Mark Hotel on Madison Avenue where someone has come forward claiming to have information about the missing witness, Mary Lou Salinger. This press conference was called by Xenia Smith, principal of the executive search firm Smith and Wetzon. She is about to give her statement."

"Do you know her, T.J.?"

"No." Do you want to know her, T.J.? No.

The woman looked directly into the camera. She held up the newspaper with Mary Lou Salinger's picture. "This is not Mary Lou Salinger. I don't know who Mary Lou Salinger is and I don't care. I know that this is a picture of my partner, who has been on a leave—"

"Your partner, Ms. Smith?" a voice called out. "How long have you been in a personal relationship with—"

Scorn, outrage marred the beautiful face. "Oh, for pity sakes, not *that* kind of partner. Do I look like one of *them?* I certainly do not. When did the word 'partner' lose its legitimate meaning?" She stabbed at the picture on the newspaper with her perfectly manicured red talon. "This woman is my business partner, Leslie Wetzon."

Chapter 19

"Leslie?" T.J. rolled the name on her tongue. It was the same name that cop had used. "What was the last name?" Her lips were numb.

"Wesson, I think. Something like that. Isn't that the name that cop at the senior center mentioned?" Zoey tilted her head. "Are you Leslie, dude?"

The camera had shifted to Roz Abrams. "There you have it. The mystery deepens. Tune in at five for more on this new development in the case of the missing witness to the explosion at Teterboro Airport."

Zoey pressed the off button. "Leslie?"

"I don't know. But that awful woman. She's Leslie's partner. What kind of person is Leslie if she's in business with that woman?"

"She's a babe," Zoey said. "And she looks like she's got money. What kind of business is it, do you suppose?"

"Do you have a phone book?"

"Under the bed." She brought it to T.J., who blew off the clumps of dust before opening it to the business section.

"If it's a partnership, want to bet she'd list herself first? God, look at all the business Smiths. Let's forget it." She closed the directory and rested her head on the back of the sofa. Lethargy enveloped her like a deep brown fog. She didn't want to know any more.

"Give it here." Zoey found the page with the Smiths and ran her finger down the names. "You're probably right . . .

wait a minute. Here's a Smith and Wetzon. With a 'tz.' That's pretty close. Come on, T.J., make the call."

T.J. shook her head. "You do it. What if they recognize my voice?"

"Well, isn't that the point? Don't you want to know who you are?" When T.J. didn't answer, Zoey punched in the numbers. "Oh, hi," she said into the phone. "Can you tell me what kind of business this is?" She listened intently. "Well, no, I'm not. I work for the IRS. An auditor." She thanked the speaker, hung up, and let out a hoot.

"You're an auditor for the IRS?"

"He asked me whether I was a stockbroker, and I just picked the most boring-sounding job."

"You're probably right, but why did he ask if you were a stockbroker?"

"I don't know. He said they're executive search consultants. Very fancy. What does it mean?"

"It means that if I'm this Leslie Wetzon, I'm a head-hunter for stockbrokers." She was sweating, jumpy, as if she'd had too much caffeine. She'd known the answer, said it without hesitation. Leslie Wetzon was a Wall Street head-hunter. Jason McLaughlin, the man whose plane had exploded, was a financier. There had to be a connection. "I have to get out of here." She got up and pulled on her jacket. "I'm due at the Big Dipper at six."

Zoey jumped up. "I'll go with you."

"No." She softened her tone. "Don't worry, Zoey. I'm not going to do anything crazy. I just need some time to think about all this."

"Listen, T.J., I'm off tonight. "Why don't I come and have a drink and we can go home together? What time do you finish?"

"Two-ish."

★ ★ ★

T.J. broke into a jog as soon as she came through the outer door. West as far as Fifth Avenue, uptown, east again, block after block, until Tompkins Square Park loomed up in front of her. Her mind was jerking her in different directions. What was she to do? She'd been relieved that Zoey hadn't insisted on coming along. If only she could talk to someone who was not one of the walking wounded, as Zoey was, as David, as was T.J. herself. She veered into the park and sat on a bench, hardly registering the dog walkers, the mothers with children.

It was this terrible aloneness, being swallowed up in quicksand and no one to help her. She felt the tears start, and she hated them. This was not like her. She didn't cry at the drop of a hat. She didn't? How did she know that?

An almost-human shriek filled the air and a small white bundle landed on her lap. A cold nose nuzzled her face and strange gutteral cries came from the animal. She held the trunk of the wriggling body away from her, its leash dangling from a red leather collar. A little white dog. A Maltese.

"Hey, I'm really sorry." A man was hurrying toward her. "She got away from me."

"It's all right," T.J. said, scratching the little dog's ears. "She's very sweet. What's her name?"

The man sat down on the bench and the dog jumped to his lap and covered his face with kisses and then came back to T.J. and did the same with her.

"Isabella," the man said. "Izz." He wore dark glasses and a Mets cap, a windbreaker, jeans, and joggers. A pepper-and-salt stubble almost hid the small cleft in his chin. He didn't look threatening. "She can get a little exuberant sometimes."

She hugged the dog. "Izz, you're very sweet. You came at just the right time."

The man seemed to be studying her from behind his dark glasses.

She buried her face in the white fur.

"Can I help?" His voice was soft, gentle. Maybe he was a shrink. He reminded her of the doctors at Mount Sinai.

No. She didn't know him. She was way too vulnerable. "I've got to get to my job." She put the dog in his lap and stood.

"Where do you work?"

"At The Big Dipper. Do you know it?"

"Yup." He got up and set the dog on her feet, unknotting the leash. He was stocky in build, about a head taller than T.J. "Maybe I'll see you around," he said.

She didn't look back, though she felt the need to. When she did, there was no sign of him or his dog. Forget them, she thought, think about your job. She planned to shower and change into the tight jeans and one of Zoey's tee-shirts that bared the belly-button. She'd make herself up with a lot of eyeliner and mascara and shiny lip gloss. Wally Dipper wanted hip, she'd give him hip.

Her thoughts veered back to the financier. He was the key. She'd been at the site of the explosion, she was sure of that now. What had she been doing there? "My name is Leslie," she said aloud, to hear how it sounded.

When the light turned green, she crossed the street, walked the short block to Fifth Street and Zoey's building. Some instinct, good self-preservation genes, she thought afterward, made her focus on the two men moving away from the building. She ducked behind the tall steps of the brownstone across the street.

The men paused, looked back to where T.J. would have

been. Acid rose in her throat, bitter and viscous. She couldn't hear what they were saying but after a moment, they appeared to exchange cards. They shook hands and separated, one man walking west toward Second Avenue, the other eastward toward Avenue A.

T.J. had no trouble recognizing either man. The one walking toward Second Avenue was Mary Lou Salinger's phony Uncle Lew, and the man he'd just parted from was David Lumare.

Chapter 20

Keeping one eye on the door, Wally Dipper whipped bottles
of beer down in front of four of the half dozen people sitting
at the counter, then filled mugs from the tap for the others.
He did a double-take when T.J. walked in, releasing a
"Whoa." In spite of the paper coasters, the bottles and
mugs sweated sloppy puddles on the old wood. The beer
drinkers were hyper, the laughter shallow as they talked
about work, a film shoot in the area. Unwinding. She could
feel their edge; it hadn't gone smoothly.

When Wally finished, he motioned her over. He wore a
blue cap with the white NY initials of the New York Yan-
kees, jeans, and a black tee-shirt that stretched tight across
his gut, distorting the foaming mug and the words: The Big
Dipper. One end of a white towel was tucked into the side
of his straining waistband.

"You can hang your jacket on one of the hooks in the
back and grab a cap. It's gonna be busy tonight because
Ellis came in drunk as a skunk and I sent him home. I'll
handle the kitchen, it's only burgers and fries, but you'll
have to tend bar."

"I've never done it."

"Don't matter. They mostly do beer and wine. Once in a
while, a martini. Just roll a little white vermouth around the
glass and fill it with gin or vodka, whatever they want, and a
coupla olives on a toothpick. Blink those pretty eyelashes at
them and tell them you're a rookie. The beer is three bucks,
wine, six, martini, seven. Cash box's under the bar. No

credit cards or checks. Make sure you card the kids. Tips are yours."

She went back where he'd pointed and hung her jacket from a hook, one of many at all different heights, on the wall outside the kitchen. From one hook hung a basket full of assorted caps and worn, crimped-up gloves. She picked out a Mets cap, put it on, pulled her hair through the back opening, and adjusted the back clip so it didn't settle over her eyes.

Where would she find another place to stay? She'd tell Zoey she was leaving when Zoey came by later. Maybe it was time to stop running and call the tall cop with the sad eyes. The decision, because that's what it was, came as a huge weight lifting from her shoulders.

"T.J., you get lost back there?"

She came rushing back, embarrassed. "Sorry."

"You have to move fast around here." Wally headed for the kitchen. "And you'd better use the stool or nobody'll see you."

T.J., looking for the so-called stool in the space behind the bar, found a raised wooden slat runner about a foot deep and a step high. It gave a bit when she stepped up. Behind her was a refrigerator case crowded with bottles of beer, mostly American but Mexican and German as well.

The film group was replaced by three NYU students on their way to the Public Theatre, which was in the neighborhood. Two tap beers, one white wine. White wine for the two burger customers. She filled the glasses and Wally picked them up and served them before he headed back to the kitchen for the burgers. She saw that while the diners waited for their burgers, they would drink the wine, then when the burgers came, they would order a refill.

Caught up in the process, she didn't have time to think about her predicament. She was learning how to fill the mugs from the taps without splashing herself. The fumes alone were intoxicating. Just when she thought it was going to be a slow evening, the barstools filled up and a waiting line formed for the first vacant table. Her calves tightened as she moved back and forth on the wood slat runner. Her hand and arm cramped over the taps. Blisters appeared on her thumb, in her palm.

She began to feel as if she were in one of those silent movies, fast motion: pour the wine, uncap the beer, pull the tap, light on the foam, serve the customer, collect the money, pocket the tips.

At one point, she thought she heard Wally say, "You're doin' great," but couldn't be sure because the noise level mixed with the rock music from the jukebox was a head-thumper. The case for the empty beer bottles was full. She picked up another empty case and put it on top. Her eyes were drooping; her hand throbbed. She thought, how long am I going to be able to do this?

"Hey, T.J." A sporty type shook an empty Corona at her. "Brewski."

"House red, T.J.," one of Wally's hamburger customers said, getting out of her seat. They all seemed to know her name now. T.J. poured a glass of wine and handed it over, making a mental note to tell Wally. But Wally knew from instinct what to charge, or maybe from looking at what was on the table.

Someone sat down on the one empty stool. "What'll you have," T.J. asked, wiping the counter and putting down a paper coaster.

"Beck's."

She reached into the case and pulled out an icy bottle,

uncapped it, and set it in front of the man who'd ordered it, glancing at him for the first time.

"What's the T.J. stand for?"

"Where's your lady friend?" She almost didn't recognize him without the dark glasses, and he'd shaved off the stubble. Even in the gauzy light, his eyes were a startling turquoise.

He didn't get it. "Lady friend?"

She turned away to take some cash off the counter, the charge into the cash box, the tip—four dollars—into her pocket. Her pocket was getting crowded. "Isabella."

His eyes teared up. What an odd reaction. "She's probably smoking a cigarette and sitting on my favorite chair."

More patrons left and T.J. got busy taking money, making change, wiping down the counter. Almost everyone was gone, or on the way out. Zoey would probably be there any minute.

The man with the striking eyes was still at the bar nursing his beer. He put some bills on the counter.

"Are you an actor?" T.J. asked. She started to give him change.

He waved his hand, rejecting her change. "I work for the city," he said.

Wally had come out of the kitchen drying his hands. He took off a grimy apron, stared after the man as he flipped them a goodnight salute. "Yeah, right," he said.

"Do you know him?" T.J. went over the counter with a damp cloth. Another minute and she would drop where she was standing.

"I've got to sit down." She came around and sat on one of the stools.

"Works for the city all right," Wally said. "Good job, T.J." He went behind the bar and unloaded the cash box, counting the proceeds, tapped himself a beer. "What'll you have?"

"Beck's. What's that guy's name?" She took a hefty swallow. She was really thirsty.

"Don't know. Never seen him in here before." He drank down half the mug and wiped his mouth with the back of his hand.

"But you knew he works for the city."

"I know a cop when I see one," Wally said.

Chapter 21

T.J. drank her brew and watched Wally replenish the beer in the refrigerator. The cold bottle eased some of the raw pain in her swollen hand, but she couldn't hold onto it. She switched it to her left hand. "You don't like cops?"

"Hangover from the sixties."

She held out her damaged hand. Her fingers wouldn't flex. "Any suggestions?"

"Ice. And next time use one of the gloves in the basket."

Of course, she thought.

He filled a metal bowl with ice cubes and set it on the counter in front of her. "Go on." When she hesitated, he took her hand and thrust it into the ice.

"Yow!"

"Swelling'll go down."

"Thanks." She looked at her hand. "What a mess." She patted it dry with a napkin. "What time is it?"

"Almost three. You live around here?"

"Staying with a friend. She was supposed to meet me here tonight. I have to find another place, if you know of anything. I just need a room." Zoey must have found something better to do, she thought. She handed Wally the empty bottle and collected her jacket. "I'm on my way. See you tomorrow."

"Six," he said, shaking the ice from the bowl into a towel. "Wrap your hand in this."

If she'd expected empty, quiet streets, she was wrong.

Groups of young people were standing in front of bars, smoking, though temperatures had dropped. It was Friday night, actually early Saturday morning. The weekend had begun. Car traffic was steady. Restaurants and cafes were beginning to empty out. She walked down Avenue B to Fifth Street, then cut west.

The side streets were deserted and she quickened her gait, looking back over her shoulder. No one seemed to be following her. Fifth Street was like a painted set she'd wandered onto. The Twilight Zone. She'd seen those old television dramas. For all she knew she could have entered another dimension. She wrapped the ice-laden towel tighter around her hand.

Avenue A was back in the real world again. Fifth Street again, more darkness and quiet. A car rolled slowly past her. She didn't realize she was running until she reached First Avenue and had to stop for the red light.

She was only a half a block from home. When the green "walk" signal came, she rushed across the wide street. The wind lifted her hat; she grabbed it. The Mets cap. She hadn't returned it.

She tucked her hair up under it to hold it tighter. All she was thinking about when she unlocked the outside door was a hot shower and washing the smell of beer from her hair.

The building was still, the lobby barren except for an empty grocery cart to the left of the elevator, which was waiting for her. Weary, her hand throbbing, she walked down the hall to Zoey's apartment, fumbling for the key.

It wasn't necessary. The door wasn't locked. It locked automatically when the door closed. She was sure she'd closed it when she left. No. Zoey was careless about the door. When she threw the garbage in the incinerator, she shifted the lock so she could get back into the apartment without her key. She'd forgotten to put it back when she went out. Damn.

T.J. pushed open the door. Something brushed her face. Zoey's coat. It was hanging where she always left it—on the hook behind the door. The lights were on. The cloying smell of orange juice mixed with others, more acrid, more terrifying.

"Zoey?" She moved past the door. The living room was trashed. Sofa cushions gutted, foam protruding. The refrigerator door hung open, food containers smashed. Orange juice underfoot. "Zoey?" The extent of the ruin stupefied her, but only for a moment. Zoey. She dropped the towel. Ice cubes spattered over the debris.

Zoey lay in a fetal position amid the devastation of the bedroom, her head against the radiator. In her rush, T.J. stepped into something slippery and came down hard only inches from Zoey. Urine, vomit, blood, the rest. "Zoey?" She rolled Zoey onto her back. Had she had a seizure when the burglars came? Her face was so battered she was unrecognizable. No pulse. Who was she kidding? These were no burglars. They were looking for T.J. And they'd killed Zoey. Dear, kind Zoey.

Beer rose bitter in her throat. Leaning over the toilet, she threw up bile. She drove back her tears. Call 911. What if Zoey was still alive?

After a quick search she found the phone under the bed and crawled under for it. Under the bed. She froze. A fragment of memory filtered through. No. Not now. She punched in 911. "She's not breathing." She gave the address, Zoey's name. "The apartment's been burglarized. She's been beaten up. And she's an epileptic."

"What is your name?"

"Please come right away." T.J. hung up. Zoey was dead.

It should have been you, she told herself. She bent down over Zoey and touched her battered face. "Dude. Oh, dude."

Where was Chat? "Chat?" She had to leave, run, get away. What if they discovered she was still alive? A plaintive meow stopped her near the door. It was coming from the kitchen. From the stove. She opened the oven door and the cat leaped into her arms, clinging to her.

The stairs were marble, steep and slippery. She plunged down and, clutching Chat, raced through the lobby and out to the deserted street. Sirens, coming close. She went back and propped the door open with the empty shopping cart.

She walked toward Second Avenue. The EMS truck rushed past her, siren wailing. Lights flashed on the roof of a police car that followed the medical service truck. Brakes squealed as they came to a halt in front of Zoey's building. They pushed the cart aside and burst into the lobby.

A man rushed past her, people in night clothes came out from brownstones across the street. Soon enough, a crowd had formed in front of the building. T.J. turned back and joined the curious. An air of excitement, anticipation, settled over them. Something about impending disasters brought this out. Was it the enjoyment of someone else's trouble? *Schadenfreude?* The Germans were so good with words like that.

Another police car and a van. A crime scene unit. Zoey was dead. She watched them unload their equipment. The cops in the second car pushed back the crowd to either side of the building, clearing the entrance. Time passed and more onlookers arrived, spilling into the street. More sirens. An ambulance. Harsh lights. *Gaudy night.*

At first, the watchers whispered to each other, but no more. Now everyone was silent, separate, sensing violence, death. A soundless Greek chorus.

The cold seeped into her legs; her hand burned. She couldn't leave. Bad enough she'd run away and left Zoey like that. The cat shifted against her. She opened her jacket and the cat crawled inside, then she zipped it up leaving Chat's head free. She sneezed twice, three times. Her eyes and cheeks itched.

More time passed. Everyone waited. Police came and went. The ambulance attendants started moving. A gurney was set up and rolled into the building. Now the crowd shifted uneasily. T.J., already on the outer edge, drifted backward. Chat began to purr.

A shudder ran through the watchers. The gurney was rolled out of the building, an almost flat blue body bag strapped to it. Zoey hardly took up any space.

"Hold it!" The shout came from a man running toward the scene. He was holding up a wallet, something. The attendants stopped. The cops came over to talk with him. He was one of them. He put the wallet away, moved toward the gurney. They gave him space.

It was like a movie, T.J. thought. But the cop was someone she knew, the one with the little white dog, the one who'd talked to her in The Big Dipper only an hour earlier. An attendant unzipped one end of the body bag. The cop bent over Zoey's body, then doubled over as if he'd been sucker-punched. Another cop touched him on the shoulder, and he straightened. He wiped his eyes, motioned to the attendant. The bag was zipped up, and Zoey was loaded into the waiting ambulance.

T.J. couldn't take her eyes from the cop. She stood with the others watching. Someone yawned. The excitement was waning. It was time for the living. T.J. sneezed again. Chat buried her head inside the jacket. Another sneeze, louder.

The cop stared into the crowd that surrounded her. His face wavered in the rolling, colored lights. He came toward her as the crowd began to disperse. She thought she should run but her feet were locked to the sidewalk.

And she was tired of running, sick to her soul about Zoey. She scrunched up her face to halt the tears, but she couldn't stop them.

When he stood in front of her, she held out her wrists. "Do you want to arrest me?"

He took her wrists, lifted them, and kissed her fingers. "Jesus Christ, Les, I'm so happy you're alive."

Chapter 22

"She's with me. I swear. No, she's okay. She will be."

She could hear him talking on the phone. Nothing wrong with her hearing. It was just the rest of her. She laughed, then couldn't stop, gasping into hiccups. The dog licked her face, cuddled into her side. Her sore hand wore an efficient bandage.

He came and sat on the bed. "Les." Tree-filtered sunlight dappled his face.

She couldn't remember much about how she'd gotten here. It was his place, of course. It was a guy place, looked as if he'd just moved in. A gun in a shoulder holster hung from the doorknob of a half-opened closet.

"Where's Chat? Hic—"

"The cat? Is that her name? She's upstairs with Patrice. She tried to eat Izz."

"She did not. This isn't funny, Sil—sil—hic—"

"Silvestri," he said. "That's me. And I agree, it's not funny."

She'd almost said Silvestri. What was there between them? "What's your first name?"

"Only my mother knows."

"Then you must have said Silvestri before—hic."

"Not till now." A kettle whistled. He got up. "I'm making you some tea."

"I don't want tea. I have amnesia—hic. I want to know who I am."

"You're Leslie Wetzon. I'm Silvestri. You scared the shit out of us."

"Us." She mulled that over. "You're a cop—hic. You thought I was on the gurney, dead, and you were very upset. Do we have a relationship?"

He got up. "Sometimes," he said, as he left the room.

She closed her eyes and saw Zoey, not as she'd last seen her, but vibrant and funny, kind and generous. Izz licked the tears from her face.

"I'm not sure I like tea," she said, eyeing the oversized mug Silvestri set down on the floor near the bed.

"There's honey in it. You look like one of those anorexic models. By rights I should have taken you to the hospital."

"But you were so glad to see me you couldn't let me out of your sight."

She'd stopped him in his tracks, and he seemed to be thinking about it. "Something like that," he said.

She choked up. "Horrible things keep happening. Now Zoey's dead. Because of me."

"Was that her name?"

"Her folks were Salinger fanatics, she said."

"Then her name would have been Zooey, and Zooey was a boy."

"We did that riff. They were expecting a boy and made the adjustment."

"The super said she came to feed the cat and water the plants, but didn't live there."

"She did live there, house-sitting. She took me in because I had no place to go. She was easy, a kind of free spirit."

"The place was a wreck. You'd better sit up." He lifted her, raised the pillow. "Slide back." She liked the way his hand felt on her back. "What were they looking for? Who are they?" He tucked the quilt around her.

"I don't know."

"Was Zoey into drugs?"

The tea was hot and sweet. Her hiccups had gone. "No. They were looking for me. One of them came to Mount Sinai—you knew I was there?" He nodded. "Anyway, he said I was this Mary Lou Salinger and he was my uncle and going to take me home. He scared me. I mean, do I look like a Mary Lou? I knew he was lying. That's why I ran away."

"You're not any Mary Lou Salinger, that's for sure. Where did T.J. come from?"

"Temporary Jane, as in Doe. I guess I can't be T.J. any more," she said with a frisson of regret.

He gave her a half smile, but he was hardly listening. "Something stinks about all this. Almost two months ago you took a leave of absence, left Izz with me, and disappeared."

"I don't live here, I take it."

"You live on the Upper West Side."

"Ah. That's what they thought at the hospital because I mentioned Zabar's." She shivered, thrust the mug at him with shaking hands. "I can't go home. They'll be watching for me."

"Les, if you were at the scene of that Teterboro explosion, what the hell were you doing there? Is this something Veeder got you into?"

"V-v-v-veeder?" Her teeth were chattering. "Who's Veeder?"

"Say that after you get your memory back. Oh, for crissakes." He set the mug on the floor again and held her, stroking her hair, until the shivering stopped.

She liked his arms, his smell, the bristles of his beard. She wanted more. He did, too, but he eased her back against the pillow. "Talk to me," he said.

112

"I was lost," she said. "I didn't know what to do. When I left you in the park yesterday, I saw Mary Lou's Uncle Lew in front of Zoey's building with someone Zoey and I trusted. David Lumare, the mime master."

"The loft on Avenue A."

"Yes. We'd told him my story. He wanted the reward. I had to find another place to stay, but I was so tired of running. There was this tall cop who saw me on the street and followed me. I was going to call him and give myself up."

"That's my old partner, Metzger. He spotted you even with all that crap on your face. He followed you to the building on Fifth Street, and called me. When I saw that picture in the paper, I knew it was you. All your friends knew it was you. And I knew you were in trouble, but you didn't call me. You always call me when you're in trouble."

She was outraged. "I do not, Silvestri! You know that's bullshit."

"Gotcha, Les." He was grinning at her.

"Hey," she said. "Now if I can only remember what happened."

"If you were at that explosion site, you were in New Jersey. How did you get back to New York?"

"Bus," she said without thinking. "Bus! I was on a bus and there was a blind man and a dog, a golden retriever." She closed her eyes. "Nora."

"Nora?"

"The dog's name was Nora." Excited, she grasped his hand. "It's coming back!" She wondered if it was because she felt safe with him, safe enough to let what had happened out of her subconscious. "I'm hungry," she said.

"Finish the tea and I'll toast a bagel." He handed her the mug.

"Silvestri, wait. There was a phone number and a reward

for information about Mary Lou Salinger. I called it, and I was patched through to someone who said she was Special Agent Blue. She must have recognized my voice because she said it was okay to come in now."

"Goddammit!" Silvestri's fist punched the bedroom door. "Goddam those Feebs!"

"The FBI?"

"Oh, yeah, I knew it stank. This is another one of their fiascos."

Izz, who'd been cocking her head back and forth, leaped off the bed, barking. She ran from the room, her tail fanning. Then came the thumping on the door.

The familiar fear swelled in her chest, crowding out air. "Are you expecting anyone?" The thumping stopped.

"No. I told Patrice to stay away." More thumping. "And you can't get upstairs without a key." He slipped his gun from its holster.

Chapter 23

"Stay still, don't speak," Silvestri said, gun long down his side. He closed the bedroom door, but the lock didn't hold, leaving a sliver opening.

She got out of bed, carrying with her a billow of stale beer. Damn, where were her clothes? She was wearing one of Silvestri's sweatshirts and her underwear, feet bare on a wood floor that desperately need sanding. What a thing to think of at a time like this.

His apartment was one floor up, the windows looking down on a tree-lined street. A fast getaway was out. The floorboards creaked as she backed away from the window. She peered through the narrow gap. A grotesque woman. No. A transvestite. Masses of black curly hair, a lot of eye makeup, and a diamond stud in a Streisand nose.

"Going to shoot me with that sexy gun, ya big Palooka?" The voice was nicotine-coated, teasing.

"What do you want, Patrice?" Silvestri parked his gun in the waistband of his jeans.

She held out a palm. Her nails were long daggers. "Moolah for cat food. The monster has a ferocious appetite. She won't let my poor Tallulah near her dish. A twenty? Dearie, that's hardly enough. That's better. How long will she be visiting?"

"I'll get her out as soon as we find her owner."

"Marvelous. What's her name?"

"Chat." He was crowding the door, not letting her inside.

"Chat," Patrice said, tasting the French of it. "How wonderfully original, dearie, don't you think?"

"Get out of here, Patrice."

"It's Les, isn't it?" Patrice was bouncing, craning her neck, trying to see beyond Silvestri. "You've found her. I can tell. You're a changed man."

The door slammed.

"Les, it's okay."

She pushed the door open all the way. "What a trip."

"Yeah. Patrice. She's okay, though. I didn't want her to see you. The fewer people who know you're here, the better."

"Does she know me?"

"She met you once, but she's sharp. She recognized your picture immediately and came down and flapped the newspaper in my face."

"Where're my pants?"

"I had to take them, and everything else. They're scene-of-the-crime evidence."

"Oh, fine. That makes me a prisoner. Is that what you want?"

He went into his tiny kitchen and took two bagels from a grocery bag, sliced them, and put them in the toaster oven. "I want to keep you safe until I find out what's going on."

"Oh, Silvestri, you're always trying to protect me, but you can't. I'm my own person." She paused, catching the look on his face, playing back what she had just said. "Ah, I see. Are you always trying to protect me? And do we fight about it?"

He put the hot bagels on paper plates, set them on a card table with a slab of cream cheese. "Come on, we can both use some food."

She sat on one of the folding chairs, the metal cold

on her thighs. "Any coffee?"

He put two cups in the microwave. "Coming up."

"Stale Starbucks, huh?"

His eyes were on the door. "Someone's out there. Go back to the bedroom." Out came the gun again.

She took the half-eaten bagel with her and closed the bedroom door. Again, the lock didn't catch. Izz whined and scratched, pushing at the door. She picked up the dog and waited. But Izz wriggled and when set down, batted the door open and squeezed out.

"I told you she was okay." Silvestri sounded exasperated.

"I had to see for myself." Izz barked. "Hello, little darling."

"How'd you get up without buzzing?"

"A babe named Patrice. Said she's your bosom buddy, Silvestri. Some bosom."

The voice. She recognized it. She really did. She threw open the door. "Carlos!"

"Oh, Birdie, Birdie-mine." He wrapped her in an enormous hug, held her at arm's length, covered her face with kisses. He was dark haired, and slim, her height, but with the build and musculature of a dancer. "You scared the shit out of us, my love."

"So I've been told." Carlos being here made it right. She was utterly safe with him.

"How come you know him and don't know me?" Silvestri took the half-eaten bagel from her and dropped it on the paper plate.

Carlos grinned. He said, with a mincing lisp, "No excess sexual baggage with me, Silvestri."

She laughed.

"What happened to your hand?" Carlos said, touching the bandage.

117

"Blisters from the on-tap handle." When he looked confused, she added, "I got a job bartending."

"You?" He was convulsed.

"My God, what day is this?"

"Saturday."

"I have to go in at six o'clock tonight."

"No way," Silvestri said.

"I have to. Wally's all alone there. On a Saturday night. I can't do that to him. Don't argue with me, either of you."

"She's back," Carlos said.

"I guess I'll be sitting on a barstool most of the night," Silvestri said.

A buzzer sounded. She caught the look between Silvestri and Carlos.

Carlos steered her back to the bedroom while Silvestri flattened himself against the window frame and looked down at the street. "It's Metzger." He pressed the button releasing the downstairs lock.

The spicy smell of Jewish deli preceded Metzger into the room.

He handed Silvestri a fat shopping bag and set the other on the floor near the door along with the roll of newspapers he'd wedged under his arm. "Leslie," he said, his basset hound eyes brimming. "You are a joy to behold."

Silvestri squinted at his former partner.

Moved by Metzger's reaction, Leslie stood on tiptoe and kissed his cheek. "I'm sorry I didn't trust you." She looked back at Silvestri. "If I had, maybe Zoey would still be alive."

"Carlos Prince," Carlos said, putting out his hand.

"Artie Metzger," Metzger said. "You're the choreographer. My wife's a big fan."

"Right. Birdie and I started out as gypsies together."

"Gypsies, yes." She felt overwhelmed. "I have to sit down." She sank onto the folding chair.

Metzger sent an inquiring look to Silvestri, who said, "Carlos is okay."

"Damn straight. Well, not really." Carlos gave Leslie a wink and looked around, seeing the apartment for the first time. "You need a decorator, Silvestri."

"From Katz's, pastrami, corned beef." Metzger began unloading the shopping bags onto the card table. "And a couple of pounds of coffee, milk, cigarettes. In for the long haul."

They settled down at the table brimming with corned beef and pastrami sandwiches on rye, mustard, sour pickles, kraut, potato salad. Silvestri had made coffee, but they were drinking beer and the coffee would come later.

She remembered the newspapers, but they weren't near the door where she'd last seen them.

"So what do we have?" Metzger asked.

"The girl, Zoey, is dead, murdered last night."

"Because of me." Izz was a warm weight in her lap, her nose twitching over the food odors. "They're looking for me. She had epilepsy. They beat her up and maybe caused a seizure. They think I have something and they want it."

"Probably thought she was Les. Same size and coloring," Silvestri said.

"What do they think you have?" Carlos mumbled through his corned beef.

"I don't know."

"And why'd you dye your hair?"

"I don't know. I didn't even know I was a blonde until Zoey told me that it was coming through."

"We ought to start at the beginning," Metzger said.

Silvestri agreed. "You're right, we're getting ahead of

ourselves. Here's what I know. Les called me a couple of months ago and asked if I would take Izz. She said she had to go out of town on business for a few weeks. I figured she was going to the Coast to be with Veeder."

"Veeder again." She was puzzled. He was a blank.

"He's trying a big murder case out there. But it turns out Veeder didn't know where she was either."

"You asked me to pick up your mail and check the apartment," Carlos said. "Wouldn't tell me what you were up to, just said that it was something you had to do for Laura Lee."

"Laura Lee?" Metzger said, reaching for another sandwich.

Leslie's eye twitched. She hid it under her hand.

Carlos said, "She's Birdie's best friend after me."

"Financial adviser," Silvestri added. "Wall Street. Come to think of it, why haven't we heard from her?"

"I called her after Birdie's picture was in the paper—"

"Laura Lee," Leslie said. She pushed back her chair, sliding a startled Izz to the floor, and stood, hugging herself and swaying. "Something's wrong. I forgot. I'm sorry."

They rushed to her. Carlos got there first. They all exchanged glances, how to protect her, understanding she might not let them.

"Here's the deal," Carlos said. "Laura Lee's office told me she's been on a leave of absence for the last three months."

Chapter 24

"I don't want a Valium," she said, pushing Carlos' hand away. "I'll fall asleep and forget the rest of my life."

"Birdie, I hate to tell you this, but you look like hell: black circles, crazy hair, and nothing but skin and bones."

"Thanks, ma." Then she wailed, "I don't have any clothes."

"Les, just lie down for a little while. Artie and I have to try to figure this out. Didn't tell you about the Feebs, Artie."

"Feebs, for crissakes? This is one of their fuck-ups?"

Carlos tucked her in and sat with her. He handed her the Valium, which she swallowed with the remains of the tea. "I've seen enough TV to know that Feebs is NYPD talk for the FBI," he said. "What does the FBI want with you?"

"It's another clue," she murmured. "I look like hell?"

He patted her head. "We have to get you blonde again. Looks weird this way. Everyone's going blonde with dark roots, you're dark with blonde roots. Rest, dear heart. Meantime, I'll go uptown and get you some clothes."

"Underwear and makeup." She was floating now. Somewhere else.

"Only if you sleep." He kissed her forehead and headed for the door.

"Carlos."

"Go to sleep."

"That awful woman who said I was her partner—"

His laugh was luscious. "I'm just going to love this," he said.

When he opened the bedroom door, she heard Silvestri say, ". . . bodies identified?"

Shaving cream. She inhaled the smell, opened her eyes.

"Les?" Silvestri, his hair damp, stood in the doorway patting his face dry. He wore jeans and a white singlet.

Things slithered back into her consciousness. His Italian wedding shirt, he called it. "What time is it?"

"Two-thirty." He hung the towel from the doorknob. "Carlos brought some stuff. If you're up to it, we'll drop in on the Feebs. And I promised the guys at the Ninth we'd make a stop there."

"I'm okay." She sat up. A guitar case was sitting on the floor near the door. "What's that?"

"Carlos' clever suitcase."

"You're joking."

"Take a look."

The guitar case held jeans, her gray blazer, two turtle-neck sweaters, charcoal and black, a long black skirt, a tangle of black pantyhose, black boots, a pair of Keds, underwear, and a plastic bag full of makeup, a comb, even moisturizer, her travel hair dryer. A soft leather shoulder bag and a black beret. "God!"

"A packing master," Silvestri said.

"All those years of touring," she said. "I'm pretty good at it, too."

"Your leather coat is in the closet. He wore it over his shoulders. Get some clothes on." Silvestri took a clean shirt from a drawer in an old bureau. "Special Agent Blue has a lot to answer for."

She eyed the old bureau whose surface was close to imperceptible, then pushed the unopened mail, books, and papers aside and arranged the collection of makeup Carlos had chosen. "Good, eyeliner, mascara, shadow . . . Will the FBI be open?"

"Those intrepid guardians of our shores? Oh, sure. And I'll bet Special Agent Blue will turn up as soon as she knows we're there." He buttoned the shirt and tucked it into his jeans.

She shook out the black skirt. Not too creased. Skirt, sweater, blazer, okay. "May I use your shower?"

A long moment passed. Her question was a stranger's question. It had unsettled him, and she was sorry. She opened her palms and shrugged.

"Make yourself at home," he said.

Dressed, her hair dried and pulled back from her face with a band, she made up her eyes. It was an imperfect job and she let it go. The bathroom was steamy, forcing her to keep wiping the clouds forming on the medicine cabinet mirror.

When she stepped into the living room, Silvestri was drinking coffee and eating another sandwich. The newspapers were spread out on the table. He folded them, put them under the table.

"Zoey?"

"Yup. The tabloids love this stuff."

"I should look." She didn't want to.

He finished the sandwich, rinsed his hands in the sink. "Later."

"What about the explosion?"

He made a tiny measure with his thumb and forefinger. "On the business page. This Jason McLaughlin guy was— is—a piece of crap. He ran a big financial empire out of a mansion surrounded by electric gates—on the Jersey shore. Secretive verging on paranoia."

His words as she was drifting into the Valium haze came back to her. "The bodies. Do we know who they were?"

"The pilot, three other bodies. The pilot and co-pilot have been identified. They were in the plane. The other two—a man and a woman."

"McLaughlin?" She opened the cabinet over the sink and took down a mug, perceiving she'd known it was there. Filled the mug halfway with coffee.

"Maybe. The man would have been around six feet."

She made a strangled sound, dropped the cup into the sink. The cup exploded, coffee splashing.

On his feet, Silvestri turned her to him. "What's wrong?"

She closed her eyes, shaking her head back and forth, back and forth. It was the not knowing that frightened her, as if the memory had skulked past, leaving only a backwash of dread.

"Les, talk to me."

"It's not Jason," she said, unable to find words for the dread. "Jason is not much taller than I am."

Chapter 25

The sun was high, brilliant. As they left Silvestri's brown-stone, he stepped out first to check the street. Leslie shaded her eyes and lifted her chin, absorbing the rays. Refueling. Until the shriek.

"Oh, fuck," Silvestri said, throwing up his hands.

"I might have known," the shrieker screamed. "I'm her best friend and I'm the last person to know. Thank God for the Tarot."

"Huh?" Was this the missing Laura Lee? "Did she say Tarot? What did Tarot cards have to do with this?" Leslie peered around Silvestri. It was the awful woman she'd seen on TV. Her partner. Decked out like a fashion model, oval-lensed shades, tight-fitting brown jodhpurs, high-heeled boots, and a dark chocolate suede jacket over a black turtle-neck, she was posed against a sable Jaguar double-parked across the street.

"I have been trying to carry on our business, doing your work as well as mine, and let me tell you, sweetie pie, it hasn't been easy. It's time you stopped this ridiculous cha-rade and got back to work. You have no idea how stressed I am." She crossed the street and stood in front of them, a Valkyrie from Fashion Week.

Leslie balled up her fist and tried to step around Silvestri. She was going to bop this bitch one right in her perfect face. Silvestri held her back.

"Shut up, Xenia. This is exactly why I didn't call you. Leslie has amnesia. She has been through some sort of trauma we don't know anything about, and her life is in danger—" He was getting edgy, as people passed by dog walking, or with laundry or shopping carts, giving them curious stares.

"I don't believe any of this. After all we've meant to each other, Wetzon, you're going to treat me this way." She burst into tears.

"I don't know you," Leslie said, softening, coming out from behind Silvestri. "I'm sorry if I caused you any pain . . . Xenia."

"Xenia? Xenia?" The Fashion Statement whipped off her sunglasses. "Oh, God help us, it's true." More tears. "You never in your life called me Xenia."

"Xenia, look," Silvestri said. "We're on our way to the Ninth Precinct. The woman who took Les in got murdered last night."

"Murder!" Smith brightened. "Perfect. You'll need me."

"What we need right now, Xenia, is for you to put up a front. You haven't seen Les, you don't know anything about this."

"But I have to be involved."

"It's the best way to keep Les alive, and you want that, don't you?"

"What a horrible question, Silvestri. How can you even ask me that?" The sunglasses were back in place.

"Then go home. If they connect you with Les, your life will be in danger, too. The longer you're here, the more dangerous it gets."

Smith turned pale, took quick glances over each shoulder, drifted a couple of steps back.

"Les needs you to be there for her."

"Well, of course, sugarbun. You can count on me." She got into her car, got out again. "Wetzon! Where is Bill in all this? I've been calling his office and they keep telling me he's out of town."

"Who is Bill?" Leslie whispered to Silvestri through her clenched smile.

"She doesn't remember him, Xenia," Silvestri said.

"How could she not remember him? He's the love of her life."

She got back in the car, gunned the motor, pulled away.

"What a major bitch."

"Big time," Silvestri said, looking down at her. Arm around her waist, he hugged her to him.

"Who is Bill?"

"Veeder." He put on his dark glasses.

"The love of my life?"

"So Xenia says. Let's get going."

"Silvestri?"

"Yeah?" He flagged down a cab, took her hand. "Come on."

"Silvestri, I think maybe you're the love of my life."

They didn't speak in the cab. He was still holding her hand.

"Stop here," he told the driver.

"It's another coupla blocks to Federal Plaza."

"S'okay." He gave the driver a ten and waved off the change, then walked her into a Rite Aid. "Sunglasses, dark," he said. "Try these."

She tucked a stray strand under the beret. "I look like a French film star."

"Fine."

Twenty-six Federal Plaza was a cold, ugly fortress of a building. Next to a security booth, a police car was a horizontal buffer across the parking entrance. Inside the huge lobby were two uniformed cops and three security guards manning the metal detectors. Silvestri showed his badge and was waved around.

"Elevator bank A for FBI," one of the guards said.

On either end of elevator bank A were two more security men, their uniforms different from the others.

"Special Agent Blue," Silvestri told the one closest to them. "She's expecting us."

Leslie was startled. When had he called her?

The guard took their names and called upstairs. "There must be some mistake. Agent Blue is not in today."

"I think she'll want to know that Leslie Wetzon is here to see her."

Ah, a surprise tactic, Leslie thought. Not bad.

"Wait here, please." The guard stepped away from them and spoke into his phone.

"This place does not look familiar to me, Silvestri," Leslie said, uneasy. "It's probably a waste of time. She's not here anyway. Maybe we should leave now."

"Take it easy, Les. Here comes security."

The guard held out two temporary visitor passes. "Please put these on. Twenty-eighth floor."

She could feel Silvestri's tension. It was like her own, but hers was mixed with fear.

A man in gray flannels and a sport jacket was waiting for them on the twenty-eighth floor. "If you'll have a seat," he said. "Special Agent Blue is on her way." He pressed his finger to a raised panel and a buzzer sounded. He passed through the door.

They sat on one of the couches. It could have been a corporate reception area, but no magazines, and the reception counter had the big FBI seal and said FBI, New York Division.

Now she allowed herself to remember the sick feeling, her reaction to Silvestri's telling her the height of the other man who'd died in the explosion. "Why did I know it wasn't Jason McLaughlin?"

"That's what Special Agent Blue is going to tell us when she gets here."

Agent Blue was black. Leslie choked back a giggle. *Blue is black and black is blue* became a refrain in her head. A short woman in a charcoal pantsuit, Agent Blue was a collection of lumps and bumps of bosom, belly, and thighs. She bustled into the reception area, a Starbucks coffee container in her hand, looked Leslie over, and said, "Welcome home."

"This is not her home," Silvestri said. "This is never going to be her home."

"Good to see you, too, Silvestri." Agent Blue pressed her finger to the panel and a buzzer sounded. "Follow me." She led them down a long hall and into a large, open room filled with cubicles containing desks, computers, and telephones. Most of the desks were unoccupied. Two agents stood talking in an aisle, one the man who'd greeted them. The agents stopped talking and watched Leslie and Silvestri. Agent Blue nodded to them.

Her cubicle was on the right side of the room, halfway down. It held a filing cabinet and a standard institutional desk, two chairs parked in front. A map of the city was Scotch-taped to one low wall. Agent Blue motioned them to the chairs. Steam rose from the coffee container when she removed the cover. She sat down at her desk, a tight squeeze, and gave Leslie a hard look.

"So, tell me, Leslie," she said, "what did you do with the diamonds?"

Chapter 26

"Excuse me?" At first Leslie was not sure she'd heard right, but it was as if a switch marked "trembling begin" had been thrown. She might have said more, but Silvestri cut her off.

He put himself between her and Agent Blue, blocking off contact. "Don't say another word, Les. You don't owe them any explanations."

"Oh, but she does." Judy Blue seemed unperturbed. "Sit down and let's talk like professionals."

"Shall I step outside?" Though Leslie'd intended irony, her voice sounded squeaky, inadequate. The room pitched.

Silvestri turning, touched her cheek. She ducked her head against him. His rage was hot. "Let's go," he said, taking her elbows, lifting her.

"Sit down," Agent Blue said.

"What for?" He was walking Leslie out. "So you can stick a gun in her face? It's not going to work like that."

"She has information we need."

"And she's been through hell and can't remember what you got her into."

The elevator came and they got on. No sign of Agent Blue.

In the lobby Silvestri returned their badges to the security guards.

"I thought I was going to pass out," she said, unsteady, leaning on him.

"I'm taking you home." He looked for a cab, but there was never much activity in the City Hall area on a Saturday.

"I don't mind walking," she said.

"I didn't like the way you looked in there." He squeezed her hand.

"I'm okay now," she said. "I don't know anything about diamonds."

"I know that."

"I would have liked to have heard what I'm involved in."

"They weren't going to give us anything. I saw that right away. That's the way they work. Shit, they're still taking credit for breaking the first World Trade Center bombing, when we did all the work." He stopped to light a cigarette, inhaled once, twice, with pleasure, then stamped it out. "I wouldn't put it past them to have the whole place up there bugged."

"What will they do now?"

"They know where I live. They'll come to us this time. It's better that way. There's a cab."

When they got into the cab, she said, "I'd like to go to the precinct and tell them about Zoey."

"Are you sure, Les? It can wait another day."

"I want to get it over with."

The Ninth Precinct was on Fifth Street across Second Avenue. No wonder the cops were there so fast.

"Stick to the murder," Silvestri said. "Nothing about the FBI crap. Keep it simple."

Squad rooms were squad rooms, she thought. The FBI had neat little cubicles for obsessive-compulsive law and order, the NYPD still smacked of a jock enclave of old desks, a few computers, typewriters, paper, chipped and scarred filing cabinets, and the pervading smell of pizza, doughnuts, and burnt coffee. The NYPD felt less surreal.

Detective Dolores Hammond came to greet them. Everything about her was taut, including her short, tight curls. She was built like a long-distance runner.

The squad room was small, if not cozy, and grubby. Hammond's partner, introduced as Zoot Kaminsky, pulled over a second chair for Silvestri. Silvestri knew him and they traded some information about people no one else knew.

"Can I get you some coffee?" Detective Hammond asked.

"I wouldn't recommend it," Silvestri said.

Hammond grinned. "It's okay. I brought the coffee maker and I make it. It's not the usual poison."

After Kaminsky served up the coffee, Hammond said, "So what's your interest in this, Silvestri?"

"Leslie Wetzon."

Kaminsky said, "Who is Leslie Wetzon?"

"I'm Leslie Wetzon."

No surprise on either detective's face, just curiosity.

"You knew that," Silvestri said. "Her prints are on file."

Kaminsky gave him a reproachful look. "What kind of nickname is T.J.?"

"She was in an accident—"

Kaminsky interrupted. "Jesus Christ, Silvestri, will you let her answer?"

"I was in an accident," Leslie said. "I lost my memory and wandered around the city for a few days until I met Zoey. She took me in and was trying to help me find out who I am. T.J. stood for Temporary Jane. Zoey got me involved with her mime troupe." She took a sip of the coffee. It was good.

Hammond was making notes. "So when did your memory come back?" A hint of disbelief colored her comment, which irritated Leslie.

"Look, I'm trying to tell you the truth and you're giving me attitude. I don't think I have to talk to you, do I, Silvestri?"

"Guys?" Silvestri took her hand. "Go on, Les."

"A friend of Silvestri's spotted me and told Silvestri—"

"Artie Metzger," Silvestri said.

"Yeah? No kidding," Kaminsky said. "Jeeze, haven't seen him in a dog's age. We were at the Academy together."

"Where were you between nine and twelve that night?" Hammond said.

"I was at my job, The Big Dipper, Avenue B, near Tenth Street. Wally Dipper can vouch for me. I was the only one tending bar all night. I got there at five and didn't leave till after two. Zoey was supposed to pick me up but she didn't show. I thought she'd probably found something better to do."

"What about her midnight to six shift at the coffee place in Grand Central? Why would she be picking you up when she was supposed to be at work?"

"She told me she was off that night."

Hammond put down her pencil. "You found her and made the call to 911."

"Yes." She felt ashamed. "I ran away. I'm sorry."

"Why didn't you wait there?"

"I was afraid. I thought maybe whoever killed her might still be there. I didn't touch anything. I'm really sorry."

"How did you get there, Silvestri?" Kaminsky said.

"I was listening to the calls and heard the address mentioned. I saw her in the crowd and took her home with me. But I cleared it with you, Kaminsky, as you know."

"Okay," Hammond said, "we'll get your statement typed up. We'll call you to come sign it. We may need to talk to you again so don't leave town."

"She'll be with me," Silvestri said. "If you need her."

"Wait," Leslie said. "How did Zoey die?"

"We don't know yet. We're waiting for the autopsy results."

"She had epilepsy. Did you know?"

Hammond made a note. "No."

"She was hiding it. It was very bad and she wouldn't take the medication. She didn't like the way it made her feel."

Kaminsky walked them to the door. "Thanks for coming in, Ms. Wesson."

"That's Wetzon," she said. "W-e-t-z-o-n."

"Right. Say hello to Metzger," Kaminsky told Silvestri.

"Let's walk," she said when they hit the street.

He flagged down a cab. "Get in, don't argue. It's been a long day."

"I'm still going to The Big Dipper, Silvestri."

"You haven't forgotten how to be a hard head."

The cab pulled up behind a double-parked car in front of Silvestri's brownstone.

"Well," Silvestri said. "Looky here."

The chunky black woman in the charcoal pantsuit climbed out of the double-parked car and stood waiting.

Chapter 27

Judy Blue cast a dubious eye on Silvestri's sagging sofa and chose one of the metal folding chairs. "You live like a cop, Silvestri." She gave the sniffing Izz a pat on the head.

"Enough with the pleasantries." He went into the bedroom with Leslie's coat and came back with a blanket. "Take the couch, Les. When she's had it, you're out of here, Blue," he said, standing, arms folded.

Boots off, Leslie, with the immediate addition of Izz, curled up on the sofa under Silvestri's blanket. She contemplated him, having trouble understanding why they'd split up. "What time is it?"

"Going somewhere?" Judy Blue asked. She walked the folding chair closer to the sofa without getting up. Her abundance spilled over the seat. She adjusted her jacket.

"My job at The Big Dipper."

"How'd you hurt your hand?"

"Bartending." She held up her hand. "The tap."

"Let's talk about the explosion."

"I don't remember anything."

Silvestri said, "Aren't you getting a little ahead of yourself, Blue?"

Judy Blue sighed. "What do you want to know, Silvestri?"

"Are you wearing a wire?"

"No."

"How about a mini recorder? Like the one in your pocket." He held out his hand.

Without an iota of shame, Judy Blue took a tiny recorder from the pocket of her jacket and removed the tape. "Okay?"

"Thanks," Silvestri said, taking the tape. "Okay, let's talk. You first."

Agent Blue dropped the empty recorder into her pocket. "Jason McLaughlin," she said. Leslie shuddered, pulled the blanket to her chin. "You know him, of course."

"I don't remember. Why do you say 'of course'?"

"You were with him the night of the explosion. You were working for him. As an assistant."

"I'm a headhunter. I have my own business. How could I possibly be working for him? It doesn't make sense. People on Wall Street know me. They'd recognize my name." She looked at Silvestri. She was doing all right.

"You took a leave of absence. And another name."

Leslie gripped the blanket as Judy Blue's words sank in. "My God," she said. Sweat beaded along her upper lip, the nape of her neck, rolled down between her breasts. "Mary Lou Salinger."

"Yes."

"She was working for you," Silvestri said.

"Look, Silvestri, this wasn't our idea. We don't put civilians undercover. She volunteered to go in on her own because her friend—"

"Laura Lee Day," Leslie said. "She was in trouble."

"This is nice," Laura Lee said. "I'm fried." Her usual buoyant spirits were deflated, her face drawn, blue smudges under her eyes.

They were in the Union Square Cafe, sitting at the bar, one of the greatest pleasures of living in New York. Caesars and a bottle of Grande Cassagne syrah. Laura

Lee had just returned from Mississippi after attending her grandfather's funeral.

"Want to talk?" Wetzon said.

"Not yet." A wan smile surfaced. "Would you believe my mother kept introducin' me as her 'unmarried daughter'?"

"No."

"How was your day?"

Wetzon took a sip of wine. "Like any other day, full of misperceptions."

"That's the subtext of our business, isn't it, Wetzon darlin'?"

"You're so right." She dug into the salad. "I love anchovies."

Uncharacteristically, Laura Lee was silent, picking at her food.

"So," Wetzon said, trying a diversion, "I sent a broker with a major WASP pedigree, a numeral three no less, good business potential, great tailor, to see Dick Malloy."

Laura Lee perked up. "If it fits, I always say."

"You know him?"

"I met The Dick at Grace Goldsmith's weddin'. He's a friend of her husband, ex now."

"God, already? How long were they married?"

"Eighteen months," Laura Lee said, taking a sip of wine. "He looked good on paper. The forged kind. Anyway, The Dick's been callin' me ever since, tryin' to get me out for a drink."

"Maybe he's trying to recruit you without having to pay a headhunter."

"I told him right upfront, Wetzon darlin'. I don't go anywhere without you."

Wetzon lifted her glass, drawling, "What a pal, what a pal."

"So anyway, you sent a numeral three to see The Dick."

"A study in contrasts. But guess what? The numeral three tells me, 'I really liked Dick. I was very comfortable with him. He left it to me to pursue. I want to.' "

"And the punchline is?"

Wetzon smiled. "Not what I expected. The Dick said no chance he'd hire him, that he was a permanent mediocrity. When The Dick asked him where he saw himself in five years, the jerk says, 'in my own business.' "

Laura Lee groaned. "WASPs are definitely missin' a gene."

Wetzon topped off their glasses.

"I think my Uncle Weaver is involved in a major fraud," Laura Lee said. "He runs the U.S. Jackson Insurance Company. It's a privately held, very successful company."

"Did he buy a slew of derivatives?"

"Not exactly. Aunt Bren says he's been investin' the company's pension with a hedge fund run by someone I swear I'd never heard of and makin' huge profits. A con man for sure."

"He never checked him out with you?"

"That side of the family, my mother's side, has never taken me seriously. He's bein' defrauded. I came back and began lookin' into this hedge fund. It's bein' run by some recluse out of his mansion on the Jersey shore, and well recommended by a priest connected to the Vatican."

"How is that possible?"

"I don't know. But I'm goin' to find out."

"Do we know this con man with the hedge fund?"

"I didn't. His name is Jason McLaughlin. Do you know him?"

"Les? Les? Hey—" He shook her shoulder.

Silvestri was sitting next to her, staring into her face. Judy Blue was leaning toward her, consternation wiping the neutrality from her face.

Leslie blinked. "What's wrong?"

"You blanked out," Silvestri said. "Where were you?"

She was puzzled. "How long?"

"A minute or so," Judy Blue said.

"I don't understand—"

A beeper went off. Both Judy Blue and Silvestri reached for theirs.

"It's mine," Judy Blue said. She took out her cell and walked into the kitchen. "Yeah. I'll be right in." She moved toward the door. "We'll have to continue this later."

Silvestri was trying to read her. "Something to do with this case?"

Judy Blue paused, weighing whether to say anything further. "I'm trusting you, Leslie, not to run away again."

"I didn't run away."

"That phone call?" Silvestri said.

Judy Blue nodded. "We have positive ID on the bodies."

Chapter 28

"So the fuzz turns you on," Wally said, jerking his head toward Silvestri at the end of the bar, his back against the wall, eyes on the door and storefront window.

Gingerly, Leslie pulled the glove on over the bandage and adjusted the Mets cap. "I knew him in another life."

"Whatever. So long as he pays for his seat and he's not made." Wally headed for the back. "Keep your head up. We'll be busy tonight, but at least Ellis is sober and in the kitchen."

She brought Silvestri a Beck's. The two Texas types in jeans and cowboy boots who'd just come in, ordered tap. They were actors talking shop. Actors always talk shop.

The place began to fill up. Wally was wearing a path in the floor taking orders, fetching burgers, serving the glasses of wine Leslie poured.

When a solitary man in a wet raincoat walked in and sat down in the empty seat next to Silvestri, the actors, who had just paid their bill and were getting ready to leave, did a double-take. They decided to stay and asked for two more cold ones, throwing what they thought were surreptitious glances toward Carlos.

"You guys are too much," Leslie said, rinsing a glass with vermouth and filling it with vodka. She added two olives on a toothpick and placed it in front of Carlos.

"I wanted onions," he said.

"I don't do onions. You want a burger?"

"Why not?"

"One down, medium rare," she told Wally as he went by.

Carlos rolled his eyes at Silvestri. "She was born for this."

A line had formed outside, people waiting to get in. Leslie worked up a sweat, moving up and down the bar, filling booze orders for Wally's tables, collecting money.

She looked up once and saw Silvestri had gone. "Where'd he go?" she asked Carlos.

"This is not a bad burger," he said.

"Carlos."

"Outside. He got a call."

"Is he coming back? I'll need his seat."

"He's not leaving you, Birdie." He wiped greasy fingers on a napkin and reached into his pocket. "Forgot to give you this." It was a man's watch, an old Porsche. "It's mine. I couldn't find one of yours."

She stopped to strap it on. It was loose, like a bracelet. "I'm keeping it."

Someone waved to her down at the other end. A multi-highlighted, rain-sprayed blonde sat sideways on the stool, two men behind her. Two cold ones and a red. The blonde said, "I'm counsel and I say we let him swing in the wind. There's no way we can look good in an arbitration."

The younger of the two men said, "He's buried more clients than an undertaker."

"Becker, Bryson's got him now. Good luck to them."

Leslie wondered if they were talking about a broker from her headhunting life. Would she recognize his name? She wiped down the counter pretending not to listen, but they never mentioned the broker's name.

The two actors had worked themselves up and approached Carlos. Carlos was gracious. Two women slipped onto the stools the actors had vacated and ordered Coronas.

Leslie set the mugs down, edged toward the front window hoping to catch a glimpse of Silvestri. The window was steamy. A wide-brimmed black hat, then the face beneath it, wavered in the condensation, gaping, rivulets of shock. Or was it tears? Whatever it was, it was gone in an instant.

She looked for Silvestri, didn't see him in the misty drizzle.

The actors left and two more people came through, waiting to be seated. Leslie hurried back to Carlos. "Find Silvestri," she said. "I just saw—" She stopped.

Silvestri was back. "You just saw?"

"David Lumare. He was staring at me through the window. He's wearing a broad-brimmed black hat."

"Christ!" Silvestri was out the door.

Wally gave her three more wine orders. "You got to keep an eye out for the refills."

Her feet hurt. Her hand was throbbing again. Silvestri came through the door, dispelling rain like a wet puppy. He shook his head. The evening wore on.

Carlos watched, worried. "Birdie, I think you should call it quits. Not just tonight, but for good. This is no way for you to live. You don't have to."

She had to agree with him. Besides, she had to begin recapturing her real life.

It was after two when Silvestri sent Carlos home.

With only Wally and Silvestri remaining, she wiped down the bar. Wally restocked the fridge. No one spoke.

She placed the Mets cap and the leather glove on the bar. "This is it for me, Wally."

"I'll see you Monday, T.J.," Wally said.

"She's quitting," Silvestri said.

"Silvestri!"

"Well, you are, aren't you?"

"Are you?" Wally said.

Leslie nodded. "Outside, Silvestri."

She waited until he closed the door. "You saved my life, Wally. Literally. And I thank you. I needed this job because I'd lost my memory. I have a whole other life I have to get back to."

"Okay, T.J., that's cool." He came around the bar and gave her a bear hug. "Any time you want, you got a job."

"Thanks, Wally."

The night was moist, but the rain had stopped. Their breaths made white puffs.

"You didn't owe him any explanations," Silvestri said.

"Yes, I did. He was nice to me."

He hailed a cab in spite of her protestations. "You look like you're about to drop, so don't give me a hard time, okay?"

The stairs were daunting. Silvestri picked her up and slung her over his shoulder.

"The blood is rushing to my head," she said, thumping his back.

"Good. Maybe you'll get smart and start taking care of yourself."

She didn't even have the strength to protest.

He lowered her to the bed and took her coat, fighting Izz off.

"The down jacket," she said. "I swiped it from a nurse—Lucy—at Mount Sinai. I have to give it back to her. And the money—sixty dollars."

"The jacket is evidence. We'll buy her a new one, or better yet, we'll send her a check for the works."

"Was that call something to do with me?"

He pulled off her boots and set them next to the bed. "Metzger."

"So?"

"He picked up the ID of one of the bodies, the woman. Natalie Nostrand, real name Natalya Nostradovich."

Leslie shook her head. "Don't know her, by either name."

"Her prints were on file."

"How come? Was she a felon?"

"She was a stockbroker."

Chapter 29

"I can get pretty close," William said, inspecting the new ash blonde leaking through the dark. "Maybe a little warmer than ash."

"What do you think, Birdie?"

She tugged at the towel William had wrapped around her neck. "I like warmer, but stop fussing."

William performed hair miracles for Broadway. They were in his tiny Village apartment where wigs and pieces, some of unearthly hues, claimed every available surface. As for William's own hair, he didn't have any. His looks were startling. He shaved his head and dyed his wooly eyebrows bright blue.

William was beaming to his own melody, tuned out, hands like a piano virtuoso, lathering Leslie's hair with glop, as Carlos said, putting the pieces of his Birdie back together.

"Fussing? Bite me."

"No, thank you."

She'd been relieved that Silvestri had to go to work. "Once I'm blonde again," she'd said, "don't you think I can go home without anyone still thinking I'm Mary Lou Salinger?"

"No. The Barracuda settled that with her news conference."

"Barracuda?"

"What Carlos calls your esteemed partner."

Leslie giggled. "It's good."

"Anyway, they may have someone watching your place, and your office. They're not stupid. They'll figure you were working inside and have something on them."

"Diamonds?"

"Only the FBI, the killers, and you know. And you can't remember."

"I guess that means I can't go to the office and see what headhunting is all about."

"No shit."

And that's how it was left.

Carlos took her to lunch at The Grange on Commerce Street. They ordered burgers, fries, and black coffee, straight. "You look like the peek-a-boo blonde, Veronica," he said.

"As in Lake, you mean?" Her hair, blonde, paler around her face, skimmed her shoulders. "Don't I wear it like this?"

"You wear it up in a tight knot."

"Oh, dear, that sounds like a rigid personality to me. Do you think Silvestri will like it this way?" She flushed at his intent look.

"You like him?"

She nodded. "Why did we break up?"

"He can be pretty rigid himself. And he's not what you would call the great communicator. Someone else came along."

"Bill Veeder."

"You remember him?"

"No. Did you meet him?" When Carlos nodded, she said, "What's he like?"

"Older. Criminal attorney. Tall, thin, very, very attractive. Smooth. Gets what he wants. He wanted you."

"And I fell for that?"

"You were vulnerable. An old girlfriend of Silvestri's had been murdered and he got into his noncommunicating shit. He moved out. Broke your heart."

"So I found someone else." The burgers arrived, thick and juicy. She went for the fries first.

With an indulgent smile, Carlos passed her the ketchup. "Well, Veeder was biding his time. You'd met him through the Barracuda."

"So that's why she said he was the love of my life."

"You had a thing going with him, but love of your life? Hardly. Veeder is rich and famous, had a lot of women falling all over him. He wanted you. You were flattered."

"I was shallow. How long could that last?"

"The sex was great."

"Do I tell you everything?"

He grinned at her. " 'Most."

"Have you left anything out?"

"He was married."

"God, Carlos, what kind of fool am I?"

"Birdie, darling, you a fool? Never. Lustful? Maybe. It wasn't an easy decision for you. And it isn't as bad as you think. Veeder's wife has some kind of Alzheimer thing that left her unmarked but mindless. He never put her in an institution, though he could have."

"Are there children?"

"No."

"Well, there's a blessing."

"Irony?"

"Better than tears. My life sounds pretty messy. Maybe I don't want it back." She polished off the burger and licked her fingers.

"Now none of that! You listen to Uncle Carlos. You have a good life. Your friends love you and you love them."

He looked up at the waiter. "Bring this urchin some rice pudding."

"I love rice pudding!"

"I know."

"Carlos," she said, feeding him a spoon of rice pudding, "I'm thinking I might like to do some detecting—"

"Uh oh. Nancy Drew lives."

"No, really. Do you have to be somewhere this afternoon?"

"I'm not sure I like that question."

"If you have something else to do, I'll go myself."

"You will not."

"Ooo, you're scary."

He reached across the table and pulled her beret over her eyes. "Whither thou go-est, I go. La dee dah."

She raised the beret and gave him a hard look. "I see. You promised Silvestri."

Smirking, he held up his hands. "Guilty as charged."

"You guys don't trust me."

"We know you, Birdie. You just gave the best example. You want to do some detecting on your own."

"Walk this way." Leslie danced on the sidewalk in front of Carlos. She knew he wouldn't be able to help himself; he was dancing in her footsteps.

"You better tell me where we're going, little witch."

"I thought we might beard David Lumare in his den."

"You mean the mime master who ratted you out and got your friend killed?"

She stopped and Carlos, a body in motion, stayed in motion.

"The very same," she said, arms around him. "I have to do this, don't you see? He's responsible for Zoey. He took

148

money for telling them where I was. I know he was looking in the window last night—at The Big Dipper."

"Silvestri said you're not going back to The Big Dipper."

"I'm not, but—Carlos, please come with me. He's a bad guy. He did a bad thing."

"And you want to make him eat it."

"Something like that."

When they arrived at Lumare's loft building, Carlos curled his lip. "What a dump."

"It's the space that's good. Laura Lee always says, in New York it's square footage that makes a relationship work."

Carlos pounced. "Laura Lee. You said Laura Lee. You're remembering."

"It just came out when I wasn't trying." She was close to joy. "It's going to happen now. I know."

As they got on the elevator, Leslie thought, Zoey was so trusting. David sold us both out, got her murdered, and I'm to blame.

"Twenty years ago," Carlos said, checking out the other open loft spaces, "I might have thought living like this was fun."

"Sheesh, you were never a bohemian, my love."

"Where is it already?"

"Here. Don't say anything, let me do the talking."

Carlos rolled his eyes, then looked past her. "And who are you going to be talking to, Birdie darling?"

"What do you mean—?"

It was easy to see what he meant. David Lumare's loft was cleaned out, bare of possessions and person. Only the mirrored wall remained to reflect their astonishment.

Chapter 30

A cell phone cut the silence. Carlos blinked. "Mine," he said, pulled it from his jacket, and answered the ring.

"It had better be since I don't have one." But she must. Didn't everyone these days? So hers must have been left behind in the lost world that was Mary Lou Salinger's.

"Where are we?" Carlos made a face at her. "Not where we should be. David Lumare's place. I'll let her explain." He passed his phone to Leslie. Sputtering noises were coming from it.

"Silvestri, stop yelling." She held the phone away from her ear. "Do you believe him?" she asked Carlos.

"He has a point," Carlos said.

"You're all against me." She handed Carlos' cell back to him.

"Yo," he said. "Not to worry. Lumare took a powder." He listened, nodding. "Okay." Folded the phone and dropped it into his pocket, took her elbow. " 'Let us go then, you and I.' "

"Where?"

"I have my instructions."

They came out on the street and Carlos began looking for a cab.

"Hey! If you don't tell me where we're going, I'm going to run away. And I can run faster than you can."

"T.J.!"

The Lumare Mimes, what was left of them, had just crossed the street. It was Eric who'd called out.

Carlos was wary. "Who's that?"

"Eric. One of the mimes. They must not know David ran out on them." Do they know, she wondered, about Zoey? They had to. The papers had been full of the news, with pictures and all.

"You've changed your hair," Eric said. "Because of what happened to Zoey?" His eyes were as sad as his mime character.

"No. This is my natural color. I'm so sorry about Zoey."

"Where were you when it happened?" Mona's demand unnerved her.

"Wait a goddam minute," Carlos said, getting between her and the mimes.

"It's okay, Carlos, they have a right to know." But she'd lost their attention. They were now staring at Carlos.

"You're Carlos Prince," Jeff said, awed.

"Yes. And Leslie Wetzon is my friend."

"Who is Leslie Wetzon?" Mona asked.

"I'm Leslie Wetzon. When Zoey took me in, I'd been in an accident and lost my memory."

Eric said, "Does David know?"

"David knew. You're on your way to the loft?"

"We have a gig—you coming with us?" Mona began moving. "Let's go. We'll be late."

"David's not there."

"Of course, he's there," Jeff said.

"He's not," Carlos said. "He cleared out."

Mona shook her head. "I don't believe it. He wouldn't do that."

Jeff hurried into the building.

"He did," Leslie said. "There was a reward for finding me. He took it and ran."

Carlos gave Leslie a nudge. "We're going to be late."

"I'm sorry about everything," Leslie said. The guilt was there and she couldn't make it go away. If she hadn't met Zoey, if Zoey hadn't introduced her to David, Zoey might still be alive.

"What are we going to do?" Mona asked Eric.

"You can audition for Carlos," Leslie said. "Can't they, Carlos?"

"Birdie—"

"Carlos, they're wonderful. Give them a chance."

Carlos knew when he was losing. "Give my stage manager a call at the Imperial. His name is Sam Barry. Tell him I said to set it up."

"All three," Leslie said. "Do you need a pen?"

"All three."

"Thank you," Mona said. She wrote down the backstage number.

"He's gone," Jeff shouted. "So's all our stuff."

"That was very nice of you, my love," Leslie said. She sat back in the cab and gave Carlos' sinewy thigh a squeeze.

"I'm just one swell guy." His sarcasm was belied by the tender cover of his hand over hers.

The cab driver's eyes were reflected in the mirror. "Where to, folks?"

"Bellevue," Carlos said.

"Bellevue? Why are we going there?" Her first thought, Zoey is alive, wonderful, they're taking me to her. But logic set in. Zoey was dead. Then, what if Silvestri was hurt?

"Silvestri said he'll meet you at the information desk in the main lobby."

He's all right, she told herself, because he's going to meet me in the lobby. "Bellevue is where they take wounded cops."

"You remember that?"

"It's events I don't remember. And people."

"Here okay?" the driver asked.

"Yeah." Carlos gave him a ten. "Wait for me, I'll be right back."

Leslie was dismayed. "You're not coming with me?"

"No, I'm just the delivery boy. Silvestri said he'd take it from here." Carlos got out of the cab and helped her out. They went into the busy lobby through a revolving door. "There's your boy," Carlos said, waving at Silvestri. "Give us a hug, dear heart. You know where to find me?"

She looked blank. He took a memo pad from his back pocket and jotted down numbers, handed it to her. Their hug was mutual. He shook hands with Silvestri and went back through the revolving doors to the cab.

"Don't yell," she said, casting an apprehensive eye at Silvestri.

"I'm not going to yell." Prickliness in his voice.

"You were. Just consider what I've been through."

"And you're milking it. Consider this. You're a material witness to murder. The Jersey cops want to talk to you. The Feebs'll be back."

She held up her hands in surrender. "Okay, okay. Why am I here?"

"I want you to meet someone." He took her hand. "You look like my Les again," he said, touching her hair, trying all the while to cover his emotion.

"Silvestri." She rested her head against him.

"Come on," he said, putting his arm around her.

They took the elevator to the fifth floor and walked down one corridor, passing doors open, half open. No hiding the hospital odors, disinfectant, and institutional food. And fear.

The floor bustled with activity. Nurses, aides, doctors, visitors. They passed a large nurses' station, then went on. At the end of another long hall, Silvestri stopped. A cop sat in front of a door, reading the *Post*. When he saw Silvestri's badge, he dropped the paper and stood.

Uneasy, she wondered why Silvestri was being so mysterious.

"How's he doing?" Silvestri said.

"He's tough."

Silvestri knocked on the door, opened it. "You up for company?"

"Sure," came a voice from within.

"Come on, Les." He pulled her in after him.

The whine of the dog didn't register at first. What she saw was riveting. The man in the bed had bandages that started at his shoulder and disappeared under the blanket. He was big and broad, almost overwhelming the bed. His hair was sprouted, disordered, thick and gray. The beginnings of a red-streaked white beard covered the lower part of his face. His eyes were turned toward them, but she realized he was blind.

"Back so soon, Silvestri?"

This time she heard the whine, saw the golden retriever leave the side of the bed and move toward her. She stood stock still for a moment, reeling, flooded with baffling sensations, then dropped to her knees, arms around the dog.

"Nora," she said.

Chapter 31

"Les," Silvestri said, offering her a hand up. "This is Marty Lawler."

"Pull over a chair for the lady, Silvestri," Marty Lawler said. "We have a lot to talk about."

Wetzon pulled off her beret. "You're the blind man from the bus," she said, sitting, trying to remember more. She looked to Silvestri. "Why is there a cop outside the door?"

"Marty was shot in the Port Authority trying to prevent your being kidnapped."

"And it helps that I was on the job for twenty-five years," Marty said.

"I'm so sorry." She stared at Marty's bandages. "You're lucky you weren't killed. Everybody who tries to help me—"

"Hey!"

Marty held up his hand. "Let her be, Silvestri. She's entitled to a little self-pity, don't you think?" The lilt in his voice ameliorated the irony.

"You were badly hurt," she said.

"I'll have to shoot lefty from now on."

"He was in bad shape but he's a tough mutha," Silvestri said.

Marty grinned. "What's a spleen among friends?"

Nora nuzzled her head into Leslie's lap and when Leslie scratched her ears, emitted a contented sigh.

"I have to admit I was out of it for the last week, but the guys hung around trying to catch me when I was copasetic enough to find out what happened. By that time, when I knew how much time had passed, I didn't think they'd find you alive."

"I got away from them," Leslie said, "but I don't know how."

"So they tell me."

"Les, I want you to hear Marty's story, and see if anything sticks. How about it?"

"I don't have much hope—"

"Just listen, okay?"

She nodded, realized that Marty couldn't see, said, "Okay."

"Here goes. It was raining, sleeting, an all-around lousy night," Marty said. "I was coming home from my daughter's, the bus was crowded. I was on the aisle, Nora sitting in the seat next to me, so people could get by. The bus always stops where it did that night."

Leslie spoke, as if relating a dream. "A gas station. It was closed. They were chasing me. The bus came and I got on."

"You came down the aisle toward me. I moved Nora back in the aisle so you could sit down. There was this acrid smell, like you'd been in a fire. You were wearing this big, wet cashmere coat—"

"You knew that?"

"Nothing wrong with my sense of touch. The coat was as big as a blanket, there was that much material. Musta been a man's overcoat. And I could feel the snow when you climbed over me."

"A man's overcoat? Where was my coat? Whose overcoat?"

"Take it easy, Les," Silvestri said, resting his hand on her shoulder.

She took a breath. "So I was wearing a man's overcoat when I was kidnapped. But when they found me in the park, I was wearing only a black dress."

"Maybe that's how you got away." With his good arm Marty reached for the water glass and sipped through a straw.

"Did I say anything to you on the bus?"

"Not at first. I did a good bit of nagging, I'll admit, because you were shaking like a leaf and it seemed like you could use some help. You finally told me that two men in a gray Mercedes were trying to kill you. You seemed sure they were following the bus and would be waiting when we got to Port Authority."

"And I guess they were."

"But we cooked up a bit of mischief between us," Marty said. "I had you get off behind me and I made a scene like I was having a seizure, fell on the ground and rolled around. You were able to sneak around the back of the bus and get away."

"But if I got away, what was I doing back in the terminal when you got shot?"

"Good question. You had time to disappear, but you hung around for some reason. And by the time I convinced everybody I didn't need an ambulance, you should have been long gone. But you weren't. Suddenly you were right there next to me, and so was the shooter. That's all I remember."

"Well, it's way more than I do," Leslie said, checking Silvestri. "Why, when I could have gotten away, did I hang around?"

"I thought you might be a Feeb or an undercover cop."

"Did I say anything that made you think that?"

"I asked if the two guys chasing you were cops. You said you didn't think they were on the job." He gave a nod in Silvestri's direction. "I guess I know now where that came from."

"Did I tell you my name?"

"No. I asked if you wanted me to call someone and you gave me part of a number—three seven four five five—then stopped like you couldn't remember the rest."

"My number at One P.P.," Silvestri said.

A nurse came through the door. "How are you feeling, Mr. Lawler? You don't want to overdo." She frowned at Leslie and Silvestri. "This is his first day out of ICU."

"We'll get going, Marty," Silvestri said. "If anything else comes to mind, you know where to find me."

Nora followed them to the door. "Thank you, Marty," Leslie said, giving Nora's snout a farewell rub.

As soon as the door closed behind them, Leslie's eyelids drooped, lead filled her veins. Sleep. That's what she needed. She slumped against Silvestri. Why hadn't she run when she had the chance? She asked Silvestri the question.

He held open the door of a cab that had just dropped a passenger in front of the hospital. "Let's go home, kid."

"Can we pick up some coffee and a Melitta?"

He squinted at her. "Is that how it's going to be?"

"Yup."

"Chelsea Market," he told the cab driver.

Which is how Judy Blue found them as they walked back to Silvestri's apartment carrying three fat shopping bags of groceries.

"Uh oh," Silvestri said spotting the special agent. "And she's got a junior with her."

"Does she know about Marty Lawler?"

"Not if our guys didn't tell them."

"Meaning she doesn't know."

Special Agent Blue introduced her associate as Special

Agent Gelber. Gelber was a tall, serious young man with a fifties haircut and an ultra-smooth shave. From his demeanor, he was definitely a second. Maybe even an agent in training, if the FBI had such a unit.

As they climbed the stairs to Silvestri's apartment, there was a flurry of activity from above. Patrice's head appeared over the stairs. Her wig was a cluster of long, yellow sausage curls. "Silvestri!" she shrieked, raining thousands of shiny bits of confetti down on them. "Hello, Little Les, I knew it was you he was hiding!"

"Hi, Patrice," Leslie said.

"Cat food is sooooo expensive, Silvestri." Patrice paused. "Aren't you going to introduce me to your friends?"

Something like a chuckle came from Silvestri. "Sure, Patrice. Special Agents Blue and Gelber. FBI. Would you like to come down and meet them?"

Patrice's head disappeared. A door slammed.

Silvestri positioned the folding chairs around the card table. "Sitting or standing?"

"I'm making coffee," Leslie said, unpacking the bags, filling the kettle. She rinsed and dried the Melitta parts, set in the brown paper filter, measured the coffee.

The agents sat down. Judy Blue said, "How's that memory?"

"No better, no worse," Leslie said.

"What kind of work was she doing for you?"

Agent Blue rested her eyes on Silvestri. "Let's let her tell us."

"We're going around in circles," Leslie said, pouring boiling water through the coffee, inhaling the intoxicating fumes.

"Identified the bodies yet?" Silvestri set a container of

milk on the table along with four unmatched mugs. He didn't mention he already knew about the dead woman with the Russian name.

"We have."

"So are you going to tell us or is it a state secret?"

Leslie filled the mugs and sat down.

Agent Blue put milk in her coffee and passed the container to her associate. "The woman has been identified as Natalie Nostrand. Born Natalya Nostradovich, Odessa, 1972. Emigrated to the U.S. with her parents in 1980. Settled in Brighton Beach. Graduated from NYU with a degree in Economics, 1994. Hired by Smith Barney in 1994 as a sales assistant, at which time she was fingerprinted. She moved to Peck, Landau in 1996, passed Series 7, and became registered as a stockbroker in 1997. Left Peck, Landau in 1999. In January, 2000, she paid two million for a condo in TriBeCa."

"And between 2000 and today?" Silvestri said.

"No one seems to know." Agent Blue's fingers tapped the card table.

"Her parents?"

"Father died. Mother remarried and moved away. No known siblings."

"Good coffee, Les," Silvestri said. He checked his watch.

The two special agents were looking at Leslie, as if expecting her to contribute to the mix. More tapping from Agent Blue.

"If you're asking me if I know her, I don't."

"You never recruited her?" Agent Gelber looked surprised.

"I don't remember if I did. My office would know, wouldn't they? Her name means nothing to me now."

"You need a cigarette?" Silvestri asked Agent Blue.

"I quit."

"So did I," Silvestri said, taking a pack of Marlboros from his shirt pocket and offering it to Agent Blue.

They both lit up and inhaled with gusto.

Leslie laughed. "You don't smoke, Agent Gelber?"

"No."

"You will," Agent Blue said with uncharacteristic good cheer.

Silvestri brought over an ashtray. "Did you identify the fourth body?"

The agent's face changed, stiffened. Her eyes moved from Silvestri to Leslie, back to Silvestri. Silvestri, puzzled, moved his chair closer to Leslie.

"We have." She stopped and waited.

Exasperated, Silvestri said, "Well, what's the big secret?"

Judy Blue's voice was flat. "We were able to identify the remains of the second body by a print. He was one of yours at one time, Silvestri."

"Fuck!" Silvestri was on his feet.

"In the past. He got his law degree and started defending the criminals—"

Silvestri's hand came down on Leslie's shoulder. Leslie jumped, startled. What was she missing here?

"Say it, Blue," Silvestri said, the cigarette sharp on his breath.

"The fourth body was an attorney by the name of William Veeder."

Chapter 32

"Motherfucker," Silvestri muttered under his breath. He shook his head as if after a blow, trying to clear his brain. "Les?" He knelt beside her, grasped her hands folded in her lap.

She thought, she should feel something, *something,* but she felt nothing. Judy Blue just observed. Leslie Wetzon: The specimen under the microscope. Gelber ditto.

"What the hell was he doing there?" Silvestri barked. He stood, hands gentle on Leslie's shoulders.

"Perhaps Ms. Wetzon can tell us? After all, he was her lover."

Silvestri's hands went rigid.

"I don't remember him," Leslie said. "I'm sorry he's dead, I'm sorry for his wife."

Agent Blue inhaled, tilted her head back, and not hiding her triumph, blew smoke into the air. "You don't remember him, but you know he was married?"

"Carlos told me about him, about the affair. It just doesn't mean anything to me." But it should, she told herself. What kind of unfeeling person are you? She looked into the middle distance, tried to conjure up a face, but others intruded: Marty Lawler, David Lumare, men in cashmere overcoats, Bruegel-faces.

The carryall was near the door when she came in. He was standing in front of the windows looking out at the view. He knew she was there but didn't turn around.

"*You're taking the case, then?*" *she said.*

"*Come with me,*" *he said.*

"*You know I can't.*"

"*We'll sell Xenia on opening a branch in L.A.*"

"*Fat chance with the economy in recession and the aftermath of 9/11.*"

"*I could be out there for months.*"

"*What about Evelyn?*"

"*She won't notice I'm gone.*"

"*And me?*"

"*I'll take a house on the beach.*" *He turned to her now.* "*I want you with me, I need you.*"

"*Here's the scenario. Bill Veeder moves to L.A. lock, stock, and mistress, to defend Dooney Bellemore, NASCAR racer, wife beater, and murderer.*"

"*Leslie—*"

"*Excuse me. Innocent until proven guilty.*"

"*If you love—*"

She cut the air with the side of her hand. "*It's not about love. I just don't see myself as a camp follower. Not in this life.*"

His response surprised her. "*Would you marry me if I was free?*"

"*That's not the way it is, is it?*"

"*You haven't answered me.*" *Cool blue eyes, sharp cheekbones. The lawyer on cross.*

True, she hadn't answered him. Would she marry him if he were free? I don't know, she thought. He was great looking, caring, sensitive, a wonderful lover, easy to talk to, established and successful, with all the collateral material like money, cars, apartment above the Museum of Modern Art. He was a whole generation older, stalwart and reliable. "*I don't know,*" *she said.*

163

"Well then maybe some distance will be good." He tipped her chin up, intent, memorizing her face. His breath was warm and Scotch-scented.

"Sounds as if you're cutting all ties." She was confused by her feelings. Disappointment? Maybe. Heartsick? Good question.

"Does it?" A gentle kiss, another, and another.

She softened. "I'll visit, but you'll be too busy to spend time on us."

"Try me, little package."

He wrapped her in voluminous black cashmere and carried her off.

The voices were distant, intrusive.

"Les, can you hear me?"

A woman said, "She remembers more than she's letting on."

"Get the hell out of here, both of you."

"Hey, catch her."

"Shit!"

"Call an ambulance, Silvestri."

"Didn't you hear me? Get out of here."

A door slammed. She was lifted, carried, on a bed, gone.

"Leslie?"

The hand was on the curtain. Not yet, she thought. It's not safe.

"Leslie, it's Sonya. Come back. You know you can trust me."

Sonya. The voice, soft, almost hypnotic, drew back the curtain. Don't open your eyes all the way. Wait till you're sure.

"Ah, there you are."

The woman called Sonya, sitting on the bed facing her, gave a tiny nod. Silvestri kissed Leslie's forehead and left the room, closing the door.

"Sonya?" Leslie said.

"Sonya Mosholu. We've known each other a long time." Broad-shouldered, short dark hair, dark eyes highlighted with mascara and taupey shadow, long dangling earrings, Sonya Mosholu looked the gypsy, exotic.

"I have interesting friends."

Sonya's laugh was deep, throaty. "Yes, you do."

The feeling was sweet, calm bunting. "I remember your laugh."

"Your memory will come back."

"But do I want it to?"

"Ah."

Knowledge intruded. "You're a therapist."

"Yes."

"My therapist?"

"When you need me."

She sighed. "I think I need you."

"Yes."

"Silvestri is trying hard, but I've screwed up his life."

"He loves you. He wants to make everything right, but he's realizing he can't do it by himself. Which is why he called me."

"Can you make everything right?"

Sonya smiled. "We can work on it together. Do you remember what happened before you passed out?"

"They were telling me that this Bill Veeder was the fourth body in the explosion."

"*This* Bill Veeder. You don't remember him?"

"Carlos told me about him so I knew who he was, but I

didn't feel anything. They were all waiting for me to react."

"You remembered something."

"Why do you say that?"

"Silvestri said you had a strange look on your face."

"I went somewhere else. You know, mentally. Into a scene from a film, starring me and a tall man with close-cropped white hair. Bill Veeder. I knew it when I saw him. He was going to L.A. to defend a murderer. It was a big case and he'd be gone a long time. He wanted me to come with him."

"Do you think it was your imagination?"

Leslie shook her head. "It was a flashback. I had one before, about Laura Lee. I know it means I'm coming back, but it's so fragmented and it doesn't make sense."

"Just let it happen. It will sort itself out. When you go somewhere else, try to hold onto where you are, too. Feel your feet on the floor."

"Did Silvestri tell you all of it? That someone is trying to kill me? That I was using another name, Mary Lou Salinger? That the FBI thinks I've hidden diamonds somewhere?"

"It appears that six weeks of your life are unaccounted for, but that's temporary."

"Sonya, the fragments scare me. I don't know when they're going to happen, and when they do, I'm afraid. Did Silvestri tell you about the blind man?"

"No."

"Some time after the explosion at Teterboro Airport I got on a bus and sat down next to him. He tried to help me when we came to the Port Authority, but was shot by a man who kidnapped me. He said I was wearing a lot of coat, maybe a man's cashmere overcoat."

"Okay."

"In the flashback, which had nothing to do with New Jersey—it was just me and Bill Veeder. He called me 'little package,' then wrapped me up in something huge and black and cashmere."

Chapter 33

Silvestri flipped a strand of spaghetti over his wooden spoon and tasted it. "Perfect," he said. He turned on the cold water and dumped the pasta into a colander, filling the small kitchen with steam. Giving the contents of the saucepan a quick stir, he emptied the colander into the saucepan, lifting and shaking the pan to coat the spaghetti with the thick tomato sauce.

The process was very familiar, comforting.

"Wine, beer, or water?" His hands kept moving, stirring, plating the mounds of spaghetti, setting everything on the table. How hard was he working not to look at her?

"Wine," she said. An open bottle of red stood on the card table next to a long sourdough baguette, a wedge of Parmesan, and a grater.

She filled the glasses while he grated cheese over the spaghetti.

"It'll get cold." He tore off the end of the baguette and handed it to her. "Your favorite."

Silvestri's dinner—which was delicious—passed without conversation though Leslie kept trying to catch his eye. It did no good so she finished the meal, savoring every morsel, and pushed her empty plate away. "I don't know," she said. "I don't know."

He stopped wiping up the last bit of tomato sauce, shocked into looking at her. "Wasn't it okay?"

Having got his attention, she thought, where do we go from here? He was doing his best to avoid talking about *it*.

It being what had come between them. But how difficult could that be, as she had no memory, little memory, of Bill Veeder.

What if now that they knew Bill Veeder was involved in whatever had happened, Silvestri was having his doubts about her honesty?

"Can we talk about Bill Veeder?" she said.

He took the plates and put them in the sink. "Sorry about this," he said, shaking a cigarette from the near-empty pack. His inhale was uneven. He leaned on the doorframe, arms folded. "So talk."

She sighed. "You think I'm faking this."

"If you are, you're really good."

"Look, I don't know why Bill Veeder was there. All I know is that he's dead, and if there was so much going on between him and me, why don't I feel anything?"

Silvestri grunted. "You remembered something before you passed out."

"It was like a scene from a movie. A man I'm assuming was Bill Veeder was going to L.A. to take over the defense in a big murder trial and wanted me to come with him."

"Did the movie give you your answer?"

"I said no."

"What a relief."

Was this, she thought, what had split us up? This sarcasm, this cold act? "I take it, then, that you don't care one way or the other." She got up and found the phone on the sofa. "So maybe I'll call Carlos and stay with him until this is settled and I can go home." Her voice wobbled, rose beyond her control.

He was at her side in a flash, taking the phone from her. "I care," he said. "Don't you know that?"

"I don't know anything any more," she screamed. "I'm

very tired. I want to stop." He tried to hold her, saying her name over and over, but she struggled in his grasp, punching, screaming, "I've been fighting to stay alive since the explosion. Now I'm fighting with you, or you're fighting with me. Maybe staying alive is just not worth it."

"Whatever," he yelled, shaking her. "Whatever!"

She fell back on the sofa, pulling him with her, a snarl of arms and legs, panting, fumbling with clothing, and wild kisses.

The insistence of Silvestri's beeper jarred them awake.

"Christ, Les," he said, eyes opening wide. He tried to sit up.

"Would you kindly remove your elbow from my stomach, Silvestri?"

He untangled himself, squinting into the semidarkness. "Keep your judgmental comments to yourself," he told Izz, who was sitting on the floor contemplating them. He gave Leslie his hand and pulled her into a sitting position.

Their discarded clothing lay scattered around the sofa.

"I guess—" she said, dislodging Izz from her sweater.

"Yeah," he said. His beeper went off again. He grunted, felt around on the floor. "Where the fuck—?"

Leslie found where it had slid behind one of the sofa cushions and handed it to him. His hand lingered on hers. Hers closed over his. "Silvestri—"

The second time was slow and gentle and in his bed.

It was pitch black when she woke to rustling noises. He wasn't lying next to her. "Silvestri?"

"Go back to sleep." The rustling noises became less amorphous. He was getting dressed.

"Where are you going?"

"Downstairs for a cigarette."

"You could smoke here."

"Too much second-hand smoke." He bent and kissed her. "I'll be up in a few minutes."

She dozed, waiting. Dozed. A motor revved. Woke with a jolt. "Silvestri?" No response. She got out of bed and turned on a lamp. Went into the living room. Izz was lying flat, her nose to the door. Her tail gave a despondent flop. "He's not back?" Shit, why was she asking the dog? She gathered up her discarded clothing and got dressed.

Downstairs, she checked the vestibule, opened the outside door, and looked up and down the street, hardly noticing the chill in the air. Night was making a slow drift into dawn. The street was quiet, dark except for the streetlamp across the way.

On the stone steps lay the pristine ash of a cigarette.

There was no sign of Silvestri.

Chapter 34

Her howl rose raw, excruciating, over the empty sidewalks, the dark and silent brownstones. It came back at her like a body blow, leaving her bent over, gasping for air. Her fingers went to the pencil of ash, all that remained of Silvestri, but it fell apart when she touched it.

She stared at her charry fingers, the shock easing, the dread pushed back a little, just a little. You're jumping to conclusions, she told herself. He's probably gone for a walk; he'll bring back bagels for breakfast.

Izz, who'd followed her, reacted to Leslie's fear with nervous little barks. Finally, the Maltese ran to the curb and did her morning routine.

"Good dog." Leslie picked her up and went back into the building, closed the door, climbed the stairs. Silvestri wouldn't have abandoned me like this, she thought. Not by choice. On the other hand, maybe he'd left a note and it was waiting upstairs and she hadn't noticed it.

Silvestri's door was open! Well, of course, Leslie Wetzon, you left it open. And good thing, too, because you don't have a key. You would have locked yourself out. She closed the door behind her and turned on the ceiling light, looking for the note.

But there was no note.

She gave Izz fresh water. There was still some food in her bowl so Silvestri must have filled it before he left. Don't panic. He's a big boy, he can look after himself. And he took time to feed Izz. But, she thought, what if he fed Izz and went down for a smoke and someone grabbed him?

The downstairs buzzer sounded. She froze. It wouldn't be Silvestri, so who was it? She edged to the window, separated a slat. Judy Blue. You couldn't miss her. She was looking up, gesturing to Leslie to let her in.

What if the FBI had taken Silvestri away so Judy Blue would be able to talk to her without his protection?

The buzzer sounded three more angry times, then stopped.

Leslie made coffee, thinking. The tall cop, his friend Metzger. He would know what to do. But she didn't have his phone number. What precinct was it? She should remember. Think of the numbers chiseled over the entry. Twenty first. Two-one.

If the FBI had Silvestri, they couldn't keep him very long. Or could they?

Information gave her the number of the Twenty-first Precinct, and she let them dial it for her. It was a spendthrift something her instinct told her Leslie Wetzon would never do, but she wasn't the same old Leslie Wetzon, and this was an emergency, or at least she thought it was, which was reason enough.

She wondered as she listened to the phone ringing, did the former Leslie Wetzon often have these searching dialogues with herself?

After about ten rings, someone responded. She asked for Metzger and waited while they transferred her call.

"Rodriguez."

"I'm looking for Detective Metzger."

"He'll be here in a couple of hours."

"It's important. Can you give me his home number?"

"He's probably on his way in. I'll give him a call and tell

him you want to talk to him, or you can leave him a message."

"Tell him to call me right away. Leslie. He knows where."

Dress and wait. But don't wait too long. "I'm a sitting target," she said out loud.

She brought the phone into the bathroom with her when she showered. No one called.

Dressed, she dried her hair and put on eye makeup. Still no call. She had another cup of coffee.

The downstairs buzzer sounded. The bulldog Judy Blue again? She edged to the window. Judy Blue was out of her car and crossing the street. What was going on?

Raised voices drifted up to Leslie. Judy Blue and a red-haired woman in a black suit were having a disagreement. Actually, the woman was doing most of the talking, along with finger-pointing gestures.

"I know her!" Leslie said. She picked up Izz, kissed her nose, danced around the room. "Oh, yes!" When she went back to the window, Judy Blue was returning to her car.

The buzzer sounded again.

"Yes?"

"It's Rita, Leslie."

Leslie buzzed Rita Silvestri in.

"God, how he lives," Rita Silvestri said. She unencumbered herself of the crimson and black cashmere shawl. "Not even a decent chair to sit on." Before setting her purse and heavy briefcase on the floor, she shooshed away some dust balls with the toe of her patent leather pump. "This is not how he was brought up."

"Just tell me—" Leslie's hands were icy on Rita's.

"He's pissed as hell, but he's okay. The Feebs picked him up and he got a message to me." She looked down at the little dog trying to get her attention. "Hello, Izz."

"I was scared the people looking for me got him. Did he tell you?"

"Only what you told him when he found you."

"Why did they pick him up? They can't go around arresting NYPD officers."

"They think they can do anything, and since 9/11, John Ashcroft, and the Patriot Act, they have all these new powers, goddammit. Thought they'd get a clear path to you. They can't hold him." She stood with her hands on her attractive hips and gave Leslie the once over. "So you remember me?"

"I do. A lot has come back and I remember more every day."

She knew Silvestri's mother was a respected civil rights attorney who specialized in spousal abuse cases. After Silvestri's father was killed on the job, Rita had put herself through law school.

"If you hadn't shown up, I probably would have left."

"And they were waiting for you. If you wouldn't let them in, they would grab you when you got to the street."

"So what do we do now?" She got the coffee pot and poured coffee into two mugs.

"First, let's have a good look at you, Leslie. Sit." Rita took a sip of coffee. "How are you dealing with this news about Billy Veeder?"

"Dealing? I'm not. I don't remember much about him, Rita. Just a few scraps that came back, but it's like there was nothing there."

"Poor Billy. He'd hate that he didn't leave a lasting impression."

"Billy. You knew him, too. Everybody knew him."

"He was something, Leslie. Larger than life. All that

stuff—power and sex. I knew him when he was just another one of the boys on the job, granted a little more ambitious. After Joey died and I decided to go to Fordham Law, who should be there, but charming Billy."

"Ah—" Leslie squinted at Rita. "So he really was a good lover."

Rita smiled. "Some things recede with time, but not that."

Leslie returned the smile. It was a girl thing, she knew. "I love your son, Rita."

She took Leslie's hand. "I know that. And he loves you."

"He told you?"

"He doesn't have to." She took another sip of coffee. "Let's get out of here."

"But if we go downstairs, Madam Special Agent Blue will pick me up."

Rita rummaged in her purse and handed Leslie two keys. "My apartment. Eighteen Fifth."

"That's new, right?"

"Yes. About six months. It's a penthouse. Four tiny rooms and a three-way terrace. My treat for reaching senior status. I told the concierge your name is Isabella."

Leslie laughed and patted Izz.

"Well, it was the first name I could think of. Here's what you do. There's a back door on the ground floor that leads to an alley. A lot of the houses in Chelsea have back alleys, just keep opening doors to the right and watch out for the garbage cans. You'll come out near Seventh Avenue. Grab a cab and go straight to my place. If you run into a problem, in case someone's blocking the alley, come back and we'll figure out something else. I'll wait a half hour and then go out the front door."

"Do you have a computer?"

"A laptop, why?"

"I need to do some research on Jason McLaughlin, because all this crap is about him and his business in an obscure way."

"Jason McLaughlin. The missing financier."

"Yes."

Rita frowned. "How odd."

"Odd?"

"I won a lawsuit for a client several years ago. We sued her former employer. He was a piece of work. Used a lot of different aliases to cover his past. Jason McLaughlin was one of them."

"Could it possibly be the same man?"

"Possibly. The one we sued was hirsute: mustache, beard, hair in ponytail. Grubby looking. The coincidence did make me wonder, but the pictures in the papers these last few weeks show someone clean cut, clean shaven."

"What did you sue him for, can you tell me?"

"Sure. Sexual harassment."

Chapter 35

The first sensation: hammering in her head. Her shoulders locked into her neck. She willed her eyes open, dreading. No one standing over her. No voices. Raise your head, she thought. Be wary. Don't let them see. Them? Pain in her chin, jaw. She was lying on her stomach, splayed, nose in the dirt, blood on her lips. Where the hell?

Groaning, she took inventory, moving each limb, spitting out dirt, not teeth, thank God. Memory came slithering back, some, soon more than she was prepared for.

It was a large emerald, sandwiched between two hearty diamonds. He'd pulled her down on his lap, taken her unsuspecting hand in his, and slipped it on her finger. She couldn't pull her eyes away. "It's beautiful." What was this with emeralds? Four years ago another powerful and attractive older man had presented her with an emerald, and the assumption of marriage, and she had tried on the first, thought about the second, felt uncomfortable with the fit of each, and rejected both.

Smith's voice lilted into her head. "If they give, you take; if they take, you scream." Would Smith scream and run from Bill Veeder? Not on your life. Not on anyone's life. Would Wetzon?

He was trying to read her, arms caging her, eyes winter blue.

"What does this mean?" she asked.

"That we have an after-life," he said.

"After-life?" After Evelyn?

Then he said it, "After Evelyn."

That could be a long time, she thought. After Silvestri? That could be forever.

"When I get back from the Coast," he said. "We'll make some decisions."

"This is to hold me for a while?" Private property, no trespassers. She'd been here before.

"Is that a problem?"

She touched her forehead. Her fingers came back red. How long had she been lying here? And where was here?

With difficulty she rotated onto her side. Pain flooded her.

Silvestri's apartment. Silvestri missing. Rita Silvestri, their plan to bypass the Feebs who were watching for Wetzon on the street.

I'm Wetzon, she thought. Of course. Smith and Wetzon. I have to get to the office. Smith will have a fit.

But here she was lying in the dirt behind a row of brownstones, one of which was Silvestri's. She remembered that all right. She'd been running. She looked back—God, she was stiff—and saw why she'd fallen. Two steps she hadn't counted on. She'd flown through the air with no ease at all and fallen on her head.

She propped herself up, steadying her hand against the fence, shading her eyes against the midday sun.

"Yoo hoo!" An apparition was hanging out a third floor window, waving at her. "Yoo hoo!" The apparition disappeared.

Wetzon held onto the fence. The ground was moving under her.

She blinked, her stomach churned.

"Les!" The apparition reappeared. Next to her. "What are you doing? Dearie, dearie, you're bleeding." Clucking sounds. "What a mess you've made of yourself." Strong hands held her. "Here now, lean on Patrice."

Bump, bump, diddly dum . . .

Candide, Wetzon thought, giving herself over to Patrice Buchanan, the transvestite who lived one flight above Silvestri. Candide, I am, I am. Take a bow. I am pure and innocent and free of malice, well mostly, as I make my way through a dangerous and mad world.

"Patrice, Silvestri's mother. She's in his apartment."

"She left a long time ago, dearie. I heard her. Are you sure that's his mother?"

"It is."

"So, mom's a babe." She fluttered long false lashes. "Hoo hah." She scrutinized Leslie in the sunlight. "You've got a bleeder on your lip, and an ugly scrape on your forehead, dearie. Would you believe I was a medic in my other life? Don't worry, Little Les, I'll clean you up."

"You saw me from your window?"

"I heard you leave the back way and figured you didn't want that fat Feebe to see you. Can you handle the stairs?"

"I'm fine." The stairs yawned above her, formidable. She took one step at a time, one solid ache.

"There's not much around here that Patrice doesn't know about. But I keep it to myself." As they passed Silvestri's door, Patrice gave it a good rap. No answer, only a pathetic whine and scratching from Izz. "See, no one home but Izz."

"Don't cry, Izz. I'll be back."

Inside, the phone began to ring.

One more flight. Hard work. Dragging.

Patrice flung open her door.

Incense and a Carly Simon CD. And cat. Cats. Chat's purr like a persistent motor.

Glitter and Be Gay, Wetzon thought. Red fringe everywhere, silky tie-dyed throws on a worn gold velvet sofa. Threadbare Orientals on the floor, an ornate gold filigreed chandelier with little red shades, crystal fringe. Styrofoam heads wearing wigs of many colors and abundant curls. Maroon velvet draperies, open. Resting on the sill, a pair of mother of pearl opera glasses.

"Opera glasses?" She sneezed once, twice.

A broad wink of the blackened lids and inch-long lashes. " 'The better to see you with, my dear.' " Patrice brought Wetzon to a tall stool and pressed her down. "Let's have the coat. Mmmm. Nice leather. Saks?"

"Filene's Basement."

Patrice's first-aid kit was pulled from a mirrored closet. "This is going to sting, but we have to clean out all the schmutz so we don't get any scars."

Wetzon eyed Patrice's long false nails with sparkly designs. "How are you going to do that with those nails?"

"Vinyl is a wonderful invention, no?" Vinyl gloves came on with a professional snap. "Now hold still."

Her face was on fire. She grabbed Patrice's hand. "Ouch, ouch, Patrice, stop!"

"Almost finished. So, dearie, you and Silvestri are back together?"

"How do you know we split up? Oh, excuse me, you know everything."

"Right. I'm going to put a thin coat of Neosporin on the scrapes and cuts and a Band-Aid on your forehead. Why'd you break up? I asked Silvestri, but you know how close-mouthed he is." She attached the clear Band-Aid and stepped back, tilting her head to look at her patient.

"Patrice—"

"You took up with that big shot lawyer, Bill Veeder. Silvestri's been in a funk. Couldn't get a smile out of him, and believe me, I tried. He's a good boy, Les, for a cop."

"I know."

"You'd better get those clothes off so we can see if we have to give you any more first aid. So you came back to him?"

"Something like that. If the FBI is still downstairs, how am I going to get out of here?"

"I know there's more to this story, but I guess I'll have to take a rain check. And don't you worry, Patrice'll get you out of here, Little Les, if you promise you'll tell me."

Dum dum dum ti di dum . . . The further adventures of Candide Wetzon.

Wetzon, facing her image in the full-length mirror, would never in a million years have recognized herself. Her skin was a heavy-on-the-creamy coffee color, lips outstanding, way larger than her swollen own, bright red covering the cut, glazed brilliant. Eyelids black and dusted glittery, extended eyeliner, and long black false lashes. A black wig curled over her bruised forehead, vast around her face, grand on her head, coursed past her shoulders, hiding everything but her thin nose.

"Big hair is an understatement," she told an admiring Patrice.

Fishnet stockings, mega platform, ankle strap shoes in gold and rhinestones. Tight gold short-shorts. A black net overskirt, trimmed with sequins.

"The air is thin up here."

"I knew you had great legs," Patrice said. "Push up those bosoms."

Wetzon reached into the sock stuffed bustier and tried to coax a little more from a lot less. "Yeah, but can I walk on these platforms?"

"It's not a question of walking. Watch me: you sashay, roll your shoulders, lead with your pelvis. You're a dancer, you'll know."

"Well, I have danced on a raked stage . . ."

"First, a little scent, Calvin." Patrice's touch on the perfume spray was heavy. "And finally, the pièce de résistance." On went a white angora, fat little jacket with huge shoulder pads. Stepping back to take it all in, Patrice said, "Opera gloves." She went into the bedroom and returned with long black leather gloves.

While Wetzon pulled them on, Patrice threw a handful of sparkles at her. "Fairy dust for good luck."

"Well, of course. Listen, Patrice, will you leave a message on Silvestri's phone that I'm okay?" Rita's key was still in the pocket of Wetzon's leather coat. She tucked it into her glove.

"Give me his cell number."

"I don't know it."

"Get with the program, Little Les. Okay, I'll take care of it." She gave Wetzon a light smack on the ass. "Now you go get 'em, girl."

"First I have to get down the stairs."

How, Wetzon thought, will I ever get a cab looking like this?

When she passed Silvestri's apartment, she heard the phone ringing, Izz whining.

Don't be tentative, she told herself, at the front door. Patrice is flamboyant. Flamboyant yourself out of here. She threw open the door with bravado.

It was dusk. Where had the day gone? Under the

streetlamp across the way, Judy Blue was leaning against her car, smoking, watching Wetzon. Her colleague sat at the wheel, nursing a Starbucks.

Wetzon rolled her shoulders, rotated her pelvis, shook her big hair. I'll bet I sparkle up a storm, she thought, sorry she couldn't stand under the streetlamp and glow.

She sashayed toward Seventh Avenue, a prayer on her lips. On the corner, traffic was heavy. She waved her hand for a cab, taking a quick glance back. Damn, Judy Blue was standing in the middle of the street, watching her.

"Hey, babe!" A man stuck his head out of a black SUV as it screeched to a stop beside her. "You wanna ride?" He made smacking sounds with his pursed lips.

The Toyota hit the SUV with a sickening crunch. Wetzon jumped back. There followed a perfect example of the domino effect. The result was pandemonium, horns blaring, drivers spilling onto the streets defending their cars, babies screaming. Was that a gunshot? A siren went off somewhere and Wetzon could see the flashing lights of two blue and whites crawling through the bumper-on-bumper field of cars.

Judy Blue, in the meantime, had made her decision and was walking toward Seventh Avenue. Time was running out, Wetzon knew. And she had to stay in character or she was lost. Still, no one, with the possible exception of Judy Blue, was paying any attention to her. She gave her shoulders a sensuous roll and began to sashay off.

"There she is! She's the one!"

They'd stopped fighting among themselves and all seemed to be pointing at her, moving toward her. She could see Judy Blue getting closer. One way or the other, she was fucked.

"She did it! Get her!"

"She's a goddam freak!" a woman yelled.

What a lot of noise they were making. Her head hurt. Forget it, she'd go down fighting. Lose the platforms and make a run for it, she told herself.

She gave no thought to the blue and white until it came up on the sidewalk and blocked her way.

Chapter 36

"For crissakes, Patrice, whaddaya wanna do, get yourself strung up?" The cop—his tag said P. Walsh—was a grizzled, bulky veteran, broad Irish face, chapped lips, jowls. The surging mob, the cacophony of horns, were enough to make him yell out the window to another cop. He jerked his thumb for her to get in the back.

She didn't need a second invitation. With Wetzon hunkered down on the backseat, the blue and white rode the sidewalk past the congestion, then edged onto the street.

And not a minute too soon. Judy Blue had reached the corner and was scanning the area. The blue and white passed her by. Soon enough the agent would ask a bystander what happened to the transvestite.

"Hey!" The cop was staring into his rearview mirror. "You're not Patrice."

"I'm her betheth fwiend, deawie," Wetzon lisped, fluttering the long lashes, flipping her big black hair.

"You oughta know better'n standing out there stopping traffic during rush hour."

"I wath only twying to get a cab. I have thith weally important appointment at Eighteen Fifth Avenue with a movie produther whothe going to make me a thtar. Could you be a lovely boy and dwop me there?"

"Chauffeuring transvestites around the city ain't part of my job description."

"Pleathe, dear boy, I'd be ever tho gwateful." She made kissy noises through fat, crimson lips. "Of courthe, I could

186

twy to find another cab . . ."

"Never mind." He drove east on Fourteenth and down Fifth to number eighteen, which turned out to be an elegant pre-War high-rise with gargoyles and carved turrets on its upper reaches.

She adjusted her accoutrements—the socks were creeping out of the bustier—catching the knowing expression of the cop in the rearview mirror. "Oh, well," she murmured. "Up and at 'em."

On the sidewalk, she wriggled her hips, adjusted the fishnet stockings with finesse, to the ogles of three teenaged boys, and set forth. She didn't get far. A swarthy doorman in a light opera uniform blocked her way.

"Where you think you're going?"

She looked back at Walsh, who hadn't pulled away. "Rita Silvestri in the Penthouse. I have a key." She took it from the palm of her glove. "See? She's expecting me."

"Oh, yeah? Well, she left here an hour ago."

"She couldn't have. She's expecting me. Just ring up."

"Stand back," the doorman said, with snooty disrespect. He held the door for a young woman pushing twins in a wide stroller, along with a champagne colored standard poodle prancing on his leash beside them.

"Is there a problem?" Walsh had gotten out of the blue and white.

The doorman said, "Yeah. She don't belong here."

"But I do. I have a key." Exasperated, weary, Wetzon stamped her foot, not an easy exercise in ankle strap, platform wedgies. "Can't you see this is a costume? Just ring up for me and it'll be okay."

Walsh gave her a sharp look.

"Okay, okay, Officer Walsh. I am a friend of Patrice's. She got me gussied up like this for a party."

"Call up," Walsh told the doorman.

Wetzon and Walsh were close on his heels as he went back into the building and called upstairs. "What name?"

They were both watching her intently. "Les."

He buzzed Rita's apartment. Someone answered. "Someone down here, name of Les, with a cop. Oh, okay." He hung up the phone and turned back, saying, to Walsh, not to Wetzon, "Coming right down."

Wetzon put a smile on for Walsh. "See? I told you. It's okay. You can leave me now."

"I think I'll just stick around a little while longer . . . Les," Walsh said.

When the elevator finally arrived, it was Silvestri who stepped out, looking delicious, no worse for the wear. He checked the lobby frowning, walked toward Walsh and the doorman. Wetzon turned her back.

"Patrice?" he said, "What the hell—?"

She swiveled, he stared, began coughing and choking. "Oh, for crissakes!"

"Easy there, big boy." Draping herself on him, she did Mae West, but Leslie Wetzon got the benefit of Silvestri's arm around her waist.

The doorman's mouth hung open.

"I'm on the job," Silvestri told Walsh, trying to keep a straight face. "I'll take it from here. Thanks for your trouble."

Wetzon blew a kiss to Walsh. "Thank you, my Galahad."

"Enough. Come on," Silvestri said, steering her onto the elevator. Back against the wood paneling, she unfastened one platform shoe and massaged her foot, then repeated the process with the other. He took out his cell and made a call, breaking up every time he glanced at her.

"She's here. Yeah. I don't know. Okay, but a little weird.

No. Go on. We'll see you later." He returned the cell to his inside pocket. "Where the hell were you? Rita went back to look for you." He was trying to be stern but was having a hard time of it.

"I took a header in the alley and knocked myself out. Patrice found me and fixed me up."

"I would never have guessed."

"I stopped traffic," she said with some pride. "That's why I got a police escort." She rolled her shoulders and tilted her pelvis at him. "Actually, I think I look pretty good—"

"For a midget transvestite." He was laughing again. "Come on, here we are."

Rita Silvestri's apartment was tiny, but choice, just as she'd described. They stepped into a small foyer, rust-glazed walls, a Hudson Valley scene, and a Shaker-style loveseat, a nice mohair throw. Galley kitchen off to the right, and straight ahead, a decent sized living room with the same rust-glazed walls, a plump sofa in a beige stripe, a wooden trunk coffee table full of empty glasses and half-read newspapers, and two small club chairs in milk chocolate velvet. On the floor a Chinese patterned rug, beige with blues and yellows. And all around, the terrace.

"Nice," she said.

He came up behind her, and she turned into him, brushing her face against his shirt. The eyelashes peeled off and fell on the rug. "Les, I went nuts when you weren't here." He removed the angora jacket and tossed it on the sofa. His gun and holster followed. Same with the black wig.

"We left a message on your machine." She unbuttoned his shirt, taking her time, fingers glancing skin, feeling little electric shocks.

He detached the black net overskirt and stepped back and circled her. "Mmmm. Hot stuff, kid. You have it all over Patrice."

"I should hope so, big boy," she said, with a pelvic grind.

"That's some boob corset. Is that all you?"

"It's a bustier."

"Good place to hide something. This is a security issue. Requires a body search," he said, pulling her into the bedroom.

"Rita," she said.

"She had an appointment." He pushed the quilt aside and pulled her down on top of him as he worked the hooks on the bustier. The laugh started deep inside him. She could feel it filling him and then her. "Socks," he said.

Elbowing him, she said, "I'll thank you to stop laughing and make love to me."

"Socks."

The bathrobe was white terry. Rita's. Silvestri had wrapped her in it after their shower. Her lip was swollen, the cuts and scrapes raw from the hot water. She doctored herself and dried her hair while Silvestri ran over to Bleecker Street for a couple of John's pizzas and a six-pack.

Now curled up on the sofa under the mohair throw, she thumbed through the latest issue of *The Voice*, the Greenwich Village newspaper that became the voice of the left in the sixties. How different Silvestri was. Or could it be she was seeing him from another dimension? Through refracted light.

When he came back lugging their dinner and saw her lying on the sofa, it was obvious. It could only be described as joy. He dumped the clutter from the coffee table onto the floor and set the boxes down, piled up napkins, opened two beers. Pizza filled the small apartment with a luscious fragrance. She set *The Voice* aside.

Handing her a slice, he said cheerfully, "You ought to stay out of the ring."

"You're different, Silvestri," she said, filling her mouth with pizza. "Oh, this is heaven."

"Different?" Cautious, he took a long swallow of beer.

"Different. Lighter, happier—"

He set the bottle down, serious, and looked at her. "It's come back."

"Most of it," she said. "When I cracked my head in back of your house. I remember Smith, the business, everything except what I was doing as Mary Lou Salinger and how I got there and how I ended up at Mount Sinai."

"You remember Veeder?"

"Yes." He tightened, the joy receded. "Don't go away, Silvestri," she said, setting down what was left of the slice and reaching out to him. "Don't put up the wall."

"Les, how do you feel about him?"

"Sad."

"Sad."

"It was comfortable being with him, and I feel terrible about how he died, but I never really thought our relationship was long-term. He was fun, Silvestri. He didn't make me crazy. That's your department. It was easy to be with him."

"He loved you, Les."

"You can't know that."

"Oh, yes, I can. I asked him what his intentions were and he told me."

She flushed, hot. "Shit, Silvestri, that's humiliating. How could you have done that?"

191

"I had to know, Les. But I wasn't sure about you." He took her hands. "I wasn't about to give up and walk away."

A key turned in the lock and Rita Silvestri came through the door, dropping her purse and coat on the loveseat in the foyer.

"So, you two . . . is it serious?"

Wetzon and Silvestri looked at each other and laughed.

"There's pizza and beer," Wetzon said. She stood, knocking *The Voice* off the sofa. The pages separated, the personals face-up. She was transfixed. "My God! The personals." She grabbed up the newspaper. "That's it! It's how Laura Lee got to him."

Silvestri leaned across her and picked up the paper. "Got to who?"

"Jason McLaughlin. He put ads in *The Voice* personals for girls and she answered one."

Chapter 37

"That does it." Wetzon was on her feet. "Rita, if you'll lend me some clothes, I'm going home."

"I think you should stay here tonight," Silvestri said, standing, consuming another slice. "I'll go home and feed Izz."

"My home, Silvestri, not yours. I'm tired of hiding out, wearing clothes that don't fit, tired of being a homeless fucking waif."

Silvestri squinted at her, raised an eyebrow at his mother.

"I'm not a waif."

Rita grinned. "Okay, I have this great pair of leather pants that I can't squeeze into any more . . ."

"Great! Lead me to them."

"It might be nice if you asked me what I think," Silvestri said.

"About leather pants?"

"You know what I mean, Les." He was dead serious.

Wetzon followed Rita into the bedroom, glad she'd straightened up the bed. "You'll want to change your sheets."

Rita's raised-eyebrow look was almost an exact duplicate of her son's. "I'm shocked, shocked."

"Hey," Silvestri yelled from the living room. "I want you to know I don't go along with this."

She yelled back, "Don't argue, Silvestri. The only people stalking me are the Feebs, and what can they do to me? I'm going home and I'm going to pick up my life and maybe the rest of the shit that happened to me will come back."

"Sure, killers, kidnappers, and all," he said.

"Consider this, if they are still looking for me, maybe we can flush them out."

"Right. God save me from amateurs," he said.

"You'll need a lawyer, Leslie," Rita said, as Wetzon zipped up the fly on the black leather pants.

They were not skin tight. She did a *grand plié*. Delicious. The leather, smooth against her skin, worked with her. "God, I'm a bone."

"You could use some fleshing out," Rita said, "But you look a whole lot better in those pants than I did. Don't return them. This should fit fine." She gave Wetzon a red cashmere sweater. "Bones always look great clothed."

"A lawyer?" The sweater looked good, felt good. "You?"

"No, not me. I don't handle criminal or federal. I know the perfect person."

Silvestri was working on a fresh slice when he appeared in the doorway. "Who?"

"Clo Hightower."

"You've got to be kidding."

"What's wrong with her?" Wetzon asked, taking the half eaten slice from Silvestri and finishing it.

"She's got a fucking chip on her shoulder, hates cops."

"Only when they don't do their job. Her clients love her and she wins her cases," Rita said, placidly plucking a black alpaca poncho from her closet. "It's chilly out there."

"And shoes," Wetzon said.

"What size are you?"

"Seven narrow. You?"

"Seven and a half."

"Close enough."

"Black slides. They pinch on me. Don't want them back either."

Wetzon slid her feet into the high-heeled slides. "Nice. What do you think, Silvestri?" Twirling for him, she didn't quite duck his hands as they settled on her leather-clad hips. She looked up at him and fluttered her lashes. "I'll have that beer now, dearie."

"I wonder," Rita asked, "Is it too late for grand-children?"

They packed Patrice's offerings into a shopping bag.

"Thank Patrice for me," Wetzon said, handing Silvestri the bag. "I'll get a cab."

"Wait a minute," he said. "We'll go together. I'll pick Izz up and—"

"I can handle being alone, you know, Silvestri." It came out sharper than she'd meant it, and there came that guarded expression back on his face. "Oh, damn it," she said. "That's not what I meant."

"Isn't it?" Arms folded, he looked belligerent.

"Okay, kids, back off," Rita said. She wrote a note on the back of her business card. "Here's Clo's phone number, Leslie. I'll alert her that you'll be calling."

"Tomorrow morning, from the office. I have a ton of catching up to do. Thanks for everything, Rita."

"You'll like Clo, Leslie."

In the elevator, she caught Silvestri's hand. "You know I have to do this. The rest of what I lost is going to come back. I want to be ready for it."

"I know. I just don't want to let you out of my sight." He took two keys off his keychain and gave them to her.

"I'm back and I'm staying," she told him. "And I'm broke."

"Yeah, right. What do you get by the hour?" He reached into his pocket and pulled out some bills.

"A couple of hundred minimum." She looked at the twenties he handed her. "But I'll consider this a down-payment."

He kissed her and put her in a cab, waited while she gave the driver her address.

As they pulled away, she told the driver, "Changed my mind." She gave him another address. She got out in front of the Museum of Modern Art, and walked to the Tower, where some years earlier MoMA had built luxury condo-miniums over the museum to cover the rising costs of exis-tence.

She stood in front of the Museum Tower building, re-membering.

A hand clamped on her arm, the smell of human waste. "I need money for food." The derelict was filthy, ragged, his breath noxious, eyes mad.

"Let go!" She tried to pull away.

"Dint I tell you to get away from here?"

Wetzon recognized Fredric, Bill's doorman. He charged at the derelict, a baseball bat in hand. The derelict let go of her and flicked open a knife.

Fredric swung the bat and hit the derelict on the arm. The knife fell to the pavement, and the derelict ran off. "I'm sorry, Miss." Fredric picked up the knife and closed it. "Oh, Ms. Wetzon, it's you."

"Good evening, Fredric. That man frightened me."

"I'm sorry about it. I've called the police, but he keeps coming back. I'm afraid he's going to hurt someone. First time he's pulled a knife."

"You're well prepared though."

"I keep the bat under the counter, just in case. First time

I've ever had to use it." He opened the door for her, and she stepped into the spacious, understated lobby. The concierge was not at his desk. Fredric put the bat back under the counter and, after a brief pause, the knife. "Are you enjoying California?"

The question caught her by surprise. He thought, perhaps all the service people thought, that she'd gone to L.A. with Bill.

No need to contradict, she thought. "It's not New York."

"Mr. Veeder will be arriving later?"

He didn't know? Of course. There'd been nothing in the media. For some devious reason, the FBI was holding back.

She smiled with a hint of a nod.

"That's good." He lowered his voice. "It was a bit awkward, you know. They wanted to get into his apartment, but—"

"They? Who?"

"You didn't know? The FBI. Mr. Markham wouldn't let them in without a warrant. We called Mr. Veeder's office and Mr. Farber came right over and sent them away. He went upstairs to make sure everything was okay."

"Oh, my." Mr. Farber, she thought. Who the hell was Mr. Farber? Bill didn't have an associate by that name. Had he brought someone new into the firm? "Have they been back?"

"Yesterday. With a warrant."

"Did Mr. Farber come back?"

"No, he was out of the office. Mr. Veeder's secretary came."

"Carolyn—"

He shook his head. "Not her, the new one."

Another shocker. Carolyn had been with Bill for years.

She would never have left him.

"I left my keys in L.A.," she said.

"Oscar will let you in." Fredric went behind the concierge desk and pressed a button. "Mr. Veeder called a couple of weeks ago and said he was coming in for a few days, but he must have changed his mind."

The contradictions played with her head. Could it be this was a hoax, an FBI sting? Could it be that Bill Veeder wasn't really dead?

Chapter 38

Oscar had evasive eyes; he never quite looked at her, yet she always felt the man was a watcher. He gave her the creeps. She'd mentioned it to Bill, who'd brushed her discomfort away, saying, "Oscar's a Muslim. They're not supposed to look at women, the poor slobs. Consider it a compliment. He knows you're something special."

A compliment she could do without.

He was standing outside Bill's door, key in hand, when she got off the elevator. Eyes averted, he unlocked the door and pushed it open.

"Thank you." She stepped around him as he showed no inclination to move out of the way. Inside, she turned to close the door and caught his direct stare of such pure venom that she slammed the door on it, shaken.

"Did you ever consider, Bill Veeder, that you might once in a while be wrong—?" She broke off her one-sided conversation. "Damnation!"

The luxurious apartment was skinned. That's the only description she could put on it. What remained was bare bones. Anything that moved had been removed. Though the sofa looked okay on first glance, closer examination showed the underside of the cushions had been sliced open, then replaced so the damage wasn't immediately visible.

Luck didn't hold for the bedroom. Although the bed was made up with its Porthault sheets and quilt, that there was something off-kilter was obvious. She pulled back the sheets. The mattress had been shredded, its horsehair fill pushing upward.

Under her feet the Berber carpet lumped, sliced and diced, ruined. At first, the assault seemed mindless, knocked her breath away. They'd made love on that mattress, on the Berber carpet. For a time their affair had been *trompe l'oeil*, then it had taken on an air of permanence.

Had the FBI done this? What the hell were they looking for? My God, it had to be the diamonds. Did they think she'd hidden them here? Well, they'd left no possible hiding place to the imagination, and what had they come up with?

The closets in the dressing room were emptied, all of Bill's elegant wardrobe, gone, carted away in those big plastic bags the FBI used to collect evidence. Evidence of what?

All those beautiful English, hand-tailored suits he loved. He was going to be pissed.

The kitchen, more deception. Everything seemed okay except someone had cleaned up. The cleansers tickled her nose. Bill's housekeeper Carmen had been here. The refrigerator was barren, sparkling. A note lay under a crystal salt shaker on the glass and chrome table in Carmen's large, round letters: *Mr. Bill—I did the best I could.*

She returned to the living room. "Oh, Bill, where the hell are you?" Her voice was flat and hung in the air as if he were still a presence here. She looked out the window at the dazzling lights of the city, as she'd stood here so often in the past. Dazzling. That was the word for Bill Veeder. That was the word for their time together. And ephemeral.

Like a Fourth of July sparkler, they had blazed briefly and then faded. It was not a hoax or a sting. She knew Bill Veeder was dead.

Finally she let the tears come.

★ ★ ★

Wetzon unlocked her own door with trepidation, needing no surprises, nothing new, no evidence of an FBI invasion. Rewarded, her nest was the same old welcoming home she couldn't live without. "I'm home," she shouted to the drunkard's path quilt. "Yes!" Dancing from room to room, she turned on the lights. "Yes!" She paused at her barre to do a *grand battement,* a very sloppy one at that, but such a release.

In the bedroom, she threw herself on her bed. "Yes."

Soon, she got up and wandered through her apartment. How clean everything was. Carlos. The blinds were drawn, the towels in the bathroom neatly arranged. No musty smell from a closed-in space.

On the kitchen counter she found a notebook listing the messages that had accumulated on her answering machine. Carlos.

And a shopping bag held her mail, a note attached, saying: *Bills paid, catalogues tossed. You owe me. XXX*

Oh, boy, did she.

Everything looked the same—except—except, what was that on the shelf near the kitchen window? A big white thing with a huge red ribbon, a gift card attached. *Dear heart, you are no longer the only person in New York without a microwave.*

Carlos!

She picked up the phone and punched in his number.

"Birdie! You're home!"

"You knew it was me. Spendthrift! You've got that caller ID thing. Boy, Verizon saw you coming."

"Indulge me, dear heart."

"Consider yourself indulged." She choked up. "Thank you for taking care of everything."

"Everything except you, Birdie."

"Carlos—"

"Birdie listen, I'm coming right over."

"No, no. I'm okay. Just more emotional than I used to be."

"Ha!"

"Ha, yourself, my dear bud. I remember everything now from my sordid past except for what happened to me. Silvestri didn't want me to come home, but I had to. I've got to get my life back."

"I know, Birdie, darling, I know. And you have to believe we're all with you in this." He paused. "I hope that doesn't mean re-enter the Barracuda, too."

"Carlos, get over it. She's part of my life."

"The worst part."

"And you gave me a microwave, you monster."

"So I did. Try it, you might like it."

She weeded through some of the papers on her desk, tossing invitations to events that had already happened, memos she'd written herself about things to do. Lists. "I'm reserving judgment for now, mostly because I've had the fight knocked out of me."

"Sure. And if I believed that, I'd be buying that bridge to Brooklyn. Listen, Birdie, be honest. Are you going to be okay by yourself tonight?"

"Of course. Do me a favor and call Silvestri and tell him I'm okay." She hung up the phone and emptied the old copper stock pot she used for paper waste into a garbage bag, which is when she saw the jagged scrap of newspaper. It must have been resting in the bottom of the pot. She reclaimed it. Personal ads from the *Village Voice*. Circled was one: *Executive seeks kindred female spirit—future guaranteed—for assistant position. Send photo and resume.* There was a post office box number in Deal, New Jersey. In the margin Wetzon had written "Laura Lee" and a phone number with a New Jersey area code.

She punched in the number.

"The number you have reached is not in service. For further information—" A new number was given. She dialed that one, but as soon as she heard the voice, she hung up, hoping it would be some time before the New Jersey branch office of the FBI shared the call-in numbers with New York, and Special Agent Judy Blue.

Laura Lee had answered an ad and had gone to work for Jason McLaughlin. This was about her uncle's insurance company and the fraud she thought McLaughlin was perpetrating. She had jumped into a snake pit of huge proportions. And somehow, for some reason, Leslie Wetzon had gone in after her. Had Laura Lee called for help? Or, was the FBI the prime instigator from the very beginning?

And what the hell did Bill Veeder have to do with all this?

She turned off most of the lights, inspected her refrigerator. Empty except for a half dozen cans of Amstel Light. She opened one, shed Rita Silvestri's sexy duds, and got into a steamy shower, balancing the can and the soap and doing a poor job with both.

The can slipped from her hand and suds mingled with suds down the drain.

The hair dryer was heavy in her hands and she had no energy to finish. She gave it up and crawled into bed.

Coffee. It floated into her senses. A small whine and a cold wet nose nuzzled hers when she came out from under the covers. "Izz!" It was all a dream, a rotten dream.

But it wasn't. She saw that on Silvestri's face when he

came into the room. "How'd you get in?"

"Made an exchange with Patrice." He parked the guitar case and a *Wall Street Journal* on the floor near her closet. "Your things. Are you awake enough to hear me?"

"Yes," she said, with trepidation. "What's happened?"

"They're releasing the news about Veeder later today. So be prepared, the press is going to come after you."

She sat up. Oops. No nightgown. Covered her breasts with the sheet, shy in front of him, though she didn't know why. "So he really is dead?"

"What did you think?"

She shrugged. "Is the FBI going to say I'm involved?"

"You'd better talk with Clo Hightower."

"I hate this!"

He sat down on the bed, moved the assertive Izz from his lap. "I've got to get to work."

"Me, too." She touched his thigh. "Don't say it."

"You're wrong this time. I'm not going to try to stop you."

"Good. Will I see you later?"

"If you want to."

"I do."

"Good." He took her face in his hands and kissed her, a slow, exploring kiss. The sheet slipped away.

"Morning mouth," she said.

"I'm tough." He sat back, watching her.

"Are you admiring my tits or do you have something else to tell me?"

"Both."

"Am I going to be upset?"

"I don't know."

She closed her eyes. "Lay it on me."

"Agent Blue called me about an hour ago. Your friend Laura Lee has surfaced."

Chapter 39

She's alive! Laura Lee's alive! Wetzon sang it as she
dressed. The wheres and the hows? The bare bones was all
that Silvestri knew at the moment, but he was going to try
to find out more.

Yikes! The skirt of her favorite basic black Donna Karan
suit was now a full size too big. She covered the gaping
waistband with a gray cotton tee-shirt and a wide belt,
brushed her hair smooth into her dancer's knot, and made
up her eyes.

"There you are," she told her reflection. Her skin had a
pink flush. Blame sex in the morning.

In the kitchen, she sat on a stool and read the *Journal*,
grumbling aloud about its "new look," and groaning as always over the far-right editorials. But there was much to
savor of the familiar things, coffee and bagel, toasted to hell
and slathered with cream cheese. Heaven. She gave the last
bit of the bagel to Izz, who was doing her pathetic, phony
please-feed-the-starving-dog act, and filled the Maltese's
bowl with fresh water.

Two quick phone calls reinstated delivery of the *Times*
and the *Journal* beginning tomorrow. Oh, joy. After fast-
forwarding all the blank date pages in her Filofax to today's
date, she tucked her cell phone into her briefcase. The Wall
Street warrior was back! Laura Lee was alive!

And as if that brought her luck, when she stepped out of
her building, her downstairs neighbor, who worked for
HBO, was standing on the sidewalk while the doorman un-

loaded two suitcases from the trunk of a cab.

Good mornings were exchanged, and Wetzon got into the cab. "Second Avenue and Forty-ninth Street," she said.

Smith and Wetzon, the partnership, owned a brownstone on Forty-ninth Street, between First and Second Avenues, closer to Second. When they first went into business together, she and Smith had rented the ground floor, garden included, but after the owner put the building on the market several years later, they'd bought it at a bargain price. At the time, the real estate market in the City was sagging. And not long afterward, as it always did, it had come roaring back.

The tenant on the second floor, a rare book dealer, moved to another location and while Wetzon cautioned they should wait to see what the climate on the Street would be, Smith pushed ahead with a renovation that would relieve their cramped quarters and give them a spacious duplex office. And as usual, Smith had been right. They'd hired a new associate, stealing her from Tom Keegen, their biggest competitor. A chubby diamond mine, Smith had called Darlene Ford. They'd had a very good year and were able to write off the business expenses.

But the chubby diamond mine had turned out to be a mole for Keegen and left them in the lurch, her parting gift, a thorough cleaning of their files.

A surge of excitement hit Wetzon as she unlocked the door. It was wonderful to be back, to know who she was and what she was doing.

She was the first in—no one, not even Leslie Wetzon, ever got to the office at seven-thirty in the morning. But she wanted to acclimate herself without Smith standing over her.

Their reception area was a neat, compact space with four

Knoll chairs and the reception desk, which was Max's territory. Max Orchard was Smith and Wetzon's receptionist and part-time cold caller. He worked four days a week, from eleven to four. A retired accountant in gumsoled shoes, Max was a thorough, if anal, worker. Smith had fought Wetzon tooth and nail against hiring him, but he'd turned out to be a cold calling wonder, setting up a virtual assembly line of qualified people for Wetzon to talk to and recruit. And the additional bonus: Max never got pulled into Smith's magnetic field of lunacy.

Behind the reception area, where Smith and Wetzon had shared an open office that looked out onto a pretty garden, was the free-standing staircase to the second floor, and a small, semi-enclosed space for two associates. Under the staircase, a high tech fridge in the drawer of a low cabinet, a sink, and on the granite top of the cabinet, a new electric two-sided, coffee/tea maker.

Wetzon found a bag of Oren's decaf in the fridge and made coffee. As she listened to the chug and burble, she wandered over to the desks in the semi-enclosed space. The black Formica top of Sean Duggen's desk was obscured by wandering stacks of suspect sheets, scraps of paper with chicken-scratch notes, and a black loose-leaf notebook of client firms, executive names and titles, and managers' names. Each person in the office had one and was responsible for keeping it up to date.

She was dismayed by the mess. How could anybody ever find anything here? Mentally, she rolled up her sleeves. She was going to have to do some management control.

Still, she was glad Sean hadn't quit. It meant that he was doing a good job, or that Smith had been afraid to fire her only recruiter. Firing Sean would have meant Smith would have to talk to brokers, and she loathed stockbrokers. On a good day she referred to them as pond scum.

They'd hired Sean after 9/11; Wetzon had trained him herself. The small firm where he'd just started working as an assistant trader had closed down in the wake of the disaster. He'd spent six years as an Army Ranger, and the trading firm had brought him on as an apprentice. But firms had cut back and he'd had trouble finding another job.

Sean was perfect material for a Wall Street headhunter, and both Smith and Wetzon had felt he could be groomed. He was aggressive in a laid back way, not too tall, therefore, not threatening to the powers on the Street, who were, for the most, short. Nor was he slick or glib. He had a steady, sincere quality about him, and then there was his impressive Army experience, which was a turn-on for both male and female brokers. But he was in the Reserve and could get called up any time.

"It's a good war," Smith had said. "We'll make the sacrifice, if we have to."

No one had occupied the second desk when Wetzon left. Now she found two neat trays, one more dense than the other. The leaner one was marked "Hot." No doubt about it, Max had trained this one. He always had a continuous run of "Hot" possibilities for Wetzon. She didn't recognize the initials C.O. on the suspect sheets.

God, it was good to be back.

She folded her coat over her arm and climbed the stairs to the former parlor floor, amazed to hear a minuscule creak on the third rung. After all they'd paid for the renovation, a creak was outrageous.

The parlor floor was now open space that Wetzon and Smith shared. And here a rude shock was waiting. Her desk was obscured by shopping bags of every size and color: Chanel, DKNY, Saks, Bloomingdale's, you name it. Her desk had become Smith's closet outpost, for God's sake.

And all over the bleached birchwood floor were those little indentations from Smith's spike heels.

With an angry sweep of her hand, the shopping bags crashed to the floor around Smith's desk with its pristine top. I'll kill her, Wetzon thought. And where were all of Wetzon's treasures that always sat on her desk? Where else but in her wire wastebasket under her desk. Typical, she thought. One by one, date book, pressed glass spooner for pens and pencils, marble peach paperweight, coffee mug: THE BEST MAN ON THE CASE IS A WOMAN.

She hung up her coat, and checked the appointments and hires on the calendar, which they kept on a portable cork board, portable so they could hide it from visitors. Three hires in January, four in February. Four brokers she'd worked with, three were Sean's. One hire so far in March. Well, she'd juice that up a little.

Inspired, she took her mug and went downstairs for coffee. No creak this time. On her way back, she emptied Max's HOT tray. Before sitting at her desk, she began reading through the suspect sheets, slipping right back into the Smith and Wetzon groove.

What Smith and Wetzon did was mysterious, in the best sense of the word, and therefore, it was glamorous. They saw themselves as detectives, searching out the best candidates for the positions their clients had to fill. It seemed appropriate that even the biographical profile forms they filled out for each prospect were known as "suspect sheets."

The Street called them and those like them, headhunters, and they didn't mind. Away from the Street, recruiting professionals were executive recruiters, or search consultants, and "headhunter" was a derogatory term. But the Street admired toughness and rewarded piracy. Success and power were what counted. And money brought both.

Smith and Wetzon's clients were not ordinary business people; they were the movers and shakers of the all-powerful financial community. The Street with a capital S.

While Smith and Wetzon were not really insiders, they were not outsiders either. Thus, they were in a perfect position to see every problem objectively and give the client an overview.

They were truly an odd couple. Smith had come out of personnel, and Wetzon had been a Broadway dancer. That together their names were memorably similar to the gunsmith's served only to amuse them, but they used it to enhance their singularity. They were women in a man's world.

They'd been together over fifteen years and had done extraordinarily well, through feast and famine, on the Street. Smith concentrated on business development—bringing in clients—and Wetzon recruited stockbrokers, the division of duties coming mainly because Smith loathed brokers and was very proprietary about their clients.

Over the years the shape of Smith and Wetzon's business had changed gradually. They found they were in demand for a fair amount of management consulting, fees paid with slightly more regularity than those for headhunting.

The phone rang. She stared at it. Oh, well, she thought.

"Smith and Wetzon, good morning."

"Les, where's your cell? I've been trying to get you."

"In my briefcase. Shit, the batteries are probably dead. What's the matter?"

"Marty Lawler called yesterday while I was entertaining the FBI. I just spoke with him."

"Is he okay?"

"They sent him home, so I guess. He has something he wants to show us."

"Us? Me and you?"

"Is there another us?"

She smiled. "Where does he live?"

"Washington Heights. Where're you going to be?"

"Dialing for dollars."

"I'll pick you up at six. And Les—"

"Yes?"

"Replace those batteries."

"Silvestri—" He'd hung up, but the line was still open. "Silvestri? Are you still there?" It went dead. She'd been about to ask when the media would get hold of the news about Bill Veeder, but it was just as well.

She dug Rita Silvestri's card from her purse and called Clo Hightower. An answering machine clicked on, announced, "Law Offices, Hightower and Claeson," and suggested leaving a message. She left her name, phone number, and Rita Silvestri's name.

A muffled sound came from below. She went to the top of the stairs expecting to see someone, but no one was there, and no other unusual sounds, muffled or otherwise, were discernable.

Extra batteries were in her desk drawer; a quick exchange brought her cell phone back to life. She opened the doors of the wall unit, turned on CNN, bracing herself for the announcement about Bill Veeder and further emotional turmoil. Mug in hand, she walked to the tall windows that looked out at the deck.

The mug bobbled; coffee and mug hit the floor, exploding china and liquid.

A man stood on the deck and he was pointing a gun at her.

Chapter 40

He opened the door, never taking his eyes—or his gun—off her. "Back against the wall with your hands up," he said, motioning with the gun. "Don't come any closer, Miss—" He was looking past Wetzon, talking to someone else.

"Oh, for pity sakes!" Smith rushed into the room, her Manolo stilettos nicking the floor. "It's Wetzon, my partner. Wetzon, you've made a mess of our floor."

"Strange how coffee trickles right into the nicks from your heels." Had Wetzon been holding the mug, there was no question in her mind she would have thrown it. Not at the man with the gun, who was doing his job for a security company that Smith had apparently engaged while Wetzon was away, but at Smith.

Smith humpfed. She dismissed the security man with one of her imperious gestures. "You may go. Your response should have been better. We could have been raped and pillaged by the time you got here."

Body language is not hard to read when it's in response to something Smith's said or done. Wetzon smothered a grin. The security man left the way he came: deck, stairs, garden.

Smith stepped aside. "Cherry, sugar, close your mouth, it's so unattractive, and clean up this mess."

It was then that Wetzon noticed the young woman who'd come up behind Smith. She was tall, taller than Wetzon anyway, but who wasn't? Athletic in build, her hair was very short, straw colored, and faintly green, chlorine sign of a swimmer. Though she wore a boxy black suit, it gave off borrowed vibes, not having made the adjustment to her body, its folds and creases conforming to another identity. Behind horn rimmed glasses, however, her eyes were bright and intelligent. She handed Smith a wad of pink message slips.

Wetzon ignored Smith and offered her hand. "Cherry? How do you do? I'm Leslie Wetzon."

"Cheryl," she said, taking Wetzon's hand with enthusiasm. "Cheryl Orchard. Max is my grandpop, and he's training me how to cold call. I'm your new junior associate." She smiled at Smith with the same indulgence her grandfather showed Smith's eccentricities, and went to the bathroom, returning with some wet towel paper. She got right to work cleaning up the broken china mug and spilled coffee. "I'm so happy to meet you. I've heard so much about you."

When Cheryl left the room, Wetzon said, "Cherry Orchard, indeed."

Smith began collecting her shopping bags from the floor around Wetzon's desk. "I see you've made yourself at home, sweetie pie."

"I do work here," Wetzon said. "My memory is back."

"Does that mean we're out of danger?" Smith stared at the message slips in her hand as if wondering how they got there. As was her wont, she tossed them unread into her wastebasket.

"Aren't you going to return the call from the White House?"

"Finally!" Smith dove into the wastebasket and pulled out the messages, tore through them. "Oh, it's one of your little jokes." Her eyes teared. She threw her arms around Wetzon. "I've even missed your terrible little jokes. It's so good to have you back."

Holding Wetzon at arm's length, she said, "You look absolutely washed out, babycakes. And I know just the thing, a stone massage. It will do wonders for you. We'll go together." She clapped her hands and probably would have made the appointment then and there had not Bill Veeder's photo flashed on the silent television screen and stopped her.

Wetzon was transfixed as well. She turned up the sound.

". . . has been identified as William M. Veeder, prominent criminal attorney heading the Dooney Bellemore defense team in Los Angeles. The FBI will not comment further on a continuing investigation." More pictures of Bill flashed on the screen, as if they'd emptied their files. A young and less suave Bill, with Evelyn. Bill with some of the beautiful women he'd romanced. Bill and Leslie Wetzon, Bill debonair in black tie, Leslie Wetzon looking like a deer caught in headlights.

". . . investigation concerning the explosion of a corporate jet belonging to reclusive financier Jason McLaughlin at Teterboro Airport six weeks ago. A total of four bodies, including William Veeder's, have now been recovered and identified: the pilot Curtis Abimi; co-pilot, Reza Gondal; McLaughlin's secretary, Natalie Nostrand—"

Wetzon turned down the sound while Smith shrieked, "I don't believe it! I don't believe it!"

Choking up, Wetzon groped in her desk drawer for a tissue. "So that's it," she murmured.

"You knew."

"Silvestri told me yesterday."

"He must have been thrilled."

"You misjudge him, Smith. He knew Bill loved me, Bill told him so. Silvestri wasn't sure how I felt."

"Well, I could have told him. You're crazy—were—I can't even say it—about Bill." Tears ran down her cheeks. "It can't be true. It's a mistake. They make mistakes all the time." Wetzon handed her a tissue and she sniffled into it. It seemed odd to Wetzon that Smith was more emotionally engaged in Bill's death than Wetzon was.

"It's no mistake," Wetzon said. "The question is, what the hell was he doing there? He was supposed to be in L.A."

"I'll never get over this," Smith said with a sob. "He was so dear to me. So kind after—"

Bill had been law partner of the late and despicable Richard Hartmann. It was through Smith, who was having a torrid affair with Hartmann, that Wetzon had first met Bill Veeder. The affair had ended badly for Smith but worse for Hartmann. As his illegal activities were being investigated by the D.A., Hartmann came to a violent end.

Something about the way Smith said "so kind" caught Wetzon's attention. "You slept with him."

Smith's tears were a torrent.

"Why didn't you tell me?"

More tears. "It was right after Dickie—we were consoling each other."

"I'll bet."

"He was a beautiful man. We didn't want you to know because I knew you'd take it this way." More tears.

"Okay, okay." Wetzon put her arm around Smith. Would it have made a difference? she wondered. It might have. But all that was history now.

"He called me only a few weeks ago," Smith said, blowing her nose into the mascara-smudged tissue. "He'd been trying to reach you and was getting worried."

"You told him I'd taken a leave of absence?"

Smith nodded. "Actually, I thought you were with him,

and when you weren't, I began to worry that you'd had some kind of breakdown. I mean, who in her right mind would reject a proposal from Bill Veeder?"

"He told you all this?" My God, Bill, she thought, how little you understood me.

"I helped him pick out the ring, which was gorgeous and wildly expensive. I do those things for you, you know, and I never even get a thank you."

"Goddammit, Smith! This was between me and Bill. Oh, never mind," she said, seeing the hurt on Smith's face. Smith would never, ever get it. "It's in the past now."

The television was showing pictures of McLaughlin's estate in New Jersey and interviews with neighbors. Wetzon turned up the sound in time to hear a wrap-up of the earlier information and was about to turn off the set when Bill's picture came up on the screen again.

"Look at him," Smith sniffled. "He can't be dead."

"Shush," Wetzon said. "They're making some kind of announcement."

". . . just received some new information in our newsroom, information you'll only see on CNN. One month ago, William Veeder notified the SEC and federal prosecutors in Manhattan that he would be representing the interests of missing financier, Jason McLaughlin."

Chapter 41

It was astonishing. Not that Bill Veeder was Jason McLaughlin's lawyer because that was logical when you thought about it. What else would Bill have been doing there?

What was astonishing were the number of phone calls for Wetzon that came surging in, as if some metaphysical entity had alerted all of Wall Street that "sheeeee's back."

"Take a message," she told Cheryl, whose job it was to cover the phones when Max wasn't there. "Tell them, I absolutely swear I will return every call before lunch." And then there were the calls from the media. "Tell them no comment."

"It's great to have you back, Wetzon." Sean rose, leaned across his desk to shake her hand. His dark gray suit was more Hugo Boss than Brooks Brothers, but his white shirt was crisp, his tie a conservative blue and red stripe.

"And you've done very well. I think you've gone way beyond rookie, Sean."

"I'll be happy when they pay their bills," he said. "I'm still working on my draw."

"Yes, well, brokerage firms don't like to pay headhunters until ninety days after the broker sits, and even then they tell us the check is in the mail. That's why we have to present them with squeaky clean brokers; otherwise, all our hard work goes down the toilet."

"But if the broker lies—"

"Believe me, it can happen, no matter how carefully we scrutinize the broker's record. We can't control that. And we can't control what happens after the broker joins the new firm. The firms say we're responsible no matter what. They've even demanded their money back after six months have gone by."

"We don't have to give it to them, do we?"

"We've returned half to keep our clients happy. But that's rare. If the broker behaves himself and there are no problems on his U5, and he does business, they'll eventually pay." She held up her hand with crossed fingers.

Sean smiled. "And if he's clean but doesn't bring over all his business?"

"If he's working on it, it'll be okay, but if he's sitting out his deal, that's another story." Since headhunters were paid by the broker's new firm a percentage of the broker's trailing twelve months with his former firm, the firms were counting on the broker continuing to do business at the same rate. And it didn't look good for the headhunter if the broker didn't hold up his end of the deal.

"No, really," Cheryl told someone on the phone. "I can't disturb her. She's in a meeting. I'll have her call you back the minute she's available." Listening, she looked over at Wetzon. "Hold on." She pressed the hold button.

"What's the matter?" Wetzon asked.

"He says he's on the lam so you can't call him back." She gave Wetzon an uncertain smile.

"On the lam? Good God, what's his name?"

"Bobby Baglia."

"Wouldn't you know," Wetzon said, holding out her hand for the phone. "Bobby? What's this business about being on the lam?"

"Wetzon, I swear to God I didn't do any of the crap they say I did. They had no reason to fire me."

"Give me a hint, Bobby."

"I didn't come in on Sunday and break into their goddam desks."

"Okay. If you didn't, you didn't."

"But I needed the evidence, and how the fuck else was I going to get it?"

"So you did break into their desks?" Both Cheryl and Sean were rapt on her one-sided conversation.

"It's no reason to throw me out of the office."

"What do you want to do, Bobby?"

"I'm tired of all these shit firms like First Franchise. I want you to get me into Goldman."

"Goldman, huh," Wetzon repeated, sucking in her cheeks to keep from laughing. "We'll have to think about that. Where can I reach you?"

"You can't. I'll call you tomorrow morning. In the meantime. start putting feelers out for me at Goldman."

Wetzon clicked off and groaned. "Unbelievable."

"Goldman?" Sean said, "And he's on the lam?"

"He wants me to put out feelers," Wetzon said, laughing. "I'd love to know the back story here. Know anyone at First Franchise?"

"Matter of fact, I do," Sean said.

The phone rang and Wetzon handed it back to Cheryl, who said, "Smith and Wetzon, good morning," listened, said, "hold on, please."

"Not Bobby again," Wetzon said.

"No," Cheryl said. "A Clotilde Hightower. She says she's returning your call."

"I want to talk to her. Put it through upstairs. Later, Sean."

Smith's head was bent over her Tarot cards, spread out on her desk. She gave Wetzon a brief, troubled glance and returned to the cards.

Pushing away the intimation of apprehension Smith's reading of the Tarot always brought on, Wetzon picked up her phone, released the hold button. "Leslie Wetzon." She walked out on the deck.

"This is Clo Hightower." Her voice was husky, with a slight hoarse quality and traces of an English accent. "I spoke with Rita this morning."

"Did she tell you what this is about?"

"The barest essentials. Just from that, the sooner we get together, the better."

"What's your schedule like today?"

"Hellish, what's yours?"

"Not easy. It's my first day back."

"How about the evening? Eight-thirty. My office is near Lincoln Center."

"That would be good, I think." Silvestri ought to be with me, she thought. "I may have Rita's son with me. He can fill in blanks I can't."

Pause. "Okay. I'm in the Reebok Sports Club building."

Wetzon clicked off, but again the line stayed open for a fraction of a second longer. Stepping inside, she caught Smith setting the phone down.

"You were listening. Goddammit, Smith, don't I have any privacy?"

Smith didn't even look guilty. "Sweetie pie, we're only trying to protect you."

"We? Who's we?"

"All of your friends," she said, at her smarmiest. "We love you and don't want anything more to happen to you. Who is Clo Hightower? And why are you going to see her tonight?"

Wetzon sighed. "She's a lawyer. Rita Silvestri thinks I need a litigator with experience in federal law."

"Humpf. I never heard of her. But the cards already told me the Queen of Wands is entering your life." Smith studied the cards again. "Who is the blind man?" she asked.

Chapter 42

Wetzon was stunned. "How on earth—"

"Wetzon!" Max's sudden appearance distracted Wetzon from Smith's uncanny question about "the blind man."

Smiling her Cheshire Cat smile, Smith murmured, "The Tarot never lies." She tilted her head to the side regarding Max Orchard. "Max, sweetie, you are such a fashion plate today. You quite outshine Wetzon and me."

Max gave Smith an indulgent smile. "Xenia, you do go on." His short neck, concave chest, and pot belly were exaggerated by suspenders that brought his trousers almost to his armpits. He looked like Tweedledum, in gumsoles. "Wetzon, it hasn't been the same without you. And no one has missed you more than Xenia."

"Max!" A ruddy flush stained Smith's cheeks.

Wetzon laughed, free out, relaxed. It was so good to be back. "Do tell."

"Now don't deny it, dear," Max said, shaking his finger at Smith.

Smith, for once, had nothing to say. She watched the little lights on the phone flash and blink. The activity meant money in the bank for Smith and Wetzon. Smith maintained that the secret to success was to get the money out of "their" pockets and into "our" pockets. And if you kept your eye on that goal, it was sure to happen.

"Max," Wetzon said, "I'm going to work on the hots you've qualified. Cheryl—I can see she's a love—" Smith rolled her eyes. "Cheryl can feed Sean."

"I saw you rolling your eyes," Wetzon told Smith after Max left.

"For pity sakes, Cherry a love?"

"As are you, my dear partner."

"Humpf." Still, Smith looked pleased. She gathered up the Tarot cards, slipped them into their silk case, the case into her purse.

Wetzon's intercom line buzzed. "Yes?"

Sean said, "I've got the skinny on Bobby Baglia."

"Come right upstairs and tell us. It will make Smith's day." She grinned at Smith and filled her in on the earlier conversation. "I have a feeling it's the tip of the iceberg. I wanted to scrub down after I spoke with him."

"Dirtbag." Smith plopped into her chair. "Isn't he the one that kept leaving Xeroxes of his penis for his manager's secretary?"

"The very one. He got fired for that, but let's face it, the firms are to blame for people like him," Wetzon said. "One firm fires him, another hires him."

"Not this time, I have a feeling," Sean said.

"Pull up a chair," Wetzon told him.

"What firm was he with?" Smith searched her purse for her bulging makeup bag, put it on her desk, and unfolded a little mirror.

Sean took a seat in front of Wetzon's desk. "First Franchise."

"Never heard of it." Using a lip pencil, Smith outlined her lips, switched to a lip brush, and reapplied her lipstick.

Hypnotized by the procedure, Sean was silent.

"It's one of those obscure, shlocky firms that keep opening, playing for a while, then folding," Wetzon said. "Right, Sean?"

"Uh, oh, yes, right."

"So, go on," Smith said, applying blush to her cheeks with an oversized brush.

"But this all started when he was with Broad Wall Partners."

"Another new one on me," Smith said. "Obscure and Schlocky Incorporated, no doubt."

"Yes," Sean said. "Bobby was hyping this little biotech stock, telling clients that Merck was going to buy them. He said he'd done the research for free instead of the big bucks the hotshot research analysts charged. He got Broad Wall Partners to push it, and this whole group of doctors and dentists in Minnesota buying."

"What did the biotech company have that would make Merck buy them?" Wetzon asked.

"Nothing," Sean said. "It was all hype."

"Doctors are the dumbest investors," Smith said.

"One of the doctors called *The Wall Street Journal*. Bobby kept talking about six-figure profits and the stock kept dropping. Broad Wall Partners got smart and dumped him."

"And First whatever hired this pond scum?"

"Yes, a few days later. And took one of those tombstone ads saying they proudly announce the appointment of Bob Baglia as a Managing Director."

"That's why this business gets a bad name," Wetzon said.

"There's more."

"For pity sakes. I'm going to have to take a shower."

"Go on, Sean," Wetzon said.

"Well, Bobby was hot, got everybody at First Franchise fired up pitching stocks, which was good, but then he started doing crazy stuff like sleeping in the office at night and breaking into brokers' desks with a tire iron, searching their stuff. When they confronted him, he said he had the boss's permission to look for irregularities."

"Lying dirtbag," Smith said.

"One of the brokers confronted him and there was a fist fight. Bobby got axed. He came in the next day and threw a brick through the plate glass entrance. The other brokers jumped him and beat the shit out of him, dragged him through the lobby, and tossed him onto the street. He was arrested for third-degree assault."

"He said he was tired of the crummy small firms and wants me to fix him up with Goldman."

Smith had a wild glint in her eyes. "If he turns up here, Sean, call the police and tell them he's harassing us."

"This is what comes," Wetzon said, "of firms opting not to give the real reason for terminating brokers. They're scared they're going to get sued, so they use words like, 'amicable departure.' And the scumbag goes on from firm to firm, leaving a trail of damaged clients."

"Of course," Smith said. "Is it too much to ask investors to be less gullible and check out the firms and the brokers and the stocks being touted before they send their life savings to them?"

After Sean left them, Wetzon said, "Now I'll bet you haven't heard anything that scummy since I went on my leave."

Smith looked at her with slitted eyes. "You love these stories. Admit it."

"Truth is more delicious than fiction," Wetzon said. She raised her hand. "I cannot tell a lie."

Sighing, Smith started to speak, stopped, stared at Wetzon.

"Yes?" Wetzon said, prompting her.

"Mmmm. I just had a thought. There must be a . . . mmm . . . will."

Wetzon frowned. "Will? What are you talking about?"

"It's the only way to explain the Ten of Pentacles in the spread I did for you, babycakes. It predicted a large inheritance."

"That's ugly, Smith. Bill's money will go to Evelyn."

"Who really needs it? That vegetable is loaded." Smith threw up her hands. "This is so like you." Bemused, she began to nod. "Carolyn will know."

"Carolyn? If you mean Bill's secretary, she retired."

"She couldn't have," Smith said. "I spoke with her two weeks ago. She never said anything about retiring."

"I called the office yesterday. There are all new people there. Could Bill have brought in a new partner—someone named Farber—before he left?"

"You're wrong, of course. Why would he do that?"

"Maybe because he was going to be in L.A. for a while?"

Phone in hand, Smith punched in some numbers. "Carolyn Dorley, please." Pause. She looked at Wetzon. "How surprising. I spoke with her recently and she never mentioned anything . . . I am. No, I'd prefer not. Thank you." She disconnected. "This is very strange. A foreign woman—when I said I was a client—wanted to connect me to a Mr. Farber, 'who has been working with Mr. Veeder's clients.' "

"Didn't I tell you?"

Smith unwrapped her cards and handed them to Wetzon. "Shuffle." Wetzon shuffled. Smith cut the cards and thrust them at Wetzon. "Blow on them."

"Oh, good grief!"

"Blow."

Wetzon blew on the cards, then watched Smith do the spread.

"I don't like the Moon turning up here," Smith said.

"What does that mean?" Wetzon asked in spite of her skepticism.

"It doesn't bode well." Smith studied the cards. "Ten of Pentacles again." The usual furrow did not appear between her brows. She closed her eyes and with her hands flat on the cards, took a slow, deep breath. "It's glitter. Jewels," she said, awed. "Lots."

Chapter 43

"How does she do it? It makes me crazy."

"Fasten your seat belt," Silvestri said.

" 'It's going to be a bumpy night'?"

Silvestri smiled at her. "Bette Davis, *All About Eve*."

"Bingo." She rested her hand on his thigh. How come, she wondered, men have such stone hard thighs?

"How was the first day?"

"Wonderful. Even Smith, though she eavesdropped when I spoke with Clo Hightower. She thinks I won't catch on when the line stays open a second or two more."

"Does it happen often?"

"Does what happen often?"

"The line staying open a second or two longer." He stopped for the red light.

"Only when she . . . wait, no, it happened when she wasn't in yet." She stared at him. "What does that mean?"

"Could mean nothing. I think I'll send someone over tomorrow to check out your phone lines."

"You've just creeped me out."

"I could be wrong."

She sighed. "I set up an appointment for tonight with Clo Hightower, eight-thirty. I told her you would be with me, that you'll be able to fill in a lot of the blanks. Okay?"

"Okay." He was driving uptown on First Avenue. "Where's her office?"

"Reebok Sports Club building. I want to stop and feed

Izz before we go to Marty Lawler."

"That's the plan."

"Where does Marty Lawler live?"

"Washington Heights, Cabrini Boulevard."

"I've never been up there, except to go to the Cloisters. Hey, we should go to the Cloisters some time."

He turned west on Eighty-fifth Street and joined the crawling crosstown rush hour traffic. As they waited for a light to change, he said, "You saw it?"

She knew he wasn't referring to the Cloisters. "Yes."

"You okay?"

"Yes. Smith wasn't, though."

"Oh?"

Wetzon watched the people on the sidewalks who were making better time than the cars. Her response was detached. "She had an affair with him, right after Hartmann died."

Silvestri made a strangling noise.

"Oh, go on, laugh out loud."

He did. "You gotta give it to him—" With an ever-so-slight shade of admiration.

"Yeah? And what does that say for me?"

"I told you how he felt about you, Les."

Silvestri double-parked in front of her building. "Feed, water, and a short walk," she said.

She picked up her mail and phoned Carlos on her way upstairs.

His answering machine took the call. She left a message: "Had a decent day, going with Silvestri to see a lawyer tonight. I know you're worrying. Stop. I'm okay about Bill. Maybe I'm still in shock. Love you, sweet thing."

As she shook dry food into Izz's bowl, she had an inspired thought. Carolyn Dorley. Why hadn't she thought of this before? She rinsed Izz's water bowl and filled it with fresh water. The phone book. If a dog could have a reproachful expression, Izz would qualify. "Go on, eat. It's perfectly good dog food, and that's all you're going to get. I suppose Silvestri's been feeding you junk food." More reproach, this with a twitching nose.

While the dog ate, Wetzon paged through the phone book. Lots of Dorleys. No Carolyns, but one C. Dorley, at Nine Hundred West End Avenue. She called the number. An answering machine picked up. Carolyn's voice.

"Carolyn, this is Leslie Wetzon. Please call me." She left her cell number.

Now the question was, should she tell Silvestri? It might be easier to talk to Carolyn woman to woman. A short bark from Izz waiting at the door drove the thought from her head.

She attached Izz's collar and leash and brought her downstairs, where Silvestri, who was leaning against the passenger side door, caught the fluffy, white guided missile as she flew at him.

"Dog food breath." He set her down to do her business. "We'll be late," he told Wetzon, as she collected Izz's outlay in the plastic bag. He opened the door and Izz sailed into the car and burrowed into a small space between the seats.

Wetzon shrugged. "We might as well take her with us. Just stop at a trash basket so I can get rid of this."

"I guess I'll have to arrest you."

"Aw, Silvestri, you wouldn't do that, would you? It's my first offense."

"I'll bet."

Izz crawled out of the space the minute the car began moving and snuggled up next to Silvestri, giving Wetzon an almost-female, he's-mine-try-and-get-him glance. "Bitch," Wetzon said.

Marty Lawler lived in Castle Village, a collection of high-rises on the cliffs in the northernmost section of Manhattan known as Washington Heights, for the colonial Fort of the same name that had stood at One Hundred Eighty-first Street. His building was well kept, the lobby clean and spacious.

When they got off the elevator on the sixth floor, a beefy woman, her streaked blonde hair in a ponytail, beckoned to them from an open door two apartments down. "Silvestri, right?" She wore tight jeans and a leather jacket. The red edge of a lightning tattoo showed above the neck of her tee. "I'm Mary Elizabeth, Marty's my dad. You're Leslie?" She shook hands. "Cute dog." Dipping into her shoulder bag for keys. "He's been going nuts waiting." Stuck her head in the door. Nora barked, Izz responded. "I'm going now, Dad. You call me if you need anything." She stepped aside, let them in, and closed the door behind them.

"My younger daughter's always rushing somewhere," Marty said. "Come on in, grab a seat." He came to meet them, swiveling his head, trying to catch what he could from his peripheral vision. "I see you brought a friend for Nora." He and Silvestri shook hands.

"Isabella, Izz for short," Wetzon said.

While the dogs circled each other, sniffing rear ends, then noses, Silvestri, Wetzon, and Marty sat down at Marty's dining table, in a windowed alcove near the kitchen.

"Wow," Wetzon said, gazing out the window. It was a spectacular view of the bridge that crossed the Hudson River, the one New Yorkers called the G.W., its brilliant lights defining it against the darkening sky. The first president was well represented up here.

"Looking good, Marty," Silvestri said.

"Yeah. Feel pretty good. Can't do much yet. They've got me with a goddam visiting nurse, would you believe? And a physical therapist. There's coffee, Leslie, and cups set up on the counter. Milk in the fridge. And bring over that envelope you see there."

"What's up?" Silvestri said.

After Wetzon filled the cups and set them on the table, Nora came over and put her head in Wetzon's lap. Izz growled and tried to push Nora away, butting one golden leg and then the other. Good-natured Nora's legs moved, but her head didn't budge.

"Okay, okay, girls," Marty said. "Nora, here."

With a jump, Izz staked her claim to Wetzon.

Marty emptied the envelope on the table. Coins, bills held with a paper clip, a Braille watch, a bunch of keys on a chain. And a single plastic card. "The hospital forgot to give me my stuff when they discharged me, and I clean forgot to ask. They took it off me when I was brought in. Lucky Mary Elizabeth has a key. Anyway, don't get antsy on me, Silvestri. I'm getting to it."

Silvestri grinned. "Well, get to it then."

"They gave Mary Elizabeth the lot when she went back." Marty held up the plastic card. "You see this? Well, it's not mine. I never seen it before."

"So what are you getting at, Marty?"

"Hold out your hand, Leslie," Marty said. Wetzon took the card. "What do you think? Seem familiar to you?"

Nothing came from the card. No vibes, tremors, nothing. "It looks like a hotel room key card, Marty."

"You think Les passed it to you before you were shot?"

"More likely slipped it into my pocket."

"Damn, I don't remember any of this."

Silvestri took the card from Wetzon. "It's for one of the Port Authority lockers."

Chapter 44

After dropping Izz off at Wetzon's apartment, they drove down Ninth Avenue to Forty-second Street. Silvestri circled the blocks near the Port Authority Bus Terminal until they got lucky: a car pulled out of a space near the Al Hirschfeld Theatre just off Eighth Avenue on Forty-fifth Street. It was quarter to eight.

Wetzon was nervous. Standing on the sidewalk waiting for Silvestri to lock the car, her knees felt fragile, as if they wouldn't hold her up. What if, she thought, what if—

"Hey," Silvestri said, hands on her shoulders, "don't keep jumping ahead. Your imagination is worse than reality."

They walked the short distance down Eighth, clogged with evening traffic, to the huge, hideous buildings that make up New York's Port Authority Bus Terminal. From here buses left for New Jersey, upstate New York, and all points of the compass, serving both commuters and long distance travelers. A continuous, though moving, line waited in front for cabs.

While technically it was past rush hour, commuters were still pouring into the terminal to catch their buses home. The main lobby ran the length of the city block, from Eighth to Ninth, and was lined with shops and indented areas for particular bus company ticket counters. People of all colors and in varieties of costume hurried to their buses, like Alice's rabbit. Her head spun.

Silvestri steered her off to the side, where he was greeted

234

by a burly, gray haired black man in a business suit standing in front of a Krispy Kreme doughnut shop. Obviously, a cop in plain clothes. They shook hands and clapped each other's backs. Like old home week, she thought. Silvestri introduced him as Jimmy Baker. "We were at the academy together."

Wetzon wanted to scream as the two exchanged bits of information. Jimmy was with security at the Port Authority. Yeah, yeah.

Something about the Krispy Kreme shop agitated her. The smell should have made her hungry, but she fought off a wave of nausea.

"Yeah, Lois . . . psychiatric social worker. Four grandkids."

"Hey," Silvestri said, doing the shoulder punch again.

Oh, yes, she thought. I'm going to scream. She edged away from the doughnut shop.

Silvestri grabbed her hand, pulled her close. He scanned the crowd while Jimmy gave her a wink. Wetzon gritted her teeth.

"He's a good man," Jimmy told her, giving Silvestri an elbow.

"You're such a kidder, Jimmy," she said. She pinched the narrow roll of flesh above Silvestri's belt, sending him a mental message: Let's fucking get going.

"Make him?" Jimmy said, smiling at Wetzon.

"Huh?" Wetzon said.

"Yeah," Silvestri said, arm tight around her waist.

"Silvestri?" Jimmy said.

"Yeah."

Wetzon looked from one to the other. "What am I missing?"

"I don't get them," Jimmy said, chucking Wetzon under

the chin. "Don't they know they stand out like shit on snow?"

Finally, Silvestri asked where the lockers were, and Jimmy pointed off to the distant left and Eighth Avenue. "Near the waiting room left of the restrooms. We're getting rid of them. Kind of stuff you could forget about till 9/11. Too easy to stash a bomb."

"Emptied them lately?" Silvestri asked.

"Last month. They get cleaned out permanently tomorrow. You got something there?"

"Les left a bag there a few weeks ago."

"Good thing you came today, then."

They exchanged handshakes again. "Stay in touch," Jimmy called.

"Christ," Wetzon said.

"Patience. Nothing's running away."

"Aren't you at all interested in what's in the locker?" They were walking toward the waiting room.

"Check out the crowd. Be cool. See anyone familiar?"

Damnation. She couldn't believe it. "We're being followed. So that's what all that dumb ass double talk was about."

"Not so dumb ass, huh?"

Judy Blue's cohort was checking out pantyhose in the window of a shop. "The pervert. What are we going to do?"

"You have your MetroCard?"

"Yes."

"First you're going to make a pit stop so he'll think that's where Jimmy was pointing. Then take the subway up to Clo's office."

"What about you?"

"I think they'll follow you. I'll find a men's room and if it's clear, I'll check the locker."

She went into the ladies' room. A matron was refilling the toilet paper in the stalls. Wetzon washed her hands and stared into the mirror over the sinks. Her chest constricted. *Déjà vu.* A terrified woman with dark hair and crusty cheeks looked back at her. In a moment the vision was gone and Wetzon was back. It was enough to shake her. She'd been here before, recently. But the vision was all there was and it was gone.

"I've been here, Silvestri," she said when she came out. "I caught a sliver of memory when I looked in the mirror."

"We've figured that." He'd turned them around and they were walking toward the staircase that led down to the Eighth Avenue subway line.

"Okay." She was disappointed not to be the one opening the locker. The act might have brought everything back.

"Give us a passionate kiss," he said.

"I'll have to psych myself," she said, but hardly got the words out because Silvestri's hands framed her face and there was nothing phony about his passion. Or hers.

He let go of her and gave her a light smack on the ass. "Be careful."

"You, too."

"Don't look around. Just go. I'll meet you there."

She ran down the stairs and slid her MetroCard into the slot. She'd have to change to the IRT at Fifty-ninth Street. Her watch said eight-twenty.

Chapter 45

Wetzon's thoughts were erratic, lurching from the contents of the locker to Laura Lee, to Carolyn Dorley, back to Laura Lee, the locker, Laura Lee. At Fifty-ninth Street, where she had to switch from the Eighth Avenue line to the Broadway line, not paying attention, she climbed the wrong staircase. Reversing herself, she caught Special Agent Gelber by surprise. She nodded to him as she passed, murmuring, "Gelber."

Well, good. He had followed her, not stayed on Silvestri.

When she got out at Sixty-sixth Street and Lincoln Center, curtains had already gone up, thus ending the rush to the theatres and the resulting bottleneck of cars and taxis ringing the glowing complex. Only the locals were on the street. And the wind had picked up, dropping temperatures.

Her cell phone went off. Silvestri. "What did you—"

"Where are you?" Smith demanded.

"On Sixty-seventh and Columbus. Why?"

"She's downstairs." Smith disconnected, leaving Wetzon seething.

What the hell is she talking about, Wetzon thought, hurrying to Clo Hightower's building. Who's downstairs? Oh, damnation! Smith must be in Clo Hightower's office waiting for her.

She was right.

Clo Hightower's office was modest compared to Smith and Wetzon's. The reception area was small and very modern with Danish-type furnishings in bright blue and

238

gold fabrics, recessed lighting, and a geometric patterned rug on dark-stained wood floors. No one sat at the reception desk, but a faint buzzer had sounded when Wetzon opened the door.

"Hello," Wetzon called.

"Leslie?" Hair, a lot of it, very blonde, in an old fashioned shoulder-length pageboy. Strong features, strong shoulders, strong woman. She wore a gray business suit, its skirt—a surprise—settling at mid thigh, a white, tailored shirt open at the throat. No question, Clo Hightower's pride was her legs, long and slim in sheer hose, and good grief, Manolo Blahnick shoes.

They shook hands. "Is my partner bothering you?" Wetzon asked, her voice dripping irony. "She's the great appropriator of the Western World."

Clo smiled. "She's a piece, all right. But we can work with her."

Oh, sure, Wetzon thought. She'll run rings around you, too, Clo Hightower.

A beaming Smith jumped up from Clo's black leather couch and gave Wetzon a hug. "Where have you been?"

"With Silvestri. He's on his way." Silvestri will have a fit if he finds Smith here.

Smith groaned. "I told dear Clo all about Silvestri."

"Smith!"

"And I told her everything that's happened to you, sweetie pie."

"You don't know everything that's happened to me. I don't even know that."

Clo motioned for Wetzon to sit. "Xenia understands that we'll need some time in private and she very graciously offered to sit outside, didn't you, Xenia?"

"Er," Smith said, her mouth half open.

Round one, Clo Hightower.

"I'm impressed," Wetzon said, once the door was closed behind Smith. "Smith doesn't handle easily." She sat down on the sofa.

Clo smiled. "She's a challenge. I love challenges." She took up a yellow legal pad and pen, rolled the sheets over to a blank page, and sat in the chair opposite Leslie. "Start at the beginning."

"You know I'm a headhunter and Smith's partner."

"Yes."

"You know I was a dancer—"

"A gypsy. Yes, Xenia made sure to tell me she taught you everything you know."

Wetzon rolled her eyes. "Why am I not surprised?"

"She told me that Bill Veeder was the love of your life and that you're devastated by his death."

"She would. She introduced us and got off on the affair, which I'll admit was hot. He was easy to be with, wealthy, generous, connected, and thought I was wonderful. It was seductive and I went with it. But I always knew it wouldn't, couldn't last."

"He radiated charm and power." Clo was making notes on her pad.

Wetzon sighed. "Don't tell me you slept with him, too."

"We ran into each other fairly often. I'm sure Rita told you we all went to Fordham together, but I assure you, Leslie, there could never have been anything between us."

Something in the way Clo phrased it, as well as her direct look, told Wetzon Clo was gay. "Thanks," she said, though she wasn't sure why. "Bill and I sort of split when he joined the Dooney Bellemore defense in L.A. and I wouldn't go with him. I think our relationship had burned out; at least I was. I am not arm candy and I was beginning to feel like that. We took a leave of absence from each other. I haven't—hadn't—seen him since Thanksgiving."

"Thanksgiving?"

"I intended to stay for a couple of days but ended up taking the red-eye back the same day."

"Why?"

"I don't know. I can't remember. One of many things I can't remember."

"You took a leave of absence from your job. Why?"

"Here's where it gets murky. I've lost that part of my life. Something to do with my friend and investment advisor, Laura Lee Day. Laura Lee also took a leave and no one knew where she'd gone either." A lump settled in Wetzon's throat and her eyes teared. "Silvestri told me this morning that he heard through channels that she's surfaced, and alive, thank God, but I don't know anything more."

"You were worried she wasn't?"

"I guess. When they found me in the park, they said I kept going on about a woman on the cliff singing a sad song."

Clo looked down at her notes. "You said your friend's name is Laura Lee Day? Laura . . . Lee . . . Lorelei."

"Laura Lee . . . Lorelei! Of course. My God, all the brilliant people around me, and we never considered—"

"What's the first thing you remember?"

"Waking up in Mount Sinai Psychiatric as a Jane Doe." She went on to tell Clo about the man who claimed to be her uncle, identified her as Mary Lou Salinger and was coming back for her, how she ran away, was taken in by Zoey, how Silvestri found her after his friend Metzger had spotted her with Zoey's mime troupe. "Sounds like a soap opera, doesn't it?"

241

"Just a bit convoluted. You never saw this so-called uncle again?"

"Once more. In front of Zoey's building the night before she was murdered." Wetzon swallowed hard several times, trying to ease the lump in her throat. "They were looking for me and they killed her."

"I'm sorry."

"Me too." She sighed. "Things began to come back; my life previous to the leave of absence has come back. Well, most of it. But the FBI—an agent named Judy Blue—thinks I'm hiding diamonds, and that I was involved in the explosion of that hedge fund manager's plane last month."

"Ah, yes. Jason McLaughlin. This has something to do with him?"

"So it appears. I have this odd feeling that I may have been working for the FBI, though it seems crazy. Why me?"

"We'll find out. I'm going to call Special Agent Judy Blue in the morning and set up a meeting. Okay?"

"Okay. But there's more. A retired cop named Marty Lawler, who was hurt in a shooting in the Port Authority and was in Bellevue recovering from surgery, heard about me from the television reports and called the police. He said he'd been on a New Jersey bus with me and that I was terrified and swore people were trying to kill me."

"You don't remember this?"

"A blank. Silvestri took me to see him. He has macular degeneration and is legally blind. His seeing eye dog knew me and I knew the dog. And Marty recognized my voice. He said a man shot him and dragged me off."

"But you got away."

"Somehow. They said I was found in that big snowstorm, half-dressed, semi-conscious, delirious, babbling about the woman on the cliff."

"Your friend Laura Lee."

"Yes. Look, Clo, people died on that plane, Bill died, and McLaughlin is missing, I'll bet with tons of investors' money, and then there are the diamonds—" Her hands shook and she folded her fingers tight to stop it.

Clo went back to her desk and took a small unopened bottle of Evian from a drawer, broke the seal, and handed it to Wetzon. Wetzon took a long, slow drink.

Seated again, Clo asked, "What did Bill Veeder have to do with this?"

"They said on TV that he was representing McLaughlin. But Bill was in L.A., on trial. What the hell would he be doing in Teterboro . . . ? And there's one more thing—Marty, the cop, found a key card with the things the hospital returned to him when he was discharged. It wasn't his. Silvestri said it was a locker keycard from the P.A. Marty and Silvestri think I slipped it into Marty's pocket before he was shot. Silvestri is late because when we went to open the locker, we spotted the FBI, so we split up."

On perfect cue, a buzzer went off. "Stay here, Leslie," Clo said. She opened the door and stepped out.

Wetzon standing, heard: "For crissakes, Xenia, what the hell are you doing here?" Silvestri didn't like surprises and even on a good day had no patience for Smith's antics.

Smith's response was muffled.

"Is she here?" Wetzon heard him ask.

"Yes," Clo said, leading him into her office and closing the door. He had no suitcase, no backpack. Nothing. So what had been in the locker?

Wetzon went to him and he held her. "I hate this," he said into her hair.

"Me, too."

"Gelber's downstairs. I told him to go home, that you're talking to a lawyer."

"Who's Gelber?" Clo asked.

"FBI."

"Well, we're going to deal with them tomorrow as soon as I reach this Judy Blue person. Have a seat, and tell us what you found in the locker."

"You told her?"

"Yes," Wetzon said.

"Okay," Silvestri said, "here's the thing." He was tense and somber. He took a crumpled Krispy Kreme bag from his pocket and set it on the coffee table in front of the leather sofa. "I'm a cop doing a personal favor for a friend. I don't want to know what's in the bag—" His beeper went off. He checked the number, took out his cell, and made a call. "Excuse me." He turned his back. "Silvestri."

Wetzon and Clo Hightower exchanged glances. A Krispy Kreme bag would have a doughnut in it. Or would it? They waited.

Silvestri said, "I'm on my way," and tucked his phone back in his inside pocket. "I've got a homicide. You don't need me." He gave Wetzon a swift kiss. "Later. Maybe." He stopped. "Take a cab."

Wetzon said, "Get out of here, Silvestri."

"Wait," Clo said. She handed Silvestri her legal pad and pen. "I'm going to need Marty Lawler's phone number. I want to give him a heads-up. When we talk to the FBI I'm going to have to bring him into it."

He flipped through some pages in his notes, found what he was looking for, wrote the number on Clo's pad, and handed it back.

They heard the outer door close.

Clo shut her office door. "Okay, let's see if what we have

here is just a stale doughnut, or—" She uncrumpled the bag and reached into it. "Uh oh." Out came her fist, knuckles powdery with sugar. She opened her hand.

Chapter 46

"God," Wetzon said.

Clo swept some papers off the coffee table and emptied the bag on the glass surface. Powdered sugar and diamonds, dozens of them, spewed every which way across the glass.

"Sugar-coated diamonds," Clo said, adding those in her hand. She shook the paper bag to make sure there were no reticents in the creases. Seven more joined their mates.

"Dirty diamonds," Wetzon said, trying to keep the horror from taking charge. "So the FBI was right. I did have them and hid them away." She sank onto the sofa, head in her hands. "What was I going to do with them?"

"Somehow I have a feeling you were going to do the right thing."

"Oh, for pity sakes!"

Neither Clo nor Wetzon had heard Smith steal in, but now there she stood, hands on hips, the picture of irritation. She came closer, like a bird dog zeroing in on her prey. For Smith, prey was the stones that couldn't hide their glitter under powdered sugar.

"Diamonds," Smith breathed, picking up a handful and blowing away the sugar dust. "Sweet babies!"

"Put them down, Xenia," Clo said. "They're evidence. I'm going to turn them over to the FBI tomorrow."

"That's right, Smith."

"But sugarbuns, finder's keepers, don't you think?" She rolled them around her palm like dice.

"Not this time," Clo said. She caught Wetzon's eye be-

fore stepping to her desk and taking out a manila clasp envelope.

I'm supposed to keep an eye on Smith. Ha, Wetzon
thought.

Smith made a little wheedling coo. It was going to be fun
watching her fork over the diamonds.

Clo opened the mouth of the Krispy Kreme bag and held
it out to Smith. "Just drop them in here, Xenia, thank you
very much."

"Humpf," Smith said, but she complied.

Gathering up the rest of the sticky stones, Wetzon
slipped them into the bag with the others.

"So are we finished?" Smith asked, impatient.

Clo said, "I think so." She put the Krispy Kreme bag
into the manila envelope and sealed it. "Leslie, I'll call you
tomorrow with the meeting time."

Looking around the room, Smith said, "Where's
Silvestri?"

"He had a homicide."

"I didn't see him leave. Must have been when I was in
the ladies'." She looked I've-got-a-secret pleased. What was
she up to? Wetzon wondered. "I'll go ahead and get the
car." Oh, yes, she was definitely up to something.

"You are a saint," Clo said, once Smith was gone.

"Thanks, Clo. She's not as bad as she seems." Wetzon
grinned. "Whatever that means. You'll want a retainer."

"You can give me a check tomorrow for twenty-five hundred dollars, and we'll take it from there."

When Wetzon came out on Columbus Avenue, Smith's
sable Jaguar was double-parked in front of Clo's building.
Smith gunned the engine; Wetzon opened the door and got
in.

"What's going on, Smith?"

"You're dawdling and we have an appointment."

"An appointment?" She fastened her seat belt. "What appointment? Dinner, I hope. I'm starving."

"Not dinner. Carolyn Dorley. Did you mention her to Silvestri?"

"No. I meant to but never got to it. What about her? I was thinking I'd go up to see her. I looked her up in the phone book and got her answering machine when I called."

"Well, I spoke to her."

"Hey! Did you ask her why she retired?"

Smith made a right on Sixty-sixth and another right to Broadway, pulling out in front of a cab. The bearded driver swerved left and, with the glare of a true killer, gave Smith the finger. "Our immigration policy is too lenient," she said.

"Smith, you'll get us both killed, and if I don't eat something soon, I'll die."

Smith parked in front of a fireplug near Gray's Papaya, the cheapest, most popular hotdogs in the city. "Get two and two papayas. Mayo on mine."

"Mayo? No New Yorker eats a hotdog with mayo."

"I do."

Shielding themselves with paper napkins, they ate the franks without getting interrupted. Smith said, "She didn't want to talk at first. Said she couldn't. She'd signed something. But she's very upset about Bill."

"She signed some kind of confidentiality agreement, do you think?" Wetzon licked the mustardy grease from her fingers.

"They must have given her a lot of money."

"Who's they?"

"Ah," Smith said. "That's what we're going to find out."

"But if she won't, can't talk about it—"

Smith rolled down her window. "Give me your garbage."

"No, you'll only throw it on the street. Give it here." Wetzon took the remains of their snack and dropped it in the trash basket. When she got back into the car, Smith had the motor running.

"So we're going up there even though she won't talk to us?"

"Babycakes, you always underestimate me."

Carolyn lived in the Columbia University area of the Upper West Side, in a pre-World War II high-rise on the corner of 104th Street. They drove up Broadway but since 104th Street ran east, they had to make the turn on 105th Street to come around via West End Avenue.

"Look for a parking place," Smith said. She made the turn onto West End and encountered flashing lights. 104th Street was blocked off. "Is that a fire?"

Wetzon peered out. "I don't think so. I see an EMS truck and some police cars. And an ambulance. Smith, I'm getting a very bad feeling."

"Wait until we find a parking spot." She turned right, toward Riverside Drive, and halfway down the block came upon an opening big enough for a scooter.

"You can't get in here," Wetzon said. Oops, famous last words, she thought, as Smith lined up the sports car with the car in front and with an expert spin of the wheel, backed right into the space. "Oh me of little faith."

"You always doubt me, sweetie pie," Smith said.

"You're absolutely right, and I'm sorry."

"It's very hurtful."

"I'll try to do better."

"Flip. You always make my feelings into a joke."

"Smith, I swear—" Abashed. Smith was right.

They got out of the car. While Smith checked the locks, Wetzon looked down the street at the increasing activity.

Two cops stood on the corner, turning away the curious. A van pulled up and was waved through.

"Crime Scene techs," Wetzon said.

"Come on." Smith, cheerful now, took Wetzon's arm and piloted her across West End Avenue, strolling them right up to the two uniforms, one a woman. She gave the man one of her radiant smiles. "Officer, what's happened?"

"There's been a homicide, Ma'am."

"Oh, dear, how dreadful. This is such a wonderful neighborhood."

The cop was polite, but young. He didn't respond to Smith in quite the way she was used to men responding. And the woman was studying both Smith and Wetzon in a way that made Wetzon uncomfortable. She was memorizing them.

Wetzon gave Smith a nudge. "Let's go."

Smith acquiesced, but didn't walk toward the car. "We'll try the Broadway side," she said.

"I think we should get out of here. This is probably where Silvestri went and I don't want him to see us."

"Carolyn lives in a dangerous neighborhood," Smith said, several paces ahead.

"How could you possibly know that? There's nothing wrong with this neighborhood. The apartments are huge, and it's only a few blocks from Columbia."

Smith had that pitying look on her face. "You'll have to trust me."

Right, Wetzon thought. She never heard the words "trust me" without remembering what a broker once told her. In brokerese, he'd said, "trust me" means "fuck you."

250

They came out on Broadway and saw the same configu-
ration on 104th Street, this time a barrier guarded by four
cops. "Give it up," Wetzon said, searching the faces in the
rubbernecking crowd that had gathered on Broadway. More
uniforms were canvassing the onlookers. Murderers sometimes stayed to watch.

She would never know what it was about the man that first
caught her attention. He stood in the shadows, in the back
part of the crowd, watching, as everyone was. He wasn't
talking to anyone. Something about the set of his shoulders.

Instead of stepping back, out of view, Wetzon felt herself
move forward.

"Wetzon!" Smith's voice. People looked for the voice.

The man turned his head. His eyes met Wetzon's.

"Oh, there you are!" Smith pounced on her, grabbing
Wetzon's arm, spinning her around.

"No!" Wetzon wrenched her arm away, searching for the
man. But he was gone and the crowd had filled in where he
had stood. "Goddammit, Smith! That man—"

"What man?"

"He was in the crowd, watching."

"You're having a relapse. Everyone's watching."

Wetzon stamped her foot. "I am not having a relapse. He
wears Gucci loafers. I know it. And he's a killer."

"Calm down," Smith said, fast-walking her toward the
car. "I thought you'd recovered. Now you have fixated on
some stranger in a crowd. Gucci loafers, for pity sakes.
Killer? Puh-leeze."

Furious, she pulled away from Smith, determined to go
back.

She was trying to stay calm, but her limbs trembled, and
she was having trouble with her knees. She steadied herself
against a mail box.

"We can talk about it later," Smith said, as if she were speaking to an insane person who had to be placated.

"No. No, Smith, you don't understand. I recognized him. And he recognized me."

Chapter 47

"You can take the girl out of the theatre," Smith said, fastening her seat belt, "but you can't take the theatre out of the girl."

"What the hell does that mean?" Anger cleared the panic from Wetzon's mind.

"As usual, you over-dramatize."

"Goddammit, Smith, Carolyn's been murdered and you are not taking this seriously."

Smith chortled, started the engine. "Carolyn's been murdered? Indeed! Why would Carolyn be murdered?"

"Because she knows something about Bill's business."

"Puh-leeze. There must be a thousand ethnic types living on that block, and you say the police are there because of Carolyn?" She rolled her eyes. "You have lost it, sweetie pie, really lost it."

"Ethnic types? What the hell does that mean?"

"Well, we are in Spanish Harlem," Smith said, with another pitying look. The Jaguar hummed an accompaniment.

"Excuse me, for what it's worth, this is not Spanish Harlem. Spanish Harlem is on your side of town."

"Oh, for pity sakes."

Wetzon opened the car door. "Thank you very much, but I'll find my own way home."

"Get back here," Smith said, shutting down the engine. "I'm going to show you how wrong you are." She took out her cell phone and punched in some numbers.

"Who are you calling?"

"You'll see." Smug. "Carolyn, my dear." She didn't bother to hide her I-told-you-so face. "This is—" Her eyes opened wide, staring at Wetzon. She disconnected, returned her cell to her pocket, and gunned the engine. "Close your door."

"Tell me," Wetzon said.

Smith pulled out and headed for Riverside Drive. "It wasn't Carolyn. Some cop, probably." She sent a sideways glance at Wetzon. "You may have been right, babycakes." Her cell phone rang. Smith's hand went to her pocket.

Staying Smith's hand, Wetzon said, "Don't answer it."

"Why not?"

"Because whoever you spoke to is calling you back."

Smith made a left on Eighty-sixth Street. "And who might that be?"

"The murderer, though I doubt that. I'd guess, the police."

"Humpf. What shall we do?"

"I don't know what you're going to do, but I'm going to take a nice hot shower and go to bed. And I suggest you do the same."

"Oh, very well. We'll plan our strategy tomorrow." Even in the dark Smith's eyes glittered.

Strategy? Wetzon shook her head. What the hell is she talking about? "I'm supposed to meet with the FBI sometime tomorrow, and my guess is they'll want to do it first thing in the morning. I'll call in and let the office know."

Smith thinks this is fun, Wetzon thought, as she unlocked her door and bent to pick up the squirming ball of white fur. I'm not the crazy one here.

Three phone messages blinked on her answering machine. Carlos. Silvestri. A hang up. Silvestri. Oops, annoyed. But he couldn't know she and Smith had been at the crime scene. He's just pissed I didn't come straight home, she assured herself. But she knew better.

After a hot shower and a short work out at her barre, she should have gone to bed, but she needed something more soothing. She took a chocolate croissant from the freezer and, with trepidation, microwaved it. Heaven in less than two minutes. Maybe there was something to be said for these modern apparati after all.

She fell asleep trying to remember the name of the man who had claimed to be her uncle. What was it? And what difference would it make if she did remember? He would never have used his real name. What had Bill gotten himself into? And was she in this mess because of him?

It was not a smooth ride. The driver—his name was Dantey, one of Jason's bodyguards—kept his foot on the gas, then took it off, on, off. He'd been watching her in the rearview mirror, but he couldn't see what she was doing. Which didn't mean that he stopped trying.

She'd spent the whole trip sorting the papers, pulling the important ones and padding with blank sheets. Sweat under her chin, the back of her neck, running down her sides. She slipped her arms out of the mink and finished the job, snapped the attaché closed. The papers she'd pulled, an inch thick, she tucked under the back waistband of her pantyhose. Cold against her bare skin. Her coat would cover the slight bulk. Dantey was paying more attention to her than the road.

A siren sounded and a New Jersey state trooper came up behind them and signaled for Dantey to pull over. Dantey let off a string of curses, but he pulled over. She rolled down her window. Snow drifted in. When had it started?

". . . *driving erratically,*" *the trooper said.*

She rolled up her window. The trooper was checking Dantey's license and the limo registration. Jesus, he was checking to see if Dantey was drunk. They'd never get out of here. She adjusted the bulk of papers in her hose. Then rolled down the window again, ready to come to Dantey's aid. But Dantey was saying something about sciatica and the trooper was nodding. Another minute and Dantey was back in the limo and they were on their way.

"Where are we? What's taking so long?"

"Another three or four miles," he said. "Fucking trooper."

Snow was giving an icy coating to the road.

"Teterboro," the driver said, coming to a stop.

As she gathered her things, the car door was yanked open. Natalie stood there in a fury, her sable coat flecked with dry flakes of snow. "Where have you been? We've been standing around waiting—give me those." Her eyes were mad. She reached into the limo, grabbed the two attachés. "Stay where you are," she said. "Don't think you're going with us." Screaming in high decibels, she ran to the plane. "I have them, I have them! Let's get going!"

Jason, his big, black cashmere coat draped over his shoulders like an old time movie star, was standing near the plane looking beyond her, where another car—a gray Mercedes—had appeared. Coming down the steps of the plane was Laura Lee, wearing dark glasses and a hat pulled down over her eyes. Her head made a slight movement toward Leslie, then she grimaced. The plan they'd made, to escape in the limo, was in trouble.

"Get on," Jason called to Natalie. "We'll be there in a

minute and we can get out of here." He waved to Leslie. "You too, Mary Lou."

You too, Mary Lou. Sing it. Why is he calling me Mary Lou, Leslie thought, but it was a dream and she knew she was Mary Lou.

"No!" Natalie screamed. "She's not coming!"

"Get on the plane, Mary Lou," Jason said. "It's about time you got here." Jason wasn't speaking to her, but to a man who'd come up behind her.

She turned around. The man was handing Jason a black box of some sort. He focused on her face. His body jerked. "Mary Lou? What the hell is this?"

Oh, my God, Bill, her mind shrieked. It was Bill Veeder standing in front of her. What was he doing here?

"You know each other?" Jason looked at Bill, then at her. Jason controlled. He didn't like surprises.

Wetzon backed away. Two men came toward them from the Mercedes. They were carrying guns.

Bill looked at them, looked back at the plane, yelled something, tore the coat from Jason's shoulders and before he threw it over Leslie, she saw anguish in his eyes. "Get down, get down," he was yelling. He picked her up, struggling under the voluminous coat, calling his name, and sent her flying into the boom with snowflakes of diamonds.

"Les." Silvestri's breath was stale cigarettes and coffee.

He was stretched out beside her, his skin warm against her chill.

"I was dreaming," she said. She laid her head against the hairy hollow of Silvestri's chest, trying to catch her breath.

"You were yelling, 'No, Bill, no.' "

"He was as surprised to see me there as I was him."

"I'll bet."

"He was handing a black box to Jason when two men with guns came up. He threw Jason's coat over me and pushed me away. He knew something had gone wrong. He saved my life, Silvestri."

"Gallant of him. Maybe his one and only good deed." He kissed her forehead, his stubble rubbed her cheek.

"I think Laura Lee and I had a getaway planned. Something screwed it up. Two men with guns, in a gray Mercedes."

"Are you awake?"

"Yes. What time is it?"

"Sixish."

"You've been up all night?"

"Yup." He stroked her hair. "You want to tell me what you and Xenia were doing up at my crime scene last night?"

"Uh oh."

"Yup. A very sharp uniform gave me a thorough description."

"And then there was the phone call."

"And then there was the phone call," he repeated. "She's some piece of work."

"It was Carolyn Dorley who got murdered?"

"How do you know her?"

"She was Bill's long-time secretary."

"Let's get some coffee," he said, sitting up and pulling her up with him. "I made it when I got in."

"What happened to Carolyn?"

"Gunshot. An execution. Through the forehead."

"Oh, God." She tied on her robe. "We were on our way up to see her."

"She'd written Xenia's name on a pad near the telephone."

"Carolyn was forcibly retired, I think. Whoever took

258

over Bill's practice brought his own people in. She was afraid to say anything for fear she might jeopardize her retirement benefit. At least I think that's why. That's what Smith said."

"There was more to it than that. Xenia wouldn't know if it hit her in the face."

They sat at the counter and drank their coffee. "Clo Hightower is going to set up a meeting for me with Judy Blue. You want to come?"

"No, thanks. You're in good hands. Rita was right."

"The diamonds—"

"Hey! Don't make me a co-conspirator."

"Sorry." Playing contrite.

Shaking his head, he got up from the counter. "I want to show you something." His leather jacket was hanging on the closet doorknob. He fished for something in an inside pocket. A photograph. He set it down on the counter in front of her and waited.

It was a three-by-five color snapshot. Carolyn, as Wetzon had last seen her, and a young man.

"Good God!" She stared at Silvestri, nonplussed.

"Thought you'd catch it."

"Who wouldn't?" She inspected the photograph again. There was no doubt. The young man seemed to be in his early twenties. And he was the image of Bill Veeder.

Chapter 48

"How can someone think she knows all about her lover know, in fact, nothing at all?" Wetzon said, slathering her bagel with cream cheese. She had roused Carlos as soon as Silvestri left and gotten him to meet her for breakfast at Barney Greengrass around the corner on Amsterdam Avenue.

He contemplated her with sleepy eyes. "Birdie, darling, it's too fucking early for me to answer a philosophical question. What can I say? Do you want some of my smoked salmon?"

"Yes." She arranged the salmon on top of the cream cheese and took a bite. "Try."

"I'm going to tell you something and I don't want you to snap my head off. Okay?" The diamond stud in his right earlobe caught in the overhead light and winked at her.

"I'm not going to like this, right?"

"It's entirely possible."

"Okay, wait till I take another bite." With her mouth full, she motioned him on.

"Here's my honest opinion. You didn't care. It was all about sex. The man had layers, but you didn't bother because you weren't interested."

"Oooph, Carlos. That hurts. It makes me very shallow."

"Dear heart, you are not shallow." He reached across the table and touched her cheek. "You know all of my layers."

"I love you."

"There you see, you didn't love him."

260

"He told Silvestri he loved me and Silvestri believed him."

"So he loved you. But look at how he lived. One compartment, his work. Another compartment, his wife. A third compartment, his fabulous digs. A fourth compartment, Leslie Wetzon."

"But he had a son. What about his son?"

"Did I mention a fifth compartment?"

"And he kept the compartments in the dark about the others." She sighed. "I don't know all of Silvestri's layers."

"But you know most of them, and he knows most of yours. We're talking a real relationship here."

A cell phone burbled. "Mine," she said, answering. "Yes. Okay." Checked her watch. "I'm on Amsterdam. I'll walk down." She hung up. "My lawyer set up a meeting with the FBI." She punched in her office number and told Cheryl to expect her in the afternoon.

"Who's your lawyer?" Carlos asked, grabbing the check.

"One Clotilde Hightower. You don't know her. Rita Silvestri got her for me."

"Arthur knows everybody." Arthur was Arthur Margolies, Esq., a trusts and estate lawyer and Carlos's loving partner. "And Clotilde Hightower is a name to conjure with."

Wetzon felt better after she and Carlos parted. He was her restorative. She called Silvestri as she walked, something she loathed doing on the street—not talking to Silvestri, but using a cell on the street. She kept getting a busy signal. When she finally got through, it wasn't Silvestri who answered. It was a Detective Gail Rosen. Silvestri was out and around. She left her cell number and disconnected.

Gelber stood in front of Clo's building watching for her

in every car and cab. She was halfway across the street before he spotted her. His gun bulked his jacket.

"Do you think," she said, "that I'm going to run away?"

He opened the door for her, checking behind him. "No."

They waited for the elevator, his back to her.

"You think I need an armed guard to get to my lawyer's office?"

"We're playing it safe."

They got on the elevator. "Gosh, you spoke. I thought you weren't allowed to speak." Damnation, she thought. She was getting as bad as Smith. "I'm sorry. I'm not usually so snippy."

Judy Blue in her dark pantsuit sat on the sofa in Clo Hightower's office, smoking. Clo sat at her desk, smoking. The atmosphere was cloudy.

"Ah, Leslie." Clo stood, taking one of the straight chairs over opposite the sofa. "Sit here." Back at her desk, she unlocked a drawer and took out the manila clasp envelope. She broke the seal, removed the grubby Krispy Kreme bag, and brought it to the coffee table. She took the other straight chair and settled near Wetzon.

Judy Blue stubbed out her cigarette. Her glance skimmed over the Krispy Kreme bag, returned for a moment, then focused on Wetzon. "Well, here we are."

"Yes," Clo said, stubbing out hers.

"The ball is in your court, Leslie." Agent Blue's face was grim as a bulldog's.

"My client would like to make a statement telling you what she's remembered since the last time she spoke with you."

Judy Blue made a rude, un-Feeb-like noise.

"Excuse me," Clo said. "You are aware that in cases of memory loss as Leslie has been suffering from, memory often steals back in bits and pieces."

"Let's get on with it," Judy Blue said. She took her small digital recorder from her pocket and set it on the table.

Clo snatched it and turned it off. "We'll have none of that."

"As you wish."

Irritated, Wetzon said, "Was I working for you?"

Clo smiled. "It might be nice to hear your answer, Agent Blue."

"I'd prefer to hear your client's statement."

"Go on, Leslie."

Wetzon began with Marty Lawler and her visit to Bellevue, how he confirmed she'd sat next to him on the New Jersey Transit bus, how frightened she'd been and how he'd tried to save her from being kidnapped in the Port Authority Terminal and had gotten shot for his trouble. "He's a retired cop," she added. "He knows people in the NYPD and called them."

Agent Blue was alert now, sitting forward. Gelber was writing notes.

Clo said, "Marty Lawler will be happy to speak with you to confirm this." Gelber took down the phone number. Clo signaled for Wetzon to continue.

"When Marty Lawler came home from the hospital," Wetzon said, "he found something with the items the hospital had taken off him when he was brought in." She told them about the key card, the locker at the Port Authority.

"What was in the locker?" Agent Blue asked. "Stale doughnuts?"

"Why don't you have a look?" Clo picked up the crumpled Krispy Kreme bag, spread the mouth, and offered it to Agent Blue.

Gelber came over from the door.

"So you had the diamonds all along," Judy Blue said. "You have a handkerchief, Gelber?" He drew a folded, white linen one from his breast pocket and handed it over.

She opened in on the coffee table, then poured the sugared diamonds onto the handkerchief. "Count them," she told Gelber.

"I do not remember anything about these diamonds," Wetzon said. "I don't remember putting them in the locker. I don't remember Marty Lawler getting shot. I don't remember Marty Lawler at all. He said a man dragged me away and that's the last he knew of me until he woke up in the hospital and heard the story about someone named Mary Lou Salinger being missing."

"Now I think it's time to tell us, was my client working for you?" Clo said.

"We had someone on the inside. Actually, she went in on her own and then notified us."

"Inside?" Clo said. "Inside what?"

"The Jason McLaughlin financial empire."

"My God," Wetzon said. "Laura Lee."

"Yes. Ms. Day was feeding us information, but suddenly it stopped. She may have been compromised. We couldn't get her out without jeopardizing the investigation."

"Which was more important than her life?" Wetzon said.

"It was her choice. She was trying to save a family member from being defrauded."

"Her Uncle Weaver." Wetzon shook her head. "But how did I get involved?"

"She called you, as if responding to a personal ad you'd placed in *The Village Voice*—"

"I placed a personal ad in *The Voice*?"

"You told us you hadn't, but that's how McLaughlin

found women to work for him. He placed some and re-sponded to others."

"Hold on now," Clo said. "How did the FBI get in-volved with Leslie?"

"We were talking to all of Ms. Day's friends, and hap-pened to speak to Ms. Wetzon only hours after she'd re-ceived the strange call from Ms. Day. After speaking with us, she agreed to interview with McLaughlin."

"It sounds to me as if Laura Lee was in trouble."

"We thought so," Judy Blue agreed, focusing a beady eye on Wetzon. "You don't remember any of this?"

"Do you want me to take a lie detector test?" Wetzon said, borrowing Smith's most steely voice.

"That will not be necessary," Clo said. "Just tell us what happened once Leslie joined the McLaughlin enterprise."

"He had a fortified mansion in Deal, with guest houses, every room wired for sound, armed guards, electric fences, armored cars, the works. His paranoia kept his eighteen em-ployees on the grounds. We arranged with Ms. Wetzon to make calls to her mother in Queens—"

"I don't have a mother—"

"I acted the part. We routed the calls to Federal Plaza. The best we could do was keep track of you and we gleaned that Ms. Day was okay, just not able to call out without compromising herself. You called the day of the explosion, saying that you were going away for a while but would try to call me from the airport before you left."

"Okay," Wetzon said. "I—or someone—was bolting."

"Exactly. We knew McLaughlin kept his private jet at Teterboro, but we got there too late."

"Can we talk about the diamonds?" Leslie asked. "Why did you think I had them? And who did they belong to?"

"McLaughlin's empire was imploding. He arranged for

fifteen million dollars' worth of diamonds to be delivered to him at Teterboro."

She was bewildered. "You're saying I was the bag man."

"No. That is not what I'm saying." Agent Blue hoisted herself up out of the sofa. "I think we've gone as far as we can go at this time. You have the count?" she asked Gelber.

"There are thirteen missing," he said.

"You know how many there were?" Wetzon asked.

Agent Blue shrugged. "We have our ways."

"That's a joke, right?" Wetzon said.

Agent Blue's face was impassive. She jerked her head to Gelber and he knotted his handkerchief around the pile of diamonds.

"You leaned on someone, either the jeweler or the person who delivered the diamonds," Clo said. "Who would that be?"

Judy Blue smiled. "Thank you for coming clean."

"Bullshit," Wetzon said. "You can't think I was stealing diamonds."

"Why not? You did hide them away."

"I don't remember doing it and when we had an inkling of where they were, I got them and gave them to you."

"And we thank you for being a good citizen."

"Where is Laura Lee?"

"She's with McLaughlin."

"Where is McLaughlin?"

"Somewhere in Germany. Ms. Day was able to get a call to us. It won't be long now."

Clo said, "Who blew up the plane?"

"We have nothing certain."

"Is it possible that your delivery person had other ideas about the diamonds?" Clo said.

"It's possible. But we'll never know."

266

"How can that be? I thought the FBI has its ways," Clo said.

Wetzon roused herself. She'd been only half listening as she tried to peel away the missing layers of her memory. It came to her as clear as the diamonds themselves. The parsimonious Agent Blue gave nothing away. But Wetzon knew. He'd been holding a black box.

"It was Bill Veeder who delivered the diamonds," she said.

Chapter 49

What did they have on Bill, Wetzon wondered, as she took a short cut to the East Side through Central Park. The park was wakening after winter. You could smell it. The sun was brilliant. And if you looked hard enough, you saw little green shoots sprouting on the trees. Bikers were everywhere, and on the bridle path joggers in their shorts and tees were pretending April was already here.

She veered east to the Fifth Avenue and Fifty-ninth Street exit, where stable smells persisted because of the horse carriages usually lined up along Central Park South. It was a crisp, clear March day, and tourists—there were always tourists—were taking the opportunity to ride in the horse carriages through Central Park.

No question now, Bill had saved her life in the advent of the explosion, this complex, shrouded man who'd been her lover, and yes, whom she had loved. The coat he'd thrown over her was the coat Marty Lawler had described, the one she'd worn on the NJ Transit bus.

So where had the diamonds come from? For certain, the Krispy Kreme bag would not have withstood the explosion. But, then, and this was becoming obvious, neither had the black box that Bill had been holding. Slivers of memory surfaced and faded. She could not be sure what was real, and what came from her fertile imagination.

She walked down Fifth Avenue, only subliminally aware of the stunning shop windows, and turned east on Forty-ninth Street, with no impulse to cruise through

Saks as she would have in the past.

What she was feeling was an indefinable urgency, an apprehension. The story was incomplete.

Had the diamonds, released from their container, been strewn every which way? Could she, Leslie Wetzon, in the aftermath, have picked diamond daisies and thrust them into the pocket of the black cashmere coat? Of course, if it had been Smith, that theory would be a foregone conclusion . . . Face it, she told herself, maybe she was just as attracted to diamonds as—

Approaching Second Avenue, she saw coming up on her right, Steve Sondheim's house. In front of his house, as she always did, she swept off her beret, clutched it to her breast, and bowed. Her tribute to his genius.

When she straightened she saw that two strolling, mink-wrapped women across the street had stopped to stare. Obviously, they were not New Yorkers.

It was almost noon when she opened the outside door and stepped into the office. She was starving.

"Good morning," she called to Cheryl, who was on the phone.

Cheryl replied by jerking her hand up several exaggerated times.

Sean came out and drew a finger across his throat. Wetzon nodded, headed for the stairs. She recognized the signs: Smith was manic.

"Someone from the NYPD came to check our phones this morning," Cheryl said. "He said Silvestri sent him."

"I forgot to warn you. I'm sorry."

"What was he looking for?" Sean said.

"A bug. Did he find anything?"

"I don't know, but he kept grunting and growling and talking to himself."

Cheryl said, "He asked me if someone had been in recently to fix the phones."

"Had someone?"

"Verizon was in last week to put in new wiring." Cheryl frowned. "They said the wires were frayed and could cause a short."

"Had Smith called them?"

"She never mentioned it to us," Sean said.

"I think we should probably not let anyone in to work on anything unless Smith and I know about it." She started up the stairs. "Any more calls from Bobby-I'm-on-the-lam-Baglia?"

"He's not on the lam anymore," Sean said. "They picked him up on Crosby Street, where he broke into his old girlfriend's loft and beat her up. So I guess we're not going to hear from him again."

"I wouldn't count on it," Wetzon said.

Smith was ranging around the room like a caged leopard. "You have no idea, no idea, what my life is like," she said, as Wetzon hung up her leather coat.

"And a cheery good morning to you, too." She set her briefcase on the floor near her desk.

"Phone calls, newspaper people, not to mention the dirtbag brokers who are demanding, demanding, demanding. Don't they know how unimportant they are? And why do they do this?" Smith pointed a dangerous, deep crimson-tipped finger at Wetzon. "Because you spoil them. You listen to all that whining and the garbage they shovel out and you believe them. They know they can count on you to be their advocate—"

"So what's wrong with that?" Wetzon picked up the pink message slips and sorted through them.

"What's wrong? What's wrong?" Smith raised her eyes to

the ceiling. "I can't believe she said that." She sat down with a long-suffering sigh. "You're a partner in their sleaze. And we become accomplices in sleaze." Back of her hand to her forehead. "Oh, I just don't know how much longer I can go on."

"You certainly get over it quickly enough when the checks come in."

"Well!" Smith pondered that. "There has to be a reward somewhere in this." Brightened. "Let's go to Saks."

"I just got here. I have calls to return and some catch-up to do on the computer. And I have something rather extraordinary to tell you—"

"We have to go to Saks, sweetie pie."

"Why?"

"Um, we might want to smarten you up a bit. A few chic accessories . . ."

Wetzon recognized the doubletalk. Did not recognize the usual frown missing from Smith's words. "I don't care that I'm not a fashion plate," she said. "It never hurt my business." She sat down at her desk and booted up her computer. Eeeks, Smith was still focusing on her with that critical eye. "Will you stop that, please. There's nothing wrong with this suit."

"Babycakes, really, the jacket is too long. You could use a scarf. Tee-shirts are passé. We've gone back to crisp cotton shirts. We can perk up that poor suit a little with one of Ralph's. And those shoes." She shuddered.

Uh oh, Wetzon thought. "Perk me up for what?"

Smith smiled. "You'll see."

"The hell with that, Smith. And what's wrong with my shoes? They're Ferragamos."

"Antique Ferragamos. The heels, sugar, are passé. Pumps are passé. Manolos are what the best women are wearing."

"I don't think Hillary Clinton is wearing Manolos, Smith."

"Oh for pity sakes. I see your memory loss hasn't made you wiser." She took out her makeup bag and, after checking her image in the small mirror, smiled at herself. No lines appeared.

Wetzon groaned. "Smith, you're having Botox."

"It's very important for us to look right for our clients." She fluffed her dark curls and put away her cosmetic bag. "It wouldn't hurt you to do it, you know."

"Put poison in my face? Start looking expressionless like Cher? Thanks, but no thanks. After forty they say you're responsible for your own face. I accept that responsibility."

The intercom buzzed. Max said, "We're getting a lot of calls for Wetzon. Good morning, girls."

"Max—" Smith said.

"What, dear?"

Smith rolled her eyes. "Never mind."

"I'd better start taking my calls," Wetzon said. "Do you have someone holding?"

"Phil Mackey. Line three. He called yesterday and I pulled his suspect sheet. It's on your desk."

"Max, you're a gem." Scanning the suspect sheet, Wetzon punched in line three. "Phil! It's been ages."

"You don't call me any more, Wetzon. After our long history together . . . I'm hurt."

"You've been with Durkin Aldrich for ten years, Phil, so a move is highly unlikely." She paused, listening for a clue, and in the silence, heard what she wanted. A fissure, giving Wetzon an advantage. Perhaps. "You know, we should have a drink and catch up—for old time's sake. What do you say?"

"Maybe," he said. "Maybe there've been some changes

here I can catch you up on."

She cleared mail and phone message slips from her desk calendar. "How about Monday, five or five-thirty? Four Seasons."

"Monday's no good. I'm doing a brown doctor seminar at the Hilton."

"Excuse me? Brown doctor?"

"Yeah, you know, Indian and Pakistani doctors. Big bucks there. I'm good on Wednesday."

"Wednesday it is then." She wrote it in, clicked off, copied it into her Filofax. Her first appointment! Wowee! And Phil was a huge producer, probably well into the millions by this time.

"Big?" A benign Smith, smiling, pleased.

"Huge."

"Line two, Xenia," Max said. "Twoey."

Smith punched in line two. "Twoey, sugar!" A pause. "That would have been divine, sugarbun, but something important's come up. I'm afraid we have to take a rain check. You know, business. An out-of-town client." Her body language gave off scheming vibes. She looked at Wetzon, pursing her lips. "Hold on, sugarplum." She gestured to Wetzon. "Twoey wants to talk to you."

Wetzon was very fond of Twoey Barnes—Twoey because of the roman numerals he was given when he was born. He was Goldman Barnes II, son of the late Wall Street legend, Goldy Barnes. Twoey had entered their lives after Smith and Wetzon were drawn into the investigation of his father's murder. He'd fallen in love with Smith, poor soul.

Twoey was a regular guy, not flashy, just nice, and Smith took him for granted. Twoey's dream had been to be a Broadway producer, and it was through Wetzon's Broadway connections that his dream was realized.

"Just tell me," Wetzon asked Smith before she talked to Twoey, "are we off again or on again?"

"Oh, for pity sakes," Smith said.

Wetzon pressed three. "Twoey!"

"Wetzon! It's sure good to hear your voice, kiddo. Xenie's been going nuts without you."

"You dream, Twoey."

"Believe me. How're you doing? I mean, since Veeder—"

"I'm okay. I still don't remember a chunk of what happened, but they tell me it'll come back. I'm not sure I want it to."

"Well, look, we were going to celebrate your return tonight, but you have that client—"

"Yes." She looked at Smith, who was making circles with her finger telling her to wind it down. "Rain check, okay?" She clicked off. "You wanna tell me what dinner with what out-of-town client?"

"It's been a really busy morning, from which as usual you chose to absent yourself."

"Smith! You know goddam well I was with the FBI."

"You gave them the diamonds." It was an accusation.

"They didn't belong to me. And that's the last thing I'm going to say about it." Steaming, Wetzon sat at her desk and began reading the suspect sheets Max had left for her.

"Ummmm, sweetie, Bill's lawyer called you about his will." She was agitating a pink message slip.

"Bill's lawyer? Smith, is that my message in your grasping paw?"

"What do you suppose he left you? That gorgeous apartment would be perfect."

Wetzon grabbed the message slip from Smith's hand. "You spoke to him?"

"His name is Lincoln Farber. Very nice, very professional. He said there were things to discuss with you relating to Bill's will."

"Oh, really. If he was so professional, why would he be telling you anything?"

"Do you know it's very hard to talk to you since you've been back? You jump down my throat for every little thing."

"Like taking my messages? Anyway, Bill's doorman told me that when the FBI came with a search warrant, he called Bill's office and a man named Farber came over."

Smith strolled to the stairs and listened to the activity in the office. Satisfied, she turned back to Wetzon. "He must be the one Bill brought in as a partner."

"The one who dumped Carolyn?"

"Well, I can see how he'd want to be surrounded by his own people, and Carolyn was too totally faithful to Bill."

What an opening Smith had just left her. "Yes, she was. She did everything for him. Even . . . gave him a son."

Smith flinched. "What? What did you say? A son?"

"He's about twenty or so and is the image of what Bill must have looked like as a young man."

"Son!" Smith said.

Wetzon glanced at the phone console. All their lines were in use.

"I don't believe it. He told me he couldn't—mm—mm—"

"Yes, he told me, too. That he'd had a vasectomy. Now we know why."

"But how do you know about the son?"

"Silvestri showed me a photograph of Junior and Carolyn, taken recently."

Smith sat down hard. "Bill didn't know about him. He wouldn't have kept that a secret."

"Bill, we're discovering, had a lot of secrets. Of course,

he knew about his son. There's no way Carolyn would have kept that from him. I'm sure Junior is in a good college and Bill was paying for everything. So I'm sure that whatever this Farber person has to say, it's not going to be about my inheritance."

"Why were you keeping this from me?" Smith looked tragic and Wetzon couldn't help herself, she felt guilty. Smith always thought she knew everything, but she was often wrong. And this latest error in character judgment had truly wrecked her.

"I wasn't keeping anything from you, you dope. I said I had something extraordinary to tell you and you wouldn't let me talk."

"He had a son," Smith said, shaking her head back and forth like a punchy prizefighter. "Then why is this Farber person calling you about a will? It means he hasn't left everything to this alleged son. Call him back this minute."

Crafty old Smith, Wetzon thought. "I don't feel like it. I've had quite enough for today. So now why don't you tell me who this out-of-town client is we're supposed to be entertaining tonight."

Smith brightened. "It's a surprise."

"Where are we having dinner?"

"That's a surprise, too."

It certainly was. When Wetzon followed Smith into hectic pre-theatre Gallagher's Steak House, she scanned the diners. A man rose from a table toward the rear of the restaurant. "Good God," she said.

Their dinner engagement was with Laura Lee Day's Uncle Weaver.

Chapter 50

Uncle Weaver, Wetzon thought. What the hell is he doing here? Somewhere in the back of Wetzon's mind lurked a memory shard missing a Post-it.

Gallagher's, too. Retro, Laura Lee would have said. Just the place to rub elbows with dentists from Iowa and Catholic priests and football stars. A great old-fashioned steak house with checked tablecloths and captain's chairs, but definitely not a restaurant either Smith or Wetzon usually found herself in. Still, it was something of a landmark, dating back to the late twenties and having been opened by a Ziegfeld girl, Helen Gallagher, who also happened to be one of Ziegfeld's former wives.

A burly man, looking for all the world like an ex-cop, steered them to the maitre d'.

Sides of beef hung aging for all the world to see in the open-to-view cold room on the right side of the entrance. And on the walls, photo after photo of sports figures, present and past.

Sitting with Uncle Weaver was an elderly priest, skin pale and dry, poreless, wispy flaxen strands plastered to his pate. Priests were not unusual in Gallagher's as it was a priestly favorite, but Uncle Weaver was a Baptist, a teetotaling, born again, pro-life, Trent-Lott-loving Baptist.

"Judge," Smith gushed, holding out her hand to Uncle Weaver, an imposing yet benign man in his sixties, carrying the extra weight of an aging athlete. She hadn't missed the bottle of champagne in the tall bucket.

He brought Smith's hand to his lips. "My dear, you are a lovely sight. Even more beautiful than I imagined after our telephone conversation this morning." Wetzon received a peck on the cheek and a whiff of Uncle Weaver's expensive cologne.

"Uncle Weaver, what a surprise," Wetzon said.

"How are you, my dear? Let's get you all seated. This is my friend, Monsignor Roberto Pietrosanta. I'm seeing him off to Rome tonight. Roberto," he said, *sotto voce* with a broad wink, "is highly connected to the you-know-what."

"George does enjoy exaggerating," the monsignor said, with a show of humility, and a modicum of mystery. "Ladies." His hands were soft as risen bread dough. He spoke American, no accent.

Champagne? Well, Laura Lee's Uncle Weaver was a flamboyant man. He'd ordered oysters and champagne at the Monkey Bar, when Laura Lee had dragged Wetzon off for drinks with him last time he was in the city. Laura Lee's aunt, Bren Weaver, was her mother's sister and Laura Lee's favorite aunt. The family tended to tolerate Uncle Weaver as a harmless sort who bumbled his way through life exploiting the success of his high school buddies.

But hadn't Laura Lee said Uncle Weaver was having money trouble?

"I didn't know you were a judge, Uncle Weaver," Wetzon said, watching Smith move her chair closer to the man.

"Retired, my dear Leslie. Happily retired. But the old titles seem to stick forever. And people do like to see Judge George Weaver on the letterhead of my company, U.S. Jackson Life."

The waiter appeared and poured champagne into Smith's glass.

"Not for me, thank you," Wetzon said, hand covering her glass.

Smith fluttered her lashes at Uncle Weaver and snuggled closer. "More for us." She was a trifle more reserved with the monsignor, only in that while her smile was seductive, she didn't flutter her lashes.

"Beck's would be perfect," Wetzon told the waiter as he handed them the menus. "So what brings you to the big city, Uncle Weaver?"

"Business, as usual. And I was hoping to see my lovely niece, but she appears to be out of town. I should have alerted her I was coming."

"She's in Europe. On business. But I think she'll be home any day now." Wetzon crossed her fingers under the table. And as if that inspired a response, her cell phone went off. Damn. She hated people who talked on cells in restaurants, and in the theatre, and on buses, anywhere, for that matter. And now she'd become one of the ugly horde.

It rang again.

"Answer it, for pity sakes," Smith said.

There was nothing for it. "Excuse me, please." Moving her chair back a few inches, Wetzon whispered, "Yes," into the cell.

"How'd it go?" Silvestri's voice shivered up the back of her neck.

"The doughnuts are in a better place."

"Xenia listening?"

"You are so intuitive. Will you be around later?"

"I had in mind a ride somewhere tonight. You and me."

"We're at Gallagher's right now. I don't know—"

"I'll pick you up there at seven-fifteen."

"Where are we going?"

"It's a surprise."

"I've had too many surprises lately," she said, but he'd already disconnected.

Smith looked disdainful. Uncle Weaver looked curious.

Wetzon apologized. "My boyfriend. He's very demanding. He's picking me up outside in an hour."

Smith flipped her hand. "Too boring," she said.

"Quite all right, Leslie, my dear. I arranged my trip in the last minute. Some things just can't be handled over the telephone. And after I put the monsignor on his plane tonight, I'm off myself. I'm honored to have the company of two such lovely ladies."

The men started with crab cakes, and went on to thick sirloins, hash browns, onion rings, and more champagne. Smith ordered the same and as Wetzon knew, could eat the men under the table and not even have to loosen her belt. Wetzon, in spite of Uncle Weaver's urging, stuck with bluepoints and a Caesar salad.

"Cognac, my dears?" Uncle Weaver seemed to have expanded as the meal progressed, as if someone were pumping air into him. He had spent the entire time talking about his company, describing its potential for gobbling up a half dozen or more other insurance companies across the country.

"So the insurance business is thriving?" Smith said.

Uncle Weaver smiled. "Thriving. My partners and I are—now ladies, this is inside information so I don't want you to let me down—we are in the process of buying three more companies."

"Really?" Smith was salivating and it wasn't over her steak.

"Of course, the monsignor here has been very helpful with his—ahem—"

"George, I'm sure the ladies do not want to clutter their

pretty heads with business." No question, the monsignor was irritated.

Wetzon dipped a piece of a roll into what was left of the Caesar's anchovy dressing. She was thinking, where was Silvestri already, when the waiter appeared.

"Ms. Wetzon, your driver is here."

"Driver?" Smith said.

"I've got to go." Wetzon dropped her napkin on the table. "I'll tell Laura Lee she missed a great dinner." Yeah, sure. Laura Lee, restaurant snob, would never show her face where tourists dined.

Uncle Weaver rose and planted a wet kiss on Wetzon's cheek. "I do so love the company of pretty ladies," he said.

"See you tomorrow," she told Smith. "My driver is waiting."

The night was cold and clear and she was thrilled to have escaped. Escaped. What a thought. Uncle Weaver was a nice enough man, and after all, he was married to Laura Lee's favorite aunt.

Silvestri was leaning against his car, talking with the burly man who'd welcomed them into Gallagher's earlier. They were both smoking.

"Mike, this is Les," Silvestri said. He ground out his cigarette and opened the door. "Slide in this way."

He joined her after shaking hands with Mike.

"Whew," she said, throwing herself at him.

"You taste good."

"Anchovies. Great Caesar. Can't say the same for the company. Did you have dinner?"

"Coupla slices." He checked his rearview mirror for a fraction too long before pulling into traffic.

"What's up?"

He shook his head, drove very slowly to the corner,

waited for the light to change, all the time checking the rearview mirror. "What the hell—" He was mumbling, frowning.

Wetzon waited. He'd tell her when he was ready.

Finally, he made a left, drove over to Ninth Avenue and headed downtown, still checking the rearview mirror.

"Where are we going, may I ask?"

"You may." He stopped at the red light. "I was over at John Jay this afternoon and spoke to a few people who are into this head stuff."

"So?" John Jay College for Criminal Justice had some of the top forensic specialists in the world on its faculty.

"So we're going to do some backtracking," he said, joining the line of traffic for the Lincoln Tunnel. "Starting in New Jersey."

"You're taking me to the airport, to Teterboro." There was that apprehensive quiver again.

"For starters," he said.

Chapter 51

"I might have a complete breakdown." She wasn't really kidding.

"You might, but I don't think you will. You're a tough cookie, cookie." Silvestri grinned at her, but as they entered the tunnel, he checked his rearview mirror again.

"We're being followed?"

"No. That's the problem."

"But that's good. Why are you saying it's a problem?"

"Because the Feebs had a car on the street near Gallagher's and they didn't move when we pulled out. And they didn't come after us."

"You mean agents Blue and Gelber—?"

"No. Two men I didn't recognize."

"So maybe it's an altogether different case. And it could have nothing to do with Gallagher's. There's that Cuban restaurant next to Gallagher's. Maybe some Cuban diplomat is in town for the U.N."

"Yeah, maybe." But she could see it bothered him. Like most cops he'd learned to trust his gut instincts.

"Teterboro's close, isn't it?" Wetzon said, as they exited the tunnel.

"Almost spitting distance." He edged right through the exiting traffic and made the turn onto Route 3 West. "You want to give me directions?"

"Is this a test?"

"You probably came this way in that limo you remembered riding in. And it would have been around this time of night."

"But I was sorting through papers, pulling out important stuff and replacing it with blank pages. I hid stuff in my pantyhose." She remembered how cold the papers had felt against her skin. "I suppose no papers were found."

"You suppose right." He made a right turn onto Route 17 North. "Count the traffic lights," he said.

"How many?" She peered out the window. Just highway and headlights. Ooops, a traffic light.

"Four."

"That's one."

At the fourth light, the airport built on New Jersey flatland became obvious only because of the control tower and the special lighting for runways. The rest of the buildings, administration and hangars, could have signified any manufacturing area.

Silvestri made a right and drove past chain-link fences that didn't look as if they could keep out anyone who wanted to get in. He punched numbers on his cell. "Silvestri," he told someone. "Yeah, okay." He clicked off and checked the road behind them.

A small plane roared over their heads as it took off.

Wetzon clenched. Nausea invaded. Get a grip, she told herself, as Silvestri checked the rearview mirror. "We still clear?"

"Yeah. The hell with it." He followed traffic onto the airport grounds, showed his badge to a security man. "Silvestri," he said. "I have a meeting with Stan Povicky."

The guard found Silvestri's name on a clipboard and pointed to a building. "Parking's over to your left."

"Listen, Les." He held her icy hands between his. "The site's still closed down so Povicky's going to take us over. He runs security for the airport, and he's probably not going to give us much space."

"Whatever that means."

He gave her a sharp look as he pulled up in front of a building that said ADMINISTRATION. "Stay cool," he said.

Povicky, a stumpy man with powerful shoulders and Sam Donaldson hair, motioned Silvestri into a private lot and had him park next to a yellow electric airport cart.

"Between the FAA and the FBI," Povicky said, as he settled them into the cart, Silvestri and Povicky up front, Wetzon behind, "there's not much left to see." He drove along the chain-link fence, passing behind several huge hangars. "We have nineteen hangars and two runways and no regularly scheduled flights. We leave that to Newark. We do lease, charter, cargo. Private and business, as well as life-saving operations."

"Four people died," Wetzon said.

Povicky turned his head to her, then back. "Someone got too cozy with a little C-4. But don't ask me, 'cause I'm only head of security here."

Silvestri whistled through his teeth. "So it wasn't an accident."

"C-4?" Wetzon shuddered.

"Volatile," Silvestri said.

"Here we are." Povicky drove around a darkened hangar. His headlights picked up the yellow crime scene tape. He parked the cart and while Silvestri helped Wetzon out, unlocked the padlock on the splintered and charred hangar doors and swept them open. He stepped inside. A moment later overhead lights came on, casting eerie shadows over the burned-out area and into the cavity created by the explosion. "I'll wait here while you look around."

Overhead, another plane took off, the sound ear-shattering. It made Wetzon's teeth and cheekbones ache. She closed her eyes. She was lying on a bed trying to keep the sound away.

The smell, carbony and metallic, was insidious. Though she covered her nose, it filled her nostrils. Silvestri caught hold of her as she swayed. "Easy," he said.

"I'm okay." She was determined to be.

Silvestri lifted the tape and they passed under. He switched on a large flashlight. The scarred tarmac was almost scrubbed clean beneath their feet.

"Not much here to see," Silvestri said.

"It's the smell. It was inside me. And the sound of the planes. I was trying to sleep."

"You were trying to sleep? On a bed?"

"Yes. Yes, it was a bed."

"Good. Where?"

"Where? I don't know. I don't know this area. I must have run away. How did I do that? There were two men with guns. They'd parked right behind my limo. The limo Laura Lee and I were going to escape in. How did I get away?"

"The explosion. It must have stopped the gunmen, too. Maybe even knocked them out." He took her arm. "Come on." They passed under the tape. "Povicky!"

"Where are we going?"

"You hid somewhere—where there was a bed—think about it."

They got back into the electric cart while Povicky shut down the lights and padlocked the hangar door.

"Get what you need?" Povicky said.

"Did we?" Wetzon asked when they were back in the car.

"Did we what?" He drove out onto Franklin Avenue.

"Get what we needed."

"Where would you find a bed close enough to the airport to get there on foot? Thought about it?"

"A motel."

"Look around. See any?"

"Flashing neon just ahead. Bergen Motor Lodge."

"Don't think so, but let's try." He drove up the circular driveway and stopped, thinking. "Hold it a minute." He took out his cell and made a call. "Silvestri. Yeah. See if you can find anything on the blotter about trouble in a motel near Teterboro Airport. Yeah. About the same time as that plane explosion." He hung up.

"You think—"

"I think you were running. You told Lawler about a gray Mercedes following you and men who were trying to kill you. If they followed you to the motel, they might have done some damage. Let's see if this is the place."

The Bergen Motor Lodge was a two tiered U-shaped affair on the upscale side in spite of the flashing hot pink neon sign.

"I'm not getting any vibes here," Wetzon said, her skin prickling under Silvestri's hand on the small of her back.

The decor of the motel office was what could be expected after the pink neon sign. On the desk was a vase with plastic pink daffodils. A woman, big pink hair sprayed and teased to the consistency of cotton candy, was propped behind the desk. She wore a multicolored tent and rhinestones imbedded in her winged glasses. Her lips bulged a glossy red; her nails rode out over an inch from the tip of her fingers and matched her lips. She was chewing gum. "Double for the night?" she said.

Silvestri showed his badge.

Her lips pursed. "New York?"

"Yeah. I have some questions about—"

"Well, we don't do that shit here."

"I don't care what you do. I just want to know if you had any problems here the night of the plane explosion at Teterboro."

She looked relieved. "Only the dust and junk that came down on us. Coupla cars got damaged."

"Thanks." They turned to leave.

"There was some trouble, I hear, over at the Golden Blossom, but them Arabs always have something going on."

"The Golden Blossom?"

"Yeah, a dump a little ways down on Route 17."

Silvestri's cell went off as soon as they got back into the car. "Yeah? Hey! I owe you."

"What?" Why had she asked? Something in the pit of her stomach was telling her this was it.

Silvestri tucked away his cell. "Guess where there was a shooting on the night of the explosion."

Chapter 52

The Golden Blossom Motel was a bleak place about a half mile, as the crow flies, through woods and brush from the airport. One of several such on Route 17, all reporting vacancies, its yellow sign, on a stilt, was lit from behind.

Wetzon was chilled. She pulled her beret down over her ears. "Someone was killed here?"

"There was a shooting, but no one died." Silvestri parked in front of a brown-shingled box marked OFFICE by a flashing sign.

"Who was shot?"

"The manager. It got put down as an attempted robbery."

"Attempted?"

"Nothing was taken." He unfastened his seat belt, then hers. She didn't move.

"I'm afraid," she said.

"I know. Bite the bullet."

She smiled at him. "Easy for you to say."

He took her hand. "Let's go."

The office was well lit. She'd been here. She knew that. "This is it," she said.

"Easy, Les." He opened the door. The whine of sitar music spilled out.

Behind the desk sat a bushy-bearded and mustached man, dark skin accentuated by a white turban. His left shoulder wore a cast, the arm in a sling. He was a Sikh, not an Arab, as his trashy competitor had labeled him. A cup sat to his right.

"You need a room?" he asked Silvestri. He pushed his registration book toward the front of his desk and spun it around for a signature. He looked up from his routine only after Silvestri stepped aside without signing the book. He stared hard at Wetzon. "Miss! You are the one!" He eased himself from his chair.

Wetzon stood immobile, looked to Silvestri. He was not helping. Her mouth was dry, but words came. "I'm sorry," she said.

"No, Miss, no. You saved my life. They said a woman called 911 for help. It was you, wasn't it? I might have bled to death otherwise." He spoke in clear American, with a faint sing-song.

"Sit down, please. You don't want a room?" He lowered himself back into his chair.

Silvestri pulled over a metal folding chair for Wetzon, but remained standing.

"No." She sat down, looked around the small office. Yes. She'd come here after the explosion. "I lost my memory after what happened. This is my friend. He's helping me remember by taking me back to places I might have been."

"You're a cop," the Sikh said to Silvestri.

"This is personal," Silvestri said. "Not police business."

Yet, Wetzon thought.

"Rajiv Singh," the Sikh said. "This is my place. I some-times get strange guests. I don't ask questions."

"Mr. Singh. You recognized me."

"You look better than you did when you came here. It was the same night as the explosion at the airport. You were afraid, I saw. You wore a big black coat and your face was . . ." His smile was apologetic. ". . . dirty."

It was as if she were watching a movie. They were going to kill her. Who was going to kill her? "Silvestri?"

"Hang in there, Les."

"Mr. Singh. My name is Leslie."

"I know that."

"You know that?"

"You signed the register." He flipped back the pages and then turned it around again for Wetzon and Silvestri to see.

"Oh, my God," she said. She had scrawled, almost illegibly, "Leslie"—just "Leslie"—in his book. It had been instinctive.

"You wanted a room, you said, for a few hours. And you asked me to ring you if men in a gray Mercedes came looking for you."

"And you did?"

"I did and they shot me." Stoic. No blame.

"They?" Silvestri said.

"Two men. When the car drove up, I rang the room like the lady said. They shot me when I wouldn't say which room."

"It's my fault you got shot," she said. "I'm so sorry."

"But I'm still here," Singh said.

"What room was she in?"

"Four. You want to have a look? They made a mess there, but they didn't get the lady, did they?"

"No," she said.

He took a key from a large keychain and handed it to Silvestri. "Go and see. Cabin Eight. They did plenty of damage. I had to put on a new door and have the mattress turned to the other side."

They drove to the last cabin, number eight.

The door was new, its paint fresh, the room, nondescript, dingy, the bed neat, awaiting a guest. Wetzon walked around the room. She remembered her fear more than any physical pain.

"They broke the door down," she said.

"You saw them?"

"No."

He scanned the small space. "Where could you hide?"

The bed. It was so close to the floor. No one could get under it. But she had. She sat on the bed to quell the residual panic, face in her hands. "Under here."

"Jesus, Les." He capped her head with his hand. "No human can fit under there."

"I wasn't feeling very human, Silvestri. When you're scared enough, and I was—"

"And they didn't look?"

"Check the bathroom. There was a window. I caught some threads on the coat on the sill to make it seem as if I'd crawled out."

"And then squeezed under the bed. With that oversized coat."

"I took it off and pulled it under after me."

He had that thoughtful look on his face again. "Singh said he had to have the mattress turned." He gave her his hand up. "Let's have a look."

"You'll mess up the bed. Ooops, I don't believe I said that."

"Here, help me." He'd pulled back the bed cover and lifted the mattress. "What do you see?"

She bent to look. "A big hole with burns around it."

"I've got to have a look. Can you stand here and hold this?"

"I'll try."

He settled the foot of the mattress on her arms, and

ducked his head under, then up, measuring her.

"I won't drop it, goddammit."

"Shit!" He began pulling on the underside of the mattress.

"What are you doing? I can't guarantee much longer."

"Okay, I got it." He backed out and stood up, his hand clenched on something.

"Got what?"

He opened his hand. "The bullet. Shot into the mattress."

She stared at the bullet. "One of them shot into the mattress. It wasn't that they thought I was under the bed. One of them was crazier than the other." She rubbed her eyes. "Not the one with the Gucci loafers. The other. They were angry I got away."

Silvestri was watching her. "Let's get out of here, Les."

She stood stock still. "The papers. They're under the bed."

"You mean McLaughlin's stuff?" He didn't wait for conformation; he was already on his knees, groping under the bed.

She held her breath, tense.

He pulled them out, put them on the bed, and got to his feet, disgusted. "Great police work. No follow-up. Attempted burglary? Bullshit." He picked up the papers and dusted them off. "Hardly the worse for wear." He gave her a searching look. "Let's go, Les."

"We have to remake the bed."

"Forget it. I'll tell Singh he has to remake the bed. You get in the car."

"Give him something, Silvestri. Twenty, I think. Please."

Sitting in the car, she felt detached, floating above herself. She leaned her head on the headrest.

After stashing the McLaughlin papers in the trunk, Silvestri got back into the car.

"What are you going to do with them?"

"I'm a cop, Les. What do you think I should do with them?"

"I guess they should go to the FBI."

A cell phone burbled. "It's mine," Wetzon said.

"Do you want me to take it?"

"No." She pulled out her cell and responded.

"Where are you!" Smith screamed in her ear.

"Stop screaming. I'm in New Jersey."

"I don't care where you are. Where is Silvestri?" Smith was hysterical. "Find him."

"He's right here."

Smith stopped screaming. "Put him on and snap to it."

Wetzon rolled her eyes. Nothing like Smith to dump one back into reality. She handed her cell phone to Silvestri. "She wants you."

"Xenia? Yes. Calm down. Just tell me what happened." He listened, comprehension dawning. He nodded at Wetzon. "Okay. Where are you?" He started the car. "We're on our way." He clicked off and returned the cell to Wetzon.

"Silvestri?"

He pulled out onto Route 17. The side of his mouth twitched.

"Are you going to tell me what that was about?"

His mouth twitched again. "It's the company she keeps."

"You're being obtuse."

"Okay, I'll tell you." He was trying to keep his face straight. "Xenia's been arrested."

Chapter 53

"Good God! Smith's really been arrested?"

Silvestri paid the toll at the Lincoln Tunnel. Traffic through the tunnel wasn't moving. "Yup." He didn't even bother suppressing his laughter.

"Stop that, Silvestri! What could she be arrested for? She's greedy and selfish, but last I heard you can't get arrested for narcissism."

"Couldn't happen to a nicer person."

"No. Don't say that. She'll be frantic. She *is* frantic."

"That she is." He looked over at Wetzon, who was picking out numbers on her cell. "Who're you calling?"

"Twoey. He'll get over there with a—Twoey! It's Wetzon. Yes, yes, I'm okay, but Smith's been arrested. I don't know. She's at—where is she, Silvestri?"

"Federal Plaza."

"Hold on, Twoey. Silvestri? Federal Plaza? The FBI?"

"Yup."

"Twoey, the FBI arrested her. She's at Federal Plaza. We're on our way there now, but we're in New Jersey and there's a back-up at the Lincoln Tunnel." She closed her cell. "That's why the FBI was waiting outside Gallagher's? For Smith, not me?"

"It's like what happens to dolphins."

"Do you have to be cryptic?"

He smiled at her. A loving, suffusing smile. "You did great, Les," he said.

And she had. She had walked over her own grave and

come through. Yes, she had . . . hadn't she?

Refutation came with the wilderness that swallowed her. The man with the Gucci loafers, the bus to the Port Authority, the kidnapping. What she didn't know, or couldn't remember.

They began to creep through the tunnel maybe five miles an hour, stopping and starting. *Silvestri. Save me!* Her arms wouldn't move. The seat belt choked. Certainty came that if you knocked on the space beneath her breasts, you would hear a hollow sound. *"Is there anybody there?" said the Traveler, Knocking on the moonlit door.* She loved that poem. "The Listeners." The empty, but not empty, house.

Only the listeners, only what's left of Leslie Wetzon . . .

They cleared the tunnel and stopped for a red light. "Les?" Silvestri said, intruding.

What was this? Resentment crept in. How could he know what she was feeling? How dare he know what she was feeling?

"You're on overload. I'm going to get you home."

"No!" The wilderness was hers. Hers to cherish. But now was not the time, she thought. She pushed it back. He was looking at her. Cars honked. "Green light, Silvestri," she said.

FBI headquarters at Federal Plaza, or the fortress, as Wetzon now called the building, was open for business, twenty-four/seven. At least the FBI section was. Silvestri showed his badge to the security guards at the private elevator, bank A.

"Agent Blue available?"

"She expecting you?"

"Why don't you phone up?" Silvestri said. "Tell her Silvestri and Leslie Wetzon."

The lead guard stepped away, turned his back, and made the call while the other guard kept his eye on them.

"She's probably gone home," Wetzon said. "I wonder if Twoey got here."

The guard got off the phone. "We have to pat you down."

Silvestri opened his jacket. "I'm carrying."

"Duh," Wetzon said. "Hey, you forgot the papers."

"Yeah, I did, didn't I. I'll put them in the mail."

They were given visitors' passes and told, "Twenty-eighth floor." The other guard pressed the button for the elevator.

"You wanna let me in on your thoughts, Mr. Enigmatic?" Wetzon opened and closed her mouth to keep her ears from clogging. They clogged anyway.

"Think about it, Les. If, and I'm saying *if,* we eliminate Xenia from the equation, what do we have?"

"Befuddled old Uncle Weaver and an elderly priest. How harmless can you get?"

"The simplicity of it."

"Silvestri, really, Uncle Weaver and the priest? Laura Lee's Uncle Weaver?"

"Two seemingly irreproachable old codgers."

"But Uncle Weaver is a victim. He's a former judge who runs an insurance company in Mississippi. I think he was heavily invested in McLaughlin's hedge fund. That's why Laura Lee got involved. Her aunt was worried about his strange behavior. Laura Lee checked McLaughlin out and said there was something really shady about him and his business."

On twenty-eight, the doors to the FBI office were locked. Silvestri pressed the bell. "Hedge funds? Mutual funds?"

Wetzon shook her head. "Private investment entities, not well regulated like mutual funds, though that's starting to change. They play with different strategies to hedge their portfolios against fluctuations in the stock market. Minimum investment, over a mil."

"I guess that lets me out."

"They're not open to the public unless you're a multi-millionaire, or you're an institution with mega bucks, like college endowments, pension funds, banks—"

"And insurance companies?"

"Yes."

Earnest Agent Gelber opened the door and ushered them into the waiting area. He shook hands with Silvestri, pressed his finger to the plate on the wall next to the door, and led them into the inner sanctum of offices.

"You don't seem surprised to see us," Wetzon said.

"Agent Blue won the pool."

Silvestri laughed.

"Very funny," Wetzon said, as they followed Gelber down the hall of closed doors.

Agent Blue's cubicle reeked of stale coffee. "She suggested you make yourselves comfortable."

"I guess that means we wait," Wetzon said. "Do you have a ladies' room?"

Gelber looked at Silvestri, who said, "I'll just wait here."

When Gelber hesitated, Wetzon said, "Don't you trust him?"

"Is he trustworthy?"

"I've always found him so. Are you, Silvestri? Tell the nice man you won't snoop."

Silvestri shrugged. "Can't make any promises."

"Go out that door, make a left, and it's the fourth or fifth door on your left," Gelber said.

She followed directions, but since the hall was empty, she pressed her ear to each closed door.

"Oh, for pity sakes!" someone screeched from behind the third door.

Wetzon burst into the room. Smith was sitting at a conference table opposite two FBI types. Smith was the only one not surprised to see Wetzon.

"What took you so long?" she demanded, standing. "Where's Dick Tracy?"

"Waiting to talk to Agent Blue."

By this time both agents were on their feet. The taller of the two asked, "Who are you?"

She bowed. "Leslie Wetzon, at your service. What are you doing here, Smith?"

"I rode out to the airport in the limo to see Judge Weaver and the monsignor off," Smith said, exasperated, her voice rising to a scream. "And we were arrested! With handcuffs! I'm going to sue, let me tell you! Can you believe they arrested a priest and a judge? And me, a card-carrying Republican patriot! What's the world coming to?"

"You can't stay, Miss," the second agent said.

"I'll take it from here," Agent Blue said, coming up behind Wetzon, clamping her elbow. She smelled like the chain smoker she was.

"Wait a minute," Smith yelled.

"I called Twoey," Wetzon said, over her shoulder as she was being propelled out of the room. "He's coming with a lawyer."

Silvestri looked a question at her when Judy Blue and Wetzon returned to the cubicle. Wetzon gave a faint nod.

Silvestri grinned, whispered in her ear, "That's my girl."

Sweeping empty cardboard cups from her desk into the

wastebasket, Agent Blue grunted, "Sit down, Leslie. Gelber, find a place."

Gelber leaned against one partition.

"Why did you arrest Smith?" Wetzon said.

"She got caught in the net. We wanted Weaver and the monsignor and she was with them." Judy Blue let a grimace pierce her otherwise neutral demeanor.

"Piece of work, huh," Silvestri said.

Wetzon elbowed him. "I'm sure, if Smith behaved badly, it was because she was scared."

"Right," Silvestri said.

"Absolutely," Judy Blue said.

"She didn't do anything wrong."

"We still have a few questions and then she can leave."

"What about Weaver and the priest?" Silvestri asked.

"They were going to leave the country."

"But Mr. Weaver is an innocent victim of Jason McLaughlin and his phony hedge fund." That was it, she thought. Phony hedge fund. Pyramid scheme. It was sinking in. Acid filled her mouth. "My God, Jason exploded the plane himself. He must have money sitting in Swiss accounts. We were all supposed to die. Laura Lee, me. He killed four people. He killed Bill."

"Les—" Silvestri reached for her hand.

"Let her talk, Silvestri," Judy Blue said.

Wetzon closed her eyes. She could hardly hear herself speaking, if she *was* speaking. "Jason was like a wild man. He yelled at me to get on the plane, then grabbed the box of diamonds, but Bill wouldn't let go. Laura Lee came off the plane, as we'd planned, moved toward the limo. Jason was screaming, telling us to get on the plane. And I saw Bill's face. He knew—" She shuddered and put her hands over her face.

Silvestri put his arm around her shoulders. "Where do Weaver and the priest come into this?"

Judy Blue stood. Her blue pantsuit was wrinkled. Coffee stained the edge of her sleeve. Her eyes were bottomless, tired. "Let's go. I don't want to have to tell this twice."

"Go where?" Silvestri was dubious.

"It's almost over, Silvestri, so for once, will you do as I say?" It was clear that Agent Blue had come to the end of her patience.

Silvestri reached into his inside pocket and opened his palm. He had a collection of tiny metal spools. He smacked them down on the conference table. "Look familiar?"

Agent Blue picked one up. "Hmmm. What do you think, Gelber?"

Gelber picked up another, rolled it between his fingers.

"Outdated," he said.

Agent Blue smiled. "Funny how these things are obsolete as soon as they're manufactured."

Leaving Agent Gelber with the spools, they followed Agent Blue through the sparsely occupied cubicle room and out a door at the far end. Gelber caught up a minute later, a bulge in his pocket.

Another corridor. Agent Blue knocked, then held a door open for them. A woman in black, pants and sweater, high heeled slides, came out of an adjoining bathroom, running her fingers through her cropped hair. Her face was drawn and pale. Her eyes, dull, took them in, not comprehending. Widened.

"Wetzon, darlin'!" she shrieked, rushing forward.

Chapter 54

"I thought you were dead." Laura Lee's face was mottled with tears.

"I thought *you* were dead," Wetzon said, hugging her friend.

Silvestri cleared his throat.

"Silvestri, darlin'," Laura Lee said, "I'm goin' to have to give you a hug, too." Which she proceeded to do. She pulled back and considered Silvestri and Wetzon. "You guys!"

"Uh huh," Wetzon said.

With a broad, absolutely boyish grin, Silvestri became almost mush with Laura Lee. He liked Carlos fine, but Wetzon knew he thought Laura Lee was special.

Agent Gelber appeared, carrying a cassette recorder. He set it on the conference table and plugged it in.

"What's up?" Silvestri said.

Judy Blue gave him a cool look. "Listen, Silvestri, you're only here out of courtesy. We've debriefed Laura Lee. We know Leslie and Laura Lee want to go over what happened. We just want to catch anything we haven't caught till now."

"I think there should be a lawyer present."

"Christ," Judy Blue said, rolling her eyes. "Would you believe a New York cop thinks there should be a lawyer present?"

"Don't say another word, Les."

"All right, Silvestri. Nothing said in this room will be

used against either Ms. Day or Ms. Wetzon in court."

"Or elsewhere."

"Or elsewhere."

"Turn it on, Gelber," Judy Blue said, pulling out a chair.

"Not so fast," Silvestri said. "I want it in writing."

Agent Blue stared daggers at him, sighed. "Gelber, get it done and I'll sign it."

"It would be nice if you would leave the room while we're waiting," Silvestri said.

"Nice try, Silvestri." Judy Blue settled herself in her chair.

Laura Lee tilted her head. Some of her old sparkle came back in her eyes. "Well, I swear, Silvestri darlin', you have even more in your genes than I figured."

Everyone looked at Silvestri, who smirked like a teenager.

"Laura Lee is a master of sexual innuendo," Wetzon told Agent Blue. "Can we have some water in here?"

"When Gelber comes back."

"May I use that bathroom?"

"Go ahead."

Wetzon went into the bathroom, held the door an extra second, enough time for Laura Lee to slip in after her. They locked the door behind them, Silvestri's guffaw ringing in their ears.

"Fuck!" Judy Blue yelled the word that was probably a no-no in the old Hoover rule book for FBI agents.

Laura Lee put her arms around Wetzon. "I'm sorry I dragged you into this mess."

"Hell, what are good friends for?" Wetzon turned on both water taps full force. She perused her friend. "You're a shadow of your former self."

"You're lookin' a little peak-ed yourself, darlin'. Consider all the gelato we can put away buildin' ourselves up again." Laura Lee became somber. "How are you about Bill Veeder?"

"When I first heard, I didn't remember—you know I had amnesia?"

"Blue told me you were fakin' it."

"I wasn't. I'm not. It's a long, scary story and pieces are just starting to come back, like coming to the airport in the limo. McLaughlin was leaving the country and not taking anyone with him."

"Yes. The shit had finally hit the fan. Jason said he couldn't leave till a delivery came—I knew he was waitin' on the diamonds—but I should get on the plane. You and I'd made up to take off in the limo so I was intent on slinkin' out of his line of sight."

"I remember that crazy Natalie, poor thing, grabbing the attachés and screaming at me that I wasn't going with them. I got out of the limo to divert them so you could hop in."

"Yes, and Jason stood there with that stupid black coat screamin' for us to get on the plane. Then up comes Bill Veeder. I swear to God I almost lost it when I saw him standin' behind you. I'm not sure he saw me, but Jason began yellin' at him to give over the box. You turned around to see who he was talkin' to. I'll never forget the look on Bill's face when he saw you."

"The look?"

"Shock, fear, despair—that's all I saw 'cause Jason dragged me to the limo and told Dantey to take us to Newark Airport. We were drivin' off when the plane exploded. He was pissed as hell because he'd lost the diamonds and that stupid black coat. The son of a bitch murderer."

"Bill grabbed that stupid black coat and dropped it over

me, picked me up, and threw me. He probably saved my life." She choked up, pressed her lips together.

Laura Lee put her arms around Wetzon. "You had somethin' with him. You couldn't *not* feel it. And we must be forever grateful to him for savin' you."

Banging on the door. "Come on out of there, you two."

"Can't a girl even tinkle in peace?" Laura Lee called.

"I remember Bill had wanted me to go to the Coast with him and I wouldn't. We were disconnecting, I think. Then I went out for a weekend and came right back. Something must have happened. I just can't remember what it was."

"I can tell you—"

Banging. "All right, ladies, that's it. If you don't come out now, I'm going to call someone to take the hinges off the door."

"Hold your horses. We're finishin' up. There are two of us, you know, and only one toilet." Laura Lee flushed for verisimilitude.

"Laura Lee, do you know they've arrested Uncle Weaver?"

"What?" She was stunned. "How could they do that? He's a victim in this fraud."

"They think he's up to his ears in it, that he's not Jason's patsy at all. They arrested him and an elderly monsignor as they were leaving the country."

Laura Lee sank down on the closed toilet seat. "No. It can't be. Why didn't they tell me? There has to be an explanation. He was leavin' the country? Oh, God, this will kill Aunt Bren."

"I think they're telling us as little as possible—" Banging on the door again. "I guess we'd better get out."

Laura Lee opened the door. "Gracious," she said. "We were just havin' a little pee."

305

A scowling Agent Blue pushed papers across the table. "Here, signed and delivered."

Silvestri was sitting at the head of the conference table, closest to the door, enjoying himself. He reached for the documents. After giving them a thorough read-through, he folded the papers and tucked them into his inside pocket.

"Record, Gelber," Judy Blue said.

"Wetzon was just tellin' me that she had amnesia after the explosion. So she doesn't remember much."

"I still have some questions," Wetzon said, looking to Agent Blue.

"Jump in," she responded.

"Laura Lee, you called me as if I'd placed some kind of ad in *The Village Voice.*"

"That's how Jason got women. He had a whole harem, mostly skinny feral types from the former Soviet Republics, all vyin' for his attention. He gave them cars, jewelry, clothes."

"I don't get it. You're my friend and you were recruiting me for his harem? Were you part of the harem?"

"No, darlin' Wetzon, I wouldn't do that to either of us. I told Jason I was an accountant. He needed me. His books were a mess. Well, actually, there were no books. I'd been able to get out to make some calls to Agent Judy, but all of a sudden Jason got crazy. He wanted me with him all the time. He was so freakin' paranoid, but who wouldn't be on all the drugs he was shovin' into his system. And people were just sendin' in money, can you imagine?"

"So the FBI recruited me to go in and help you."

"You're such a good friend, Wetzon darlin'. I was beginnin' to see I'd gotten in over my head. I thought you'd stay about a week and we'd get out together."

"But it didn't work that way."

"No. I told Jason we were lesbians and he let us alone. You told him that as a dancer, you knew people in show business with lots of money. In particular, Agent Judy here played Madam Moneybags. God, Jason was just dyin' to meet you, Agent Judy, and get your three million into his bogus hedge fund."

"Make-believe money for a make-believe hedge fund," Silvestri said.

"Well, Jason didn't even question that, Silvestri darlin'. He was a greedy prick."

"Where is he, by the way?" Silvestri asked.

"In a Brussels jail," Agent Blue said. "Fighting extradition. But it's only a matter of time."

"The awful thing is everyone was supposed to die on that plane," Laura Lee said. "He was just goin' to take those diamonds and disappear. He'd already set up all those Swiss accounts. But now Bill Veeder—there was a surprise."

"The news broadcasts said that he was Jason's attorney," Wetzon said.

"I don't know about that. What I do know is that he was the delivery boy for the diamonds. Jason went loony havin' to leave without them." Laura Lee shifted in her chair and looked at Agent Blue. "Wetzon told me that you arrested my poor Uncle Weaver. I think you owe me an explanation, Agent Judy."

"We're building a case against McLaughlin. Your uncle is with the federal prosecutor."

Laura Lee jumped to her feet. "He's got to have a lawyer. He may be a judge, but he can't represent himself. He's just a country boy from Mississippi."

"Well, I wouldn't waste any time worrying about the country boy from Mississippi. Your uncle pulled out his cell and lawyered himself up the minute he saw us coming."

Laura Lee sank into her chair. "I still don't understand."

"We've been working with a Mississippi insurance fraud investigator. Your uncle was buying up small insurance companies with money fed from McLaughlin, then cleaning them out. He's being charged with participation in a four-hundred-million-dollar fraud by transferring ten million dollars from the New Natchez Insurance Company to U.S. Jackson, the mother company, then to McLaughlin and out of the country. McLaughlin promised him a glorious life in a country from which he wouldn't be extradited." Judy Blue shook her head in disgust. "Con men are always suckers for other con men."

"My poor Aunt Bren," Laura Lee said.

"And the priest?" Wetzon asked. "What does he have to do with this? He can't be a real priest."

"The monsignor—he's real all right. He went along with McLaughlin's plan to set up a religious foundation, using the monsignor's Vatican connections to raise huge amounts of money to defraud both contributors and insurance companies. The money was used to buy the insurance companies, and the foundation contributors were told that profits from the insurance companies would go to various charities, including a charity that McLaughlin had set up."

"Was there ever a foundation?" Silvestri asked.

"Phony stationery, with a phony board of bishops, monsignors, and wealthy lay people, phony tax exempt acknowledgments, all in the name of the St. Anne de Roma Charitable Foundation. The works. McLaughlin gave the old man sixty thousand dollars in cash and put him up at the Regency, wined and dined him, promised him fame and power. Another fairy tale. The federal complaint is for wire fraud and money laundering. The money raised for St.

Anne's was transferred to McLaughlin's phony charity and used to buy the insurance companies."

Wetzon asked, "The proof I was gathering—the papers—" She looked at Silvestri.

"Lost in the explosion it appears," Blue said, "but we can build a case anyway . . ."

"How?" Laura Lee said.

Judy Blue smiled.

"You might check with the New Jersey cops who responded to a shooting at a motel near the airport the night of the explosion," Silvestri said. He stood, ignoring the piercing stare from Blue. "Let's go home, Les."

"What about Laura Lee?" Wetzon said, standing as well.

"I want to see my uncle, then I'm sure Agent Judy will have someone drive me home."

"Gelber will drive you home. No one can see your uncle except his lawyer."

"So you'll give me the name of his lawyer, like the nice lady you are."

Judy Blue nodded. "It's finished. McLaughlin and his co-conspirators will be in jail for a long time."

"You said some of the diamonds were still missing," Wetzon said.

"The New Jersey police were able to account for the thirteen missing gems."

"I don't understand," Wetzon said. "What about the two men who drove up in the gray Mercedes, the ones who were trying to kill me?"

"What men?" Laura Lee asked.

Wetzon was shocked. "You must have seen them. They drove up and parked right behind the limo."

Laura Lee shook her head. "Jason, Natalie, and I came

in a limo, and he sent the limo away before you got there, Wetzon."

Agent Blue hauled herself up. "I'm tired," she said. "It's been a long day."

"Two men," Silvestri said. His voice was tight. "One of them grabbed Les in the Port Authority the same night as the explosion."

"Get the tape recorder, Gelber."

"Was there a car found on the site?" Silvestri said.

"No. The pilot and copilot parked their cars on the lot."

"One of those men from the gray Mercedes tried to take me out of the hospital," Wetzon said, a sick feeling in her gut. "He killed Carolyn Dorley."

Silvestri was flummoxed. "Les, for crissakes—"

"I saw him, Silvestri. Outside Carolyn Dorley's building—and he saw me."

"That's not our problem," Judy Blue said with finality. "It has nothing to do with us."

Chapter 55

"You don't believe the gray Mercedes, or any of it, do you?" Wetzon asked, as they rode up the elevator.

They'd driven uptown, Wetzon confused and defiant, Silvestri, silent. A parking space was vacant on the east side of Amsterdam, near Eighty-sixth Street. Silvestri grabbed it.

"I believe you, Les, because how else did Veeder get there?"

The thought staggered her. Bill with those murderers? No. Impossible. But Silvestri was right, how else had he gotten there?

While Silvestri fed Izz, Wetzon stripped off her clothes and got under a hot shower. She needed to think, reason. It didn't add up. Her brain was dense, too much information, too little to work with.

Wrapped in her fuzzy robe, she brushed her wet hair forward over her face, and as she blow-dried it, felt Silvestri in the bathroom doorway before she saw him. Did he have something to tell her? Was he telling her everything he knew? She turned off the dryer and flipped back her hair.

"Harpo," the crusader for truth and justice said.

Her hair was a fright wig until she smoothed it into shape with the brush and tucked it behind her ears.

"Feeling better?" He offered his can of Beck's.

"I need something stronger," she said, as Izz wriggled past him into the still steamy bathroom and looked up at her with eyes wheedling for love and attention. "I'm—I don't know—"

"I'll take her out and be right back. Don't do anything—"

"What would I do?"

What she did was look at the light blinking five messages on her answering machine and turn her back. Tonight demanded comfort: a spoon and the container of Häagen Dazs cappuccino gelato from the freezer and a crawl into bed.

She contemplated what she knew for sure.

Out of the corner of her eye she'd seen the gray car pull up, but she was getting out of the limo, intent on giving Jason the briefcase and hooking up with Laura Lee. Intent on escaping.

A door slammed, locks clicked into place.

"There's no other explanation," she told Silvestri when he sat down on the bed. Izz nuzzled her nose into the gelato. Wetzon popped the greedy nose with her spoon. "Dogs don't eat ice cream."

"Boys do," Silvestri said. He took off his shoes.

They alternated spoonfuls until the container was empty. Comfort didn't last long. "Oh, Silvestri, what's going to happen?"

"I don't know. You saw the man near Carolyn Dorley's building?"

"He was in the crowd. He saw me. But he couldn't know who I was. If anything, he knows me by the name Jason knew me—Mary Lou Salinger. If he knew who I really was, he could have grabbed me going or coming from the office. Or here."

"Makes sense. Why would you think he killed Carolyn Dorley?"

"What else would he be doing there? This is connected to Bill, isn't it?"

"Has to be. There's a common denominator: the diamonds. He must have made a deal with someone. Was he into the shylocks?"

"How would I know? He never talked about money or business things like that."

"But he always had a lot of it."

"Yes. Evelyn was rich enough for ten people." She paused. "Loan sharks? Wouldn't he know better? On the other hand, he would know where to go, wouldn't he?"

"He was a cop before he jumped to the other side."

"What if Evelyn's money was in a family-run trust? What if she got the interest but couldn't touch the principal? They each lived rather sumptuously in different apartments."

"I'll see what I can find out about that tomorrow."

She yawned. "What are you going to do now?"

"I'm going to take a shower and come to bed."

"You'd better hurry because I can't keep my eyes open."

In her sleep she thought she knew, was sure she knew and that when she woke up, she would tell Silvestri. But like fluff from a dandelion it was gone even before Silvestri, smelling of soap and shaving cream, untangled her from the robe and pulled her close.

"Sit tight and let me handle this," Silvestri had told her, dropping her on Second Avenue and Forty-ninth on his way downtown. "Don't instigate anything."

"Instigate? What would I instigate?" No matter how she said it, it sounded as if she was not telling him everything. But this time, she was being flat-out honest. She wasn't looking for any more trouble.

He chucked her under the chin. "I wish I could believe you." But he was cheerful when he said it, so maybe he did.

"Why do I feel you know more than I do?"

"Because I do." Silvestri pulled away from the curb and drove off. Good God, she thought, Silvestri was smiling.

He was going to look into Evelyn Veeder's financial background. Bill's taking on big cases for wealthy clients might have allowed him to live in the style he did without Evelyn's money, but, Wetzon realized, he hadn't had a big case for a while. Which must have played into his decision to take the Dooney Bellemore murder case in L.A.

She didn't really expect to see Smith in the office this early, but when Wetzon had tried her at home, there'd been no answer.

As she opened the door to the office, the realization jolted her. Bill had never planned to return. She could come with him, or not. But he'd known all along she wouldn't come with him. Her whole life was here. Silvestri was here. Bill had understood that whatever her denial, Silvestri was always between them.

"Good morning, everyone. Smith in yet?"

"Not yet." Cheryl handed Wetzon a thin sheaf of pink message slips. Sean, phone wedged between neck and shoulder, waved.

"Anyone heard from her?"

"No. I put your mail on your desk. One envelope was delivered by messenger about ten minutes ago. Do you want coffee?"

"Yes, yes, yes." Wetzon headed up the stairs. "Any problems or potential problems?"

"Do you know someone named Solly Morganstern? Go on up, I'll follow."

Wetzon hung her leather trench coat in the closet and sat down at her desk, noting, but not really registering, the messenger-delivered envelope. She took the mug of coffee from Cheryl. "Solly Morganstern. Old timer. OTC guy.

Started with Luwisher Brothers. Where is he now?"

"Bliss Norderman. Sixth Avenue."

"What about him?"

Cheryl handed Wetzon a pink message slip. "He just missed you yesterday. Can you call him first? He seemed pretty upset and wouldn't talk to me."

"Okay. Get on Smith's phone if you want to listen." Wetzon punched in Solly's direct number.

"This is Solly," he said.

His voice invoked his image. They'd met for a drink a few years back. He had the tough, lined face of a man older than he actually was. Streetwise, yet not more than five and a half feet tall. Hair dyed too dark, combed straight back, and gelled to death. Moe Ginsberg suit. Nicotine-yellowed fingers. A very successful Over the Counter broker, specializing in inexpensive NASDAQ-listed stocks, riding them up and selling to protect profits. He did his own research.

"The market goes up, the market goes down. We take our profits where we find them. No profit in being greedy," he'd tell his clients. They loved him.

But these days firms were nervous about brokers doing their own research. They were terrified of lawsuits, so brokers were under orders to sell only stock that the firm's research department pushed. This could also lead to lawsuits, as when UBS PaineWebber fired a broker for telling his clients to get out of Enron two months before Enron imploded, while PaineWebber analysts still had a buy on the company.

It wasn't just UBS; Merrill Lynch, Citigroup, and the rest had run into a similar problem with their research recommendations and what brokers were told to sell. It had troubled the New York attorney general enough to start an investigation.

"Solly, this is Wetzon. You called?"

"Wetzon. Good. Here's the story." He was brusque, spare, no fat in his conversation. "You know I don't make trouble."

"I know you're quality, Solly."

"So my clients start telling me they're getting calls from another broker in my office. Whaddaya think of that?"

"Unethical."

"So I get up and I go talk to this other broker, Brian Armstrong, like a gentleman. Maybe he got the names from a service and didn't check to see if the accounts were with someone here. You know. It's unusual, but it could happen."

"You did right."

"Yeah. So you know what this big fat putz Armstrong says to me? He says, 'Listen, you old fart, you're not working these accounts enough. Your clients are loaded.' I got mad, Wetzon. I say, 'Stay away from my clients. I'm not going to tell you again.' He starts screaming, 'Or else? Or else, asshole? I'm going to come across this desk and kick the shit outa you.' "

"Jeeze, Solly, what did you do?"

"I don't like to complain, but I knew he wasn't going to stay away from my clients. I went to Jay, Jay Olson, you know, he's my manager, and I tell him what's going on. I says, 'What are you going to do about this slug?' And he says right in my face, 'Nothing.' And I says, 'Why the hell not?' And he says, 'Because Armstrong does well over two mil, and I'm not gonna make him mad. Besides, Armstrong is right. You're sitting on a lot of cash.' "

"That's disgusting." She gave the listening Cheryl a thumbs up. It was disgusting. When big producers behave badly, most firms tend to make excuses for them. Were

Armstrong a borderline producer, he would have been fired.

"I'm outa here, Wetzon. I want you to find me a firm with a good OTC desk where people act decent."

"Give me your trailing twelve so I have an idea what we're working with."

"You know the market's been crazy so I'm a little off. Let's see, trailing twelve months, and this is approximate, three hundred seventy-five."

"I'm afraid three seventy-five is not great in this climate, Solly. Would you consider a smaller firm, a good regional, like A.G. Edwards or Legg Mason?"

"Why not?"

"Okay, today is Friday. I want to do some research on their OTC desks. I'll call you on Tuesday and we can sit down and talk."

"I love how you get stuff out of them," Cheryl said, "and without half trying."

"I love my job," Wetzon said.

"Hello, hello, all my sweetie pies!" Smith's voice came from below.

"Uh oh," Wetzon said. After the events of last night, Smith should not have been elated, but there was no accounting for Smith and her moods.

She arrived in their shared office, filling it to the bursting with manic. After throwing off her voluminous cashmere wrap in the direction of her desk, she launched herself at Wetzon, shaking her perfect, scarlet-tipped finger in Wetzon's face.

"Lunch will be delivered, so don't make any plans, sugarbun." Her dark curls were flecked with gold highlights, her skin glowed. She was perfectly made up, elegant in a black and white checked Chanel suit, her long legs

317

gleaming in sheer hose, her Manolos a few black leather strips on five-inch heels.

"I see you've recovered from last night's trauma."

Smith waved Wetzon off. "Oh, they were down on their knees apologizing. You should have seen them, sugar. You'd have loved it." She winked and Wetzon cringed. "Twoey was at Yale with the prosecutor leading the investigation. The groveling was delicious."

"I'll bet."

"I, of course, was suitably gracious. You wouldn't believe how gracious I was." She flounced to her desk and picked up the pink message slips awaiting her, dropped them in the wastebasket, her usual frown replaced by Botox immobility.

"I guess I wouldn't."

Smith looked up. "Wouldn't what?"

"Believe how gracious you were. How gracious were you?"

"I told them I wouldn't sue them for false arrest."

"They are indicting George Weaver and the monsignor for stuff like money laundering and fraud."

"The FBI has totally lost its mind. Terrorists, they should be chasing terrorists. Instead, they single out a sweet, innocent judge and an addled old priest. I don't know what this world is coming to. Enough of that, however." She flashed her brilliant smile at Wetzon. "A little celebration is in order." She fished her Tarot cards from her purse and kissed them, then planted them on her desk. "Precious babies, I rely on you."

"Well, I'm glad you're okay, Smith. That's worth celebrating." Wetzon moved the suspect sheets on her desk, uncovering the envelope that had come by messenger. It was from Veeder, Farber, & Gorodet, its return address, Bill's office in Rockefeller Center.

"But sweetie, I'm not the one we're celebrating."

"Who then?" Wetzon sliced open the envelope. It was a legal letter requesting her appearance at the reading of the last will and testament of William M. Veeder, Esq. at four o'clock this afternoon at Bill's apartment in the Museum Tower. It was signed Lincoln N. Farber, Esq. Her hand shook. She dropped the letter.

Smith perched on her desk, crossing one fabulous leg over the other. She blew on her fingers and rubbed them on her lapel. "You were not returning Lincoln's phone calls, so I had to take the bull by the horns, and lead you, as I always do."

"Wait a minute, Smith. Lincoln?" Wetzon was too confused to be outraged, but that would come.

"Listen carefully, sweetie pie. I was at Saks. Just a hop, skip, and jump from Bill's office in Rockefeller Center."

"Smith, tell me you didn't go over there and introduce yourself."

"Well—"

"This is humiliating. You are not my keeper."

"Humpf. Someone has to be and I at least have your best interests at heart. They are reading the will this afternoon and we have to be there."

"No, we don't. Watch this." She crumpled the letter and threw it across the room. She was angry, angry at Smith's use of the word "we," at her interference, angry at Bill Veeder for dying the way he did, angry with herself for not being able to control the frightening turmoil rushing through her, as if the air was being sucked out of her.

"You are such a child," Smith was saying, oblivious to Wetzon's plight. "Of course, we have to be there. It appears that our darling Bill has left you a sizable inheritance."

Chapter 56

"A caviar pie, would you believe? And champagne, which she drinks and seems to always forget I don't." While Smith was in the bathroom brushing caviar and hard boiled egg out of her teeth, Wetzon gave Carlos the short version of everything that had happened the day before.

"Birdie, she's up to something," Carlos said. "I can smell it all the way across town."

"Yes, it's my inheritance from Bill Veeder. She's set on it. Boy, will she be disappointed. Even if he doesn't leave anything to Evelyn, he does have a son."

"When will you know for sure?"

"This afternoon at four, at the reading of his will. I got a special invitation by messenger this morning. So I guess I'm named." She swished her tongue over her teeth, relishing the sweet-salty tang of the caviar. No toothbrush for her.

"And where, dear heart, is this extraordinary event going to take place?"

"Carlos love, are you keeping track of me?"

"I'm thinking maybe I should tag along and hold your hand."

"Smith's going to do that, I'm afraid."

"Well, Birdie darling, this is what I think: you should keep everyone informed as to your whereabouts until the men who tried to kill you are put away."

"Bill's apartment in the Museum Tower."

"What about it?"

"That's where the reading is going to be."

"Make sure your cell is working, oh intrepid one."

Wetzon disconnected, picked up the suspect sheets Max had left for her, and walked downstairs.

"Wetzon," Max said, "I have Silvestri on line three. Where do you want to take it?"

Cheryl was in her office, on the phone. Sean was not around.

"Sean had a lunch appointment," Max said.

"Put Silvestri through here." She sat down at Sean's desk, pressed three. "Hi."

"How are you?"

"Holding up."

"How bad is Xenia?"

"You wouldn't believe her. She's manic. Twoey knows someone in the federal prosecutor's office. She spent three hours at Saks this morning recovering." Should she mention the will? No. What was the point? It would raise Bill's presence between them again. It didn't matter anyway.

"I did some checking into Veeder's finances," Silvestri said.

She heard just the barest of hesitation in his voice.

"What is it? Was he keeping half a dozen mistresses?" Her joke fell flat.

"His wife's money is in a family trust, run by her brothers and parceled out monthly for her care. Before she got sick and he set himself up in his own place, and a separate life, the interest from her share of the trust was an annual gusher. The family didn't approve of his other life. They were sympathetic with his situation but—"

"They didn't like the public flaunting."

"You could say that. They're old-line money. They hated the gossip."

She swiveled in Sean's chair and looked out at their

321

garden. The magnolia tree was showing winey buds. "What about his practice? It was always high profile."

"Sometimes high profile cases pay, sometimes they're just high profile, but in the last six months he was turning down cases. He never talked to you about it?"

"No. Not much of a relationship, was it?"

Silvestri kept his speech noncommittal. "He had an expensive apartment and an expensive office and staff."

"A nice way of saying he was broke?"

"The Bellemore case came at the right time. He put his apartment on the market, sold his practice—"

"He was selling his apartment? And his practice? Silvestri, Bill would never have done that." She thought, I was right. He never intended to come back, and wasn't going to tell her. It hurt. How could it not? What exactly was it that she and Bill Veeder had had? Did it have no meaning at all?

"Maybe you didn't know him as well as you thought, Les."

"I guess I didn't. The son, selling the apartment—he loved that place—selling the practice . . ."

"He owed money everywhere, and my guess is he was into the sharks big time. He represented McLaughlin, who asked him to convert cash into diamonds through a dealer on the Coast, and you can guess the rest."

"God, Silvestri, you're telling me Bill made a deal for the diamonds with those thugs in the gray Mercedes?"

"There was no other car, Les. He came with them, and it was probably going to be a hold-up. Come on, ten million in diamonds? They'd make it look as if they were taking him hostage and drive away with the diamonds. It would be the great payoff. They'd rough him up a little and let him out somewhere so he could call the police."

"And he was off the hook to the loan sharks. Or they would kill him and close their books."

"But they didn't get the diamonds and Veeder was dead, so they were out a bundle."

"Which is why they were looking for me. They thought I had the diamonds."

"You did."

"I must have been deaf, blind, and dumb not to see Bill's problems. There was something really final about his going to L.A. I wouldn't go with him, and I don't think he was surprised. I certainly never met anyone with him who seemed like a thug . . ."

"They have some veneer on them these days. Especially the second-generation Russians. They even wear Gucci loafers. You wouldn't have known."

"The men in the Mercedes were the Russian mob?"

"Word on the street is, Veeder was into their loan sharks."

She shivered. "I guess the son won't get anything in Bill's will."

"Not unless he had money stashed away offshore. The will, if there is one, has to be filed for probate, and you can bet the IRS will be checking that out."

"There is a will. I had a call from a Mr. Farber, who must be the lawyer he sold the firm to. About a reading of the will."

"You're mentioned?"

"So it appears." She waited for him to ask more, but he didn't so she didn't offer the when and where. "Will I see you later?"

"Yup. I still have to do some checking on this Farber and Gorodet, who bought Veeder's practice. One of my detectives went up to see them about the Dorley murder. She said they were smooth and tanned and manicured."

"They're probably criminal defense attorneys Bill knew from the courts. Is there anything new on Carolyn's murder?"

"Veeder paid her two thou a week salary."

"That's not out of line for a good legal secretary."

"But how does it line up for the mother of your child? Her severance was a hundred thousand dollars. We found the deposit slip and a torn-up signed agreement of confidentiality in her effects."

"She was petrified. I guess of losing the hundred thou." Sean was standing in the doorway.

"Or more. I gotta go. Keep your cell on." He hung up.

Okay, okay, guys, I'll keep my cell on. She thanked Sean for the use of his office, and urged him to clean up his desk. "If you called in sick, we wouldn't know where to find anything."

"What's up, Max?" she asked.

"A broker just told me that they have to be really careful who they take on as clients these days because there are professional suers."

"Do you suppose these days that brokers are checking out their clients any more carefully than clients check out their brokers?" She held up her hand as Max started to speak. "Don't answer that, it's rhetorical. Clients never seem to check out the broker who cold calls them. They just give him their hard-earned money. They don't even check out the mystery firm he works for."

She patted Max on the shoulder and climbed the stairs. Smith was on the phone doing what she did best, charming a potential client.

In the time it took to climb the stairs and listen to Smith's seductive sell on the advantages of working with Smith and Wetzon, Wetzon forgot about her cell phone.

Chapter 57

The sun pushed through the tall windows and gilded their office with yellow light. Smith opened the door to the deck and lifted her chin and announced, "At last, spring." She turned back to Wetzon. "I forget, does Bill's apartment have a terrace?"

Wetzon crumpled the refuse from the caviar pie and dropped it in the trash. There was only a smidgeon of coffee left, and she did that in. The Starbucks container went the way of the other refuse. "What difference does it make?"

"Because, sugarbun," she wriggled her shoulders, "it's going to be your place. You'll see. We can have such lovely parties on the terrace."

"There is no terrace, and there is no apartment. Silvestri told me Bill put it on the market before he left for L.A."

Smith faltered. "Impossible! Why would he do that?"

"He was broke. And he wasn't coming back to New York."

"I really don't understand any of this." She deflated like a pin-pricked balloon.

"Welcome to the club."

The intercom crackled. "Laura Lee for you, Wetzon. Line two."

"I certainly haven't missed *her*," Smith said.

"Shut up, Smith." Wetzon stabbed line two. "How are you?"

"Bearin' up, darlin'. It was so good to spend the night in my own little bed."

"Have you spoken to your Aunt Bren?"

"She's a wreck, can't understand any of it. He's posted bail, but they're screamin' for his blood in Tallahatchie County and he's fightin' going back to Mississippi. I'll tell you, for me, it's a mighty hangover that won't go away. And once Jason's been extradited . . ."

"We'll have to testify at the trial. Shit." She thought, Bill could have handled this, and then, Bill would have been representing Jason. Would Bill have given up his client? She sighed. What was the point? "Do you have a lawyer?"

"Yes. I talked to him before I got myself into this, and left a letter in case somethin' happened. Do you need someone?"

"Silvestri's mother found me a sharp woman who helped me deal with the FBI."

"You'd better alert her that there's a *Wall Street Journal* reporter nosin' around. I wouldn't talk to him, but he's picked up some chit chat among the traders and he's good."

"He hasn't found me yet. What's his name?"

"Fred Klein."

"Thanks for the heads up. When are you going back to work?"

"Monday. I'm rarin' to go, crossin' fingers and toes that my clients haven't given up on me. And I'm hearin' the clarion call for Century 21."

Wetzon laughed. Century 21, the big designer discounter on Cortlandt Street in the heart of the financial district, was a Mecca for Wall Street denizens. It had suffered peripheral damage to its building and had to dump its contents after the 9/11 terror, but it was back in operation less than six months later.

While Smith sat out on the deck coaxing an early suntan,

and perhaps basal cells, Wetzon set up her to-do list for the coming week.

On her legal pad, she put Monday's date on top of the page, and listed calls to be made, appointments to confirm. Eleven items. She went through the suspect sheets and set them up in the order she would call them.

"I'm going to do a spread," Smith said, coming back into the room. She closed and locked the door to the terrace.

"Don't involve me." In the bathroom, Wetzon unpinned her hair, brushed it smooth, and redid it in the dancer's knot.

When she came out, Smith was making little moaning noises. "I don't want to know."

"Look, the Tower. Catastrophe! Failure!"

Wetzon sighed. "Stay calm. Whose catastrophe? Maybe you're reading Bill's spread."

"Oh, no, here's the Nine of Swords. It's the worst. Ruin. What are we going to do?" She bent over as if in pain. "I won't have it. This is someone else's spread. You see, the King of Swords, reversed." She sent the cards flying from her desk and stamped her foot. "Evil."

"They're only cards, for godsakes," Wetzon said. Smith was scary when she got like this. "Why let them upset you?" She was stooping to pick them up when Smith shrieked.

"Don't touch them! It's bad karma."

Wetzon held up her hands. "Okay, okay."

"Better that they cool where they are. I may have to put this deck to sleep."

Smith's dread was contagious. Wetzon tried to shake it off. Chocolate. That was what she needed. "Powder your nose, we have to get going. We don't want to be late for my inheritance."

Smith brightened. Out came her makeup mirror and the accoutrements.

"You look beautiful, Smith. Let's go." When Smith began on her eyes, Wetzon went downstairs. The crew were taking a coffee break as most brokers did not want to talk in the last thirty minutes before the close.

"We're off," Wetzon said. "Have a good weekend." She called up to Smith. "Come on, Smith." No response. "Tell Smith when she gets her ass down here, that I've started walking."

Smith caught up with her crossing Second Avenue. "We have to get a cab."

There were barricades and police. No traffic. "And where do you think we'll get one? The president is at the U.N. today."

"Oh, for pity sakes."

"You'd think your president would check with you when he's coming to town, wouldn't you?" Wetzon laughed. "Manolos aren't made for walking, eh?"

"Oh, you just think you're hilarious."

They walked up to Fifty-third Street and headed west. It was not quite four when they came to the Museum of Modern Art. Smith was trying not to hobble.

"Come with me." Wetzon took Smith's arm and guided her to the museum and a bench just inside the museum bookshop. "Just sit here for a few minutes."

"I can't believe you made me walk the whole way," Smith said. She leaned back against the travertine wall and slipped her tender feet out of her heels.

"Think what good exercise it was."

Smith rolled her eyes. She never exercised, ate whatever she wanted, never put on weight. She scorned personal trainers as being for fat people.

Outside, along Fifty-third Street, a scraggly-haired young man was playing his guitar. A small crowd surrounded him.

"Oh, look," Smith said, sitting up. "There's Lincoln."

Wetzon followed Smith's pointed finger. Her chest compressed.

"Lincoln? You mean Lincoln Farber?"

"Yes." Feet back into her Manolos. "Hurry and we'll catch up to him."

"Don't move," Wetzon said, holding Smith down, keeping Smith in front of her, though there was no reason to any more as Lincoln Farber was no longer in sight.

It didn't matter.

She was never going to be in the same room as Lincoln Farber because Lincoln Farber was the man in the gray Mercedes, the man who'd claimed to be her uncle, the man who was trying to kill her.

Chapter 58

"What's gotten into you?" Smith said, trying to shake off Wetzon's iron grip and failing. "You're hurting me."

"Smith, listen to me." The wilderness was back. She fought to control it, one word at a time. "Lincoln Farber is the man who killed Carolyn Dorley and tried to kill me. He was at the site of the explosion."

"Oh, for pity sakes. You've lost your mind. I don't know what I'm going to do with you."

"This time you have to believe me. We're not going up there. I'm calling Silvestri." She released Smith and dug in her bag for her cell. "We can't go anywhere near Farber."

"Oh, puh-leeze, this is a simple reading of Bill's will. We won't be the only ones there." Flexing her toes as if to prepare them, she stood, smoothed her skirt.

Wetzon stared at her cell, stunned. How could she have forgotten? The minute she turned it on, it rang. "Yes?"

Silvestri's voice, tight and anxious. "Your cell was not on."

"I forgot."

"If you're going to chit chat, I'll meet you in the lobby," Smith said.

"Smith! Whatever you do, don't go upstairs. If he sees you, tell him I was delayed and you're waiting for me." Smith rolled her eyes. "Listen to me!" Wetzon followed Smith out the door, Smith acting as if she was trying to get away from a crazy person. Good thing it was New York. No one paid any attention.

"You wanna tell me what's going on?" Silvestri said.

"Hold on, Silvestri. Promise me that much, Smith."

"Okay, okay, but don't keep me waiting. My patience with your craziness is wearing thin."

Wetzon's hands fisted. She clenched them to her sides or she might have smacked Smith. "You'd better stop me before I kill her," she told Silvestri.

"Take a deep breath. Let her go. I want to talk to you about something important."

"Silvestri, she's going to the Museum Tower—we were both going—until I caught a glimpse of Lincoln Farber—".

"Stay away from him, Les. The family name is Farbricov. He's bad news."

"You're telling me?" She leaned against the outside of the building, turning her head away from eavesdroppers. Her voice was a decibel higher than normal. "He's the man from the gray Mercedes who's been trying to kill me, the man I saw outside Carolyn Dorley's building."

"I don't want you anywhere near him, Les."

"But what about Smith? She promised she wouldn't go up—"

"Up? Les, you're worrying me. You're not making any sense."

"She thinks I'm crazy. I told her I'm not in the will."

"Les, hello. Stay grounded. Christ! Will?"

"They're reading it in Bill's apartment, any minute now. God, do you think she'll go upstairs? She promised." Wetzon heard herself babbling, but couldn't make sense of it.

"Les! Stay right there. Where are you, goddammit?"

"Near Bill's. Are you going to come for me?" Her voice had settled into a squeak.

"I'm on my way. Don't turn off your cell."

She dropped her live cell into her bag and walked to the Museum Tower, peering into the lobby. The concierge was not at his desk. No one was in the lobby except the doorman, Fredric, who tipped his hat to her. Oh, God, she thought, Smith—what had she done? But maybe she hadn't—

"Evening, Ms. Wetzon." Fredric held the door for her. "We were shocked and saddened by Mr. Veeder's passing."

"Thank you, Fredric. It was a terrible loss, not just for me but for everyone who knew him." Words. Cliché words. They just came out. So glib. She gave herself a mental shake. "I was looking for Ms. Smith. She's supposed to meet me here."

"Mr. Farber's associate came in right after her and took her upstairs with him. Mr. Farber called down that you're to come right up. He said be sure to tell you Ms. Smith was with them."

Wetzon lost her air, coughing, choking. Fredric guided her to a chair. "Are you all right, Ms. Wetzon? I'm sorry I upset you talking about Mr. Veeder and all."

She waved him off. "Not that." Short, choppy breaths. "Farber and his associate, they're killers. They're going to hurt Ms. Smith. The cops—I called them—" Get a grip, she told herself.

His mouth hung open. "I'm the only one here right now. I can't do anything."

A buzzer sounded. He went to answer it. "It's the intercom," he said. "Mr. Veeder's apartment."

"Don't tell them I'm here."

He answered the intercom. "I haven't seen her yet, Mr. Farber. Okay. I will, Mr. Farber." He disconnected, staring at her.

"Thank you. Did you hear anything in the background?"

"No."

A thought came to her. "Fredric, you said you kept the baseball bat behind the desk."

He opened the door for a man in a business suit, carrying an attaché. "Good evening, Mr. Simkus."

The man got on the elevator and Wetzon and Fredric were alone in the lobby again.

"The bat," she said. She was going upstairs. They would hurt Smith, if they hadn't already. Maybe she could distract them until Silvestri rode to the rescue. She wouldn't do anything stupid like the heroines in mystery novels. But stupid was subjective.

"Yes," he said. He went behind the desk and pulled out the wooden bat. A pen knife clattered to the floor. The knife he'd taken from the derelict. "The police should be here by now. I'll make another call."

Whatever, she thought, giving in to the wilderness. She took the bat and, while he made the phone call, she picked up the pen knife, got on the elevator. A little distraction. She wouldn't have to do more than that. Just enough to buy time for Silvestri to get here.

She pressed the up button.

Chapter 59

How can I do this, she thought, the smooth warm neck of the bat in both hands. Bill's door opens in. No place to hide.

The elevator stopped on thirty-nine. Put up or shut up, she told herself. The door slid open. A man of width more than height, not expecting her, prepared to get on. The wilderness grabbed her, feral. The bat came alive in her hand. A battery ram into his groin. Every bit of strength, and more.

The man groaned, folded over. Holding his balls, he fell hard, sprawling across to the carpeted floor of the hallway, half in the path of the elevator door.

Wetzon stepped over him, bat raised—cold bitch—and cracked him on the skull. And again. Blood spattered. Her. Carpet. Wallpaper. The smell filled her nostrils. She was somewhere else. Listen to the crunch. Raised the bat again. He was the other man in the car. He'd shot the mattress. She remembered everything.

"Drop it. Slowly."

She glanced over her shoulder. Oscar of the shifty eyes. His eyes were not shifty now. He was looking directly at her and he was holding a gun. He was just far enough away from her so that she couldn't reach him. She lowered the bat.

"Set it flat on the floor."

"What are you doing, Oscar?" He didn't answer. She looked down at the bloodied face of her kidnapper. What had she done?

Oscar leaned over the fallen man, checked his pulse, patted him down, and collected two more guns.

"Did I kill him?"

"Did you want to?"

"Yes."

"Well, you didn't make it." He motioned to Wetzon with his gun. "Roll him into the elevator and press B."

It wasn't easy. "Okay." She stood in the door to keep it from closing. Could she press the button before he shot her?

"Press B and get out."

She got out. She'd lost her mind. She wanted to run away, but Smith was still in that apartment with Farber.

Oscar spoke into a radio. Where had that come from? "Package coming down. Yeah. I've got company. The Wetzon woman."

"You won't get away with this, Oscar. I called the police."

He motioned for her to move down the hall in front of him. Stopped her in front of Bill's door. "Ring the bell, see if he checks who it is, then step aside."

"If you want the diamonds, he doesn't have them. And I don't have them. The FBI has them."

"Ring the bell."

"He has Xenia Smith in there. I don't want her to get hurt."

"Ring the bell and step aside."

She rang the bell and stepped aside.

Farber opened the door. "Ms. Wetzon, at last—" He stepped back when he saw Oscar's gun in his face. "What are you doing here?"

Wetzon hugged the wall. It was another double cross. How was she going to get Smith out of there without getting caught in the crossfire?

"Back in. Keep your hands where I can see them." Oscar pushed into the apartment.

Wetzon checked the elevator. It had reached B, waited a minute or so, then started up. It stopped at L. For the police, she hoped. She picked up the bat.

Bill's door stood open. A shot, a shout. Farber ran through the doorway. He didn't see her. She swung the bat across the back of his knees. The sharp crack anointed her. His cry of pain was a Broadway overture. He went down, cursing. Struggled to get up. His legs wouldn't hold him.

"You miserable fucking bastard!" She breathed blood. Raised the bat.

The door to the elevator opened and Silvestri rushed out, along with two uniforms and some men in blue jackets. And Judy Blue.

"Les!" Silvestri yelled, grabbing the bat from her hands.

"Where's my man, slugger?" Judy Blue said.

One of the detectives nudged Farber with the toe of his shoe. "Read him his rights," he told the uniforms. He followed Judy Blue and the blue jackets, back stamped FBI, into the apartment.

Silvestri handed the bat to the uniforms and put his arms around Wetzon. She was wired tight. "Boy, you scare me."

"*I* scare me." She was weak, rattled. "Smith's in there, Silvestri."

"Come on." Arm around her shoulders, he drew her into the apartment where all kinds of electronic communications were going down, including a call for a couple of ambulances.

Oscar lay on the floor blood seeping from his shoulder. One of the blue jackets had done a makeshift bandage to stop the flow. When Oscar caught sight of Wetzon, he said,

"I'd hate to make that girl mad."

Judy Blue, crouched next to Oscar, rumpled his hair. "Yeah," she said.

Silvestri held Wetzon tighter.

Wetzon moved her lips, finally words came. "Oscar's one of yours?"

"He's been undercover here last eight months. Oscar Rashid, Leslie Wetzon, and this is Silvestri, Lieutenant, NYPD."

"I hate emptying the trash," Oscar said.

Wetzon roused herself. "Where's Smith?"

Disgusted, Judy Blue said, "Don't tell me she's here, too?"

"The other guy forced her to come up. I think that's what happened." She eased from Silvestri's grasp. "Oscar, did you see her?"

"No."

Wetzon raced into the bedroom. "Smith!" Thumping. She opened the door to Bill's dressing room closet. Smith was trussed up like a pork roast. Her mouth was taped. Her eyes burned holes into Wetzon. "Didn't I tell you not to go upstairs?"

Silvestri lifted Smith out of the closet and dumped her on the bed. "This is going to hurt, Xenia." He took hold of the tape over her mouth and pulled it off.

"Oh, for pity sakes!" Smith screamed at Wetzon. "This is all your fault." She flopped around on the bed. "Get me out of this!"

Silvestri offered Wetzon his arm. "How about we leave her to the FBI?"

"Don't tempt me," Wetzon said.

Chapter 60

The city was blooming, yellows, fuchsias, pinks, tree and bush awash with color: forsythia, golden and white daffodils, the gift from the Dutch people after 9/11. Iris and tulips filled the center islands between up and downtown traffic on Broadway's Upper West Side route and Park Avenue. In front of apartment buildings, floral plantings surrounded trees.

And they say New York is all concrete, Wetzon thought. My city is beautiful all year round, but especially in the spring.

She'd cut through Central Park, not hurrying, stopping to watch the volleyball pick-up games, strolled past Sheep Meadow, crowded with sunbathers and quiet because no radios or CD players were allowed, up Lilac Walk, where lilac buds were peeking.

Two weeks had passed, and as the earliest city cops, the New Amsterdam Night Watch, had called on the hour, all was well. With a few albeits. Smith's ego had healed faster than her bruises and bumps, mainly because the *Post* had published a huge picture of her in front of Bill's building, dishevelment and all, and called her a heroine.

Wetzon didn't care. She didn't want credit. It was terrifying to her that she'd almost killed a man, evil as he was. And she had to live with the knowledge that given the same set of circumstances she would probably do it again. Sometimes, when she least expected it, she saw herself raise the bat and heard the crunch as it connected.

And then there was Bill Veeder. There had been a will, but he had little to leave but debts. He had, however, acknowledged his son and had set up an inviolable trust in his behalf.

Still, there were bits and pieces of Bill's life that she would never know. Her hand went to the message slip she'd folded and tucked into the pocket of her suit. Bill's doctor friend and tennis partner, Steve Levy, had called her this morning.

"I was hoping we could meet for a drink," he'd said, after they'd exchanged somewhat awkward condolences. When she hesitated, wondering if he was making a move on her, he said, "It's not what you're thinking."

"Everybody knows what I'm thinking."

"I'm not going to hit on you, Leslie."

"Okay. I'm meeting a friend for an early drink tonight, at Cafe des Artistes. How about seven o'clock, same place?"

So that was the plan.

"A wee drinkie, darlin'," Laura Lee said. "Tonight's *Falstaff* night." They'd both plunged back into their lives with such enthusiasm, neither had been able to coordinate schedules until now, though they'd talked on the phone daily. And Laura Lee had chosen Cafe des Artistes because: "I feel the need for some lush, romantic, and decidedly retro ambience."

Wetzon walked past Tavern on the Green, which even in daylight and in spite of the cars parked out front, looked like a sketch from a fairy tale. She crossed Central Park West. Cafe des Artistes was in a Beaux Arts building just off Sixty-seventh Street.

Laura Lee was sitting, her back to the bar, a glass of red wine in hand, chatting up a distinguished old gentleman to her right and charming two attractive Frenchmen with hair grazing their collars. "Ah, here she is! Wetzon, darlin' say hello to Jeremy," she tilted to the right, "and these two adorables," pronouncing it in French, "are Pierre and Marc, who are here to make a documentary."

Jeremy's wife arrived just behind Wetzon, a little stiff-necked to see him with Laura Lee, and dragged him off to their table. As for Pierre and Marc, Laura Lee told them Wetzon was an important client there to talk business.

Wetzon ordered a California cabernet. The naked nymphs in the famous mural behind the bar frolicked. "Well," she said.

"Yes," Laura Lee agreed.

"How is Aunt Bren and the mistress business?"

"Which one?"

"Which one what? You mean he had more than one?"

"In Shreveport, a stripper by the name—would you be-lieve—of Tomasina de Lay."

Wetzon laughed. "Ooo la, that's some Uncle Weaver."

"The Tallahatchie Republican Club is in a state, let me tell you."

"Oh, the judge was a Republican?"

"Well, of course, darlin', and a teetotallin' member of the Christian Right."

"He shed the teetotal when he came to New York."

"A wolf in sheep's clothin'. Poor Aunt Bren thought all the while she was married to the sheep. So it goes. And how are you doin'?"

"Recovering. Smith's thrilled with herself and has no time for me, which is good."

"And you have Silvestri home again."

"I do. I really do."

"And—"

"And. And the guy I clobbered was in a coma till yesterday. The other one, Farber, has a torn Achilles and a fractured femur. I must have had an episode of superhuman strength."

"Rage cooked up your adrenalin."

"Laura Lee, did you ever think you could kill someone? I mean, not just to say, as I say about Smith, but for real."

"It could happen. Can't ever say never, darlin'." She put her hand over Wetzon's. "You were defendin' yourself. Everyone knows that."

"I know." Wetzon set down her glass. "That guy, Oscar, the handyman in Bill's building, the one I thought was creepy, like a would-be rapist or something, turned out to be FBI."

"Takes all kinds."

"If he hadn't stopped me, I would have killed that thug."

"Speakin' about killin', the prosecutor called to tell me that Jason should be back in the country to face charges by the middle of May."

"Ugh."

"What have we decided about Bill Veeder?"

"He was in financial trouble. Deep, with Russian mobster loan sharks." She toyed with her glass. "Laura Lee, one of the things I can't remember . . . with Bill and me . . . you said you knew what had happened."

"Ah, you mean when you went out to the Coast for Thanksgivin'."

"Yes."

"Okay. You got out to the airport early and they put you on an earlier flight. He had to be in court, so he'd given you the number of the limo service in case the flight was delayed. The limo picked you up when you got in and took you to the Four Seasons."

Wetzon closed her eyes. "He left a key card for me at the

desk. I remember opening the door."

"You found an actress type in a towel, blow dryin' her red hair as if she lived there. You'd gotten there a couple of hours early."

"I was furious."

"She said, bold as brass, 'Oops, it was a late night.' "

" 'Oops, it was a late night'? What a hell of a nerve!"

"You never even unpacked. You dropped the key card on the side table, walked out of there, and got on the next plane for New York."

"I'm proud of myself."

"He kept callin' but you told him fuhgeddaboudit."

Wetzon sighed. "I wonder if I'll ever remember any more of it."

"Sometimes the mind protects the bod."

"I don't understand why he took such a chance. He knew I'd never tolerate it."

"He liked pushin' the envelope, so to speak."

"I guess so. I think Oscar was put in place so the FBI could keep an eye on Bill, and when they got what they wanted, they turned him."

"Bill was working for the FBI?"

"Judy Blue wouldn't say. I'm hoping he was on the right side at the end. I have to."

"Listen, darlin', for me, he'll always be on the right side because he saved your life. Now enough of the serious stuff. Drink up, and let me tell you about my haul at Century 21."

It was not quite seven when Steve Levy arrived. She had met him only a few times, but had always liked him. He was an internist, a former ranking tennis pro, with a Park Avenue practice weighted with athletes and former athletes. A well-built man in his late forties, Steve had curly brown hair and a tan that enunciated his white teeth and warm smile.

Laura Lee watched him approach. "Well, look at this picture comin' right toward us as if he knows us."

"He does. Not us, me."

"I thought you said—"

"He wants to talk to me about Bill."

"I'll bet."

"No, I believe him."

"Leslie." Steve took her hand and kissed her on the cheek.

"This is my friend Laura Lee Day. Laura Lee, Dr. Steve Levy."

Pow! Wetzon blinked. She could feel the energy like an electric shock. They were shaking hands, eyes locked.

"Hello, guys," Wetzon said. "Laura Lee, don't you have to leave?"

"Oh, right." Laura Lee smiled at Steve Levy. "*Falstaff.*"

"Really?" Steve Levy smiled at Laura Lee. "I'm going to the Met tonight, too."

"You like opera?" Laura Lee asked in disbelief.

"Love it."

"Get out of here, Laura Lee. I have the check.."

Laura Lee grinned. "Okay. I'm sure we'll run into each other again, Dr. Steve."

"Count on it, Laura Lee." He sat down next to Wetzon and smiled at the naked nymphs. "I haven't been here in ages. Stoly martini, straight up," he told the bartender. Looked at her near-empty glass. "Another, Leslie?"

"No, I'm fine." She waited. He drank his martini. She waited.

"I wanted to talk to you about Bill," he said at last.

"Okay. Shoot."

"You're angry."

343

"I don't know what I am. He lied to me about everything, and then he saved my life."

"He loved you. He wanted to protect you."

She stared into her empty wine glass. "From what? His mob connections? His being broke? His son? God, Steve, he'd put his apartment on the market and sold his law firm and never said a word to me."

"He was dying, Leslie."

What had he said? She snapped around to him. "What?"

"Lymphoma. Very aggressive. It's why he took the Dooney Bellemore case, why he sold everything and moved to L.A."

"Oh, God, Steve, why didn't he tell me? Did he think I would leave him because he was sick?" The tightness in her chest shattered into a thousand pieces.

"You know him, Leslie, he wanted to be the big guy, the strong one, the one always in control. He could never show that he was weak. If he could, he'd have gone up to the mountains when he thought he was close and waited it out like an Indian."

"Why are you telling me this now?" Sorrow forced her voice into a small place in her throat.

"Not to make you feel guilty. He was my friend. I didn't want you to remember him in a bad way."

"He saved my life, Steve. I'll always remember how he looked in that instant."

She could smell the pizza before she even opened the door.

"There you are," Silvestri said, as Izz gave her a raucous greeting. He was wearing jeans and a singlet. Sexy, with his thick muscular arms.

Think about the pizza, she told herself.

"How's Laura Lee?"

"Good. Uncle Weaver had a second mistress in Shreveport, a stripper named Tomasina de Lay."

Silvestri's laugh was full out.

She dropped her briefcase and purse near the door, and kicked off her shoes. "I sent Lucy, the nurse at Mount Sinai, a check for a thousand, with my deepest apologies."

He gave her a searching look. "You okay?"

She nodded. She'd packed sorrow away on her walk home. Zoey. Bill. The pain would recede in time and find its place in the fabric of her life, with the joys and other sorrows.

The pizza went into the oven. He handed her a beer.

"Silvestri." Parking the beer on the counter, she put her arms around his waist, nestled her face in the hollow of his chest.

He kissed the top of her head, her forehead. "It's okay, Les. You don't have to say anything."

"I love you, Silvestri. I have to say that. I never want you to go away again."

"Then you'll have to promise me something." His lips behind her ear made tingly shocks.

Her hands crawled under his shirt. "Mmmm, anything."

"Promise me you'll never keep anything from me again."

She squinted up at him. "All right. If you'll make me the same promise?"

He squinted back at her.

"Gotcha," she said.

He gave her a big, bearish hug and laughed. "No question," he said.

About the Author

Annette Meyers has a long history on both Broadway and Wall Street. On Wall Street, she spent sixteen years as an executive search consultant, and since 1996, has been an arbitrator with the National Association of Securities Dealers (NASD). On Broadway, she was assistant to Broadway director-producer Hal Prince for sixteen years, working with him on such productions as: *A Funny Thing Happened on the Way to the Forum, Fiddler on the Roof, Cabaret, A Little Night Music, Company,* and *Follies.*

Meyers is also the author of seven published Smith and Wetzon mysteries, *The Big Killing, Tender Death, The Deadliest Option, Blood on the Street, Murder: The Musical, These Bones Were Made for Dancin',* and *The Groaning Board.*

Her most recent work, published in 2004, is *Repentances,* a stand-alone psychological suspense novel set in 1936, in the Jewish immigrant community of New York.

Meyers is also the author of two novels—*Free Love* and *Murder Me Now*—set in Greenwich Village, in 1920, featuring Olivia Brown, a young woman poet based loosely on Edna St. Vincent Millay.

She is a former president of Sisters in Crime and is current president of the International Association of Crime Writers, North America. Other organization memberships include: Mystery Writers of America, The Authors Guild, Private Eye Writers of America.

Her website address is: www.meyersmysteries.com